A Place Called

Bliss

The Saskatchewan Saga

A Place Called

Bliss

A NOVEL

RUTH GLOVER

Fleming H. Revell
A Division of Baker Book House Co
Grand Rapids, Michigan 49516

Published by Fleming H. Revell
a division of Baker Book House Company
P.O. Box 6287, Grand Rapids, MI 49516-6287

Printed in the United States of America

Library of Congress Cataloging-in-Publication Data

Glover, Ruth.
    A place called bliss : a novel / Ruth Glover.
        p.   cm. — (The Saskatchewan Saga)
    ISBN 0-8007-5743-2
      1. Frontier and pioneer life—Fiction. 2. Scots—Canada—Fiction. 3. Social classes—Fiction. 4. Saskatchewan—Fiction. I. Title.

PS3557.L678 P55 2001
813'.54—dc21
                                            00-053349

Scripture quotations are from the King James Version of the Bible.

For current information about all releases from Baker Book House, visit our web site:
http://www.bakerbooks.com

To
the dear people
of First Christian Church
in The Dalles, Oregon:

Thank you for nine wonderful years!

Scotland—1878

Sophia Galloway had been assured by the best medical advice in Kirkcudbright that her child would not be born on board ship. Whether on land or on sea, its safe arrival came first, of course. But land, with her own doctor officiating, was imperative; Sophia was no heroine, and the comfort would be best assured at home in Heatherstone, in her own bed. And it wouldn't hurt to have Hugh standing dutifully by, helpless, as she went down into the vale of death for the sake of a Galloway heir.

But Sophia was not selfless in her desire for a child. For as long as she could remember, she had wanted a child, someone to call her own. Wanted it more than the wealth, which, she had been informed constantly across the years by her debt-ridden brother, was imperative for the Gowrie family coffers and could be obtained only if she married well. Wanted it more than the marriage itself, though, as she understood it, marriage was necessary.

Because of the urgent demands that she marry money, if not a title, and because she had no marriage proportion whatsoever due to her brother Preston's profligacy—his licentiousness and dissipation had all but impoverished the Gowrie estate—marriage proposals had been few and far between. The two or three young gallants who had shown an interest in Preston's charming sister had backed off quickly when her lack of a dowry was discovered.

And so Sophia, restless and frustrated and chafing sorely under the limitations placed on women of her station, had reached the less than acceptable age of twenty-five before marrying.

Her marriage, then, was stunning; all the more so if one considered money a factor. And of the importance of this she had been reminded often and pointedly by her graceless brother.

It was more than a marriage for Sophia; it was an escape. An escape from a disintegrating house that had been plundered by Preston of its saleable items, an escape from the shire of Wigtown where the Gowrie fall from pride and position to poverty and humiliation was well known and where no bachelor would look her way except with embarrassment and, sometimes, faint regret.

Be it said forever in his favor, Hugh Galloway, with magnificent aplomb, seemed never to see the signs of faded fortune in the Gowrie estate. He treated Sophia not as a bargain but as a prize. Though she could not say she was in love with the forty-five-year-old Scot, and though she fretted over the fact that his previous marriage of fifteen years was childless, she liked him and respected him. That was enough. And surely children would follow!

Though she thought it a waste of money, Hugh Galloway, without hesitation, transferred a generous dowry into Preston's pockets.

Sophia knew the Galloway name, of course, from the adjoining shire of Kirkcudbright, and it was an old and honored one. Hugh Galloway had been a widower for several years. Now, for some reason, he had decided to remarry.

Secretly, at first, Sophia wondered what had fixed the Galloway man's attention on her—overage, impoverished, and with a brother whose reputation had dimmed any earlier glory obtained through centuries of Gowrie ancestors and their notable services to king and country.

Hugh Galloway, quite frankly, told her why she had been his choice. Any lesser quality of person than Sophia Gowrie might have been chagrined, perhaps offended, but Sophia took it as a compliment from a man whose opinion she was beginning to prize.

Hugh Galloway's future included living on the Canadian frontier. "Ontario, where we'll be, is no longer the frontier," he explained, visiting with Sophia one Sunday afternoon in the ravished hall of the Gowrie manor, "but it certainly is far removed from the culture and customs to which you have been accustomed."

Canada! Something in Sophia, as in Hugh himself, was challenged.

"And you, my dear," Hugh had said, fixing her with measuring eyes, "strike me as just the woman to face it with me."

Unexpected color had surged into Sophia's cheeks, for she felt elevated in his—as well as her own—opinion.

"My departure date is a year and more away," he said, adding with a smile, "I thought I should get this important part of the preparation struck from my list."

And even then Sophia felt no part of any list. Or, if she did, it was to feel contentment that she was at the top of it.

The banns were read and the marriage performed. Preston, in his cups as usual, bade his one sibling farewell with a maudlin display of affection that would have been missing if he had been sober. As for Sophia, she stepped into the Galloway carriage, waved to the few friends standing by, turned to her husband, and said, with a smile, "Now for the great adventure."

It seemed to please the ordinarily taciturn, often dour, Scot. Along with these characteristics and the frankness he had already

9

exhibited, Sophia was to learn of his impatience with ineptness, pride of name and position, a certain ruthlessness. But all of it was tempered with a rigid sense of fair play.

At her comment, Hugh took her hand in the first show of intimacy between them, and somehow it conveyed the regard of which he had yet to speak and which he was to demonstrate by his actions rather than by his words.

An apartment at Heatherstone became their first home. Hugh had little time for the games society played, and though he only rarely introduced Sophia to the aristocratic circle of which he was undoubtedly an accepted part, she never felt it was to her detriment. It was, simply, that Hugh was fixed on the move to Canada and regretted meaningless interruptions.

"After all," he said, "we'll have it all to do over when we settle in Toronto. On my brief trips there I've made a few acquaintances; we won't be entirely strangers in a strange land." He explained to her that his business ventures there were under way, property purchased, and a home, even now, under construction.

"It will be almost a mirror image of Heatherstone," he said fondly, "but better planned. After all these years I know what can be eliminated, what changed, and what improved." He had planned for the same awe-inspiring impression but with more comfort and utility.

The next few months were not wasted time for Sophia. Slowly she began to understand the man who was her husband, and to adapt herself to his way of life and to pleasing him. With Hugh's encouragement and guidance, an entire wardrobe was designed and most of it packed.

"The ladies in Toronto," Hugh said dryly, "will study the newest styles avidly. We're not going to a savage place, by any means. Now as for Angus—"

This was Sophia's introduction to the Morrison family, who was to accompany them. Accompany them, and yet only temporarily.

"Angus Morrison was born at Heatherstone," Hugh explained. "His father was groundskeeper until his death. Angus was a favorite of my father's, who saw the boy's intelligence and character and invested in his education. After all that, Angus came right back here and went to work as overseer—a keen farmer is our Angus. He married Mary Skye, also born and raised at Heatherstone. Mary's mother, Kezzie—" Hugh's patrician face softened. "Kezzie has been like a mother to me." Sophia already knew, and appreciated, the cherished Kezzie.

"And Angus?" Sophia pursued his earlier comment on savagery in the new land. "You seemed to indicate Angus might be going to Canada, too."

"Angus and Mary and the children. Angus wants to be his own master, and I don't blame him. It's hard to resist the call of free land, freedom from the serfdom and servitude that has plagued his strata of society for generations. It's a chance to break loose, even as it is for me."

Hugh's face darkened slightly. Being a second son, the grand Heatherstone estate had gone to his older brother. Fortunately his grandmother's vast and extensive holdings had been left to him. But to be out from his brother's shadow—Sophia could see an independent and arrogant man like Hugh would chafe under imperious authority, be it family or sovereign who held sway.

It had been while riding that Sophia had first met Angus Morrison. Her attention sharpened at her first glimpse of him.

Pulling her mount to a stop, Sophia asked, rather abruptly, "Who's that man?"

The groom who was accompanying her, a youth from the stables—and another who had been born and raised at Heatherstone—shaded his eyes, glanced at the man who had vaulted a low stone wall and was proceeding toward a field where sheep were grazing. "Why, Mum," he said, "it's no' but Angus, our overseer."

Overseer and employee, perhaps; nevertheless there was in the man's entire demeanor an air of authority. Perhaps *freedom* was a better word. He walked tall, strode easily; his head sat with some pride on his broad shoulders. His clothes, though suitable for a worker and somewhat worn, were quality and fit him well.

Some impulse drove Sophia's heels into the side of her horse. It bounded forward, over the wall, and toward the man, who turned at the sound of approaching hooves.

Breathless, though there was no need for it—it was the mare who had done the running—Sophia looked down into the craggy face of Angus Morrison. Instantly, joltingly, unexpectedly and heart-shakingly, came the thought: *Has love come, too late?*

Surely her face didn't reflect the fact that, momentarily, sound faded and sight dimmed; surely her grip of the reins was not because she felt a reeling sensation. Perhaps the strange physical reaction whitened her face.

At any rate the man's face sobered; his hand came out spontaneously toward her, and he asked, "Are you all right?"

"It was the jump—" Sophia managed.

The young groom, by that time, had found a way through the wall and was coming alongside.

"You all right, Mrs. Hugh?"

Angus Morrison stepped back immediately. "So you're Hugh's bride. I apologize for not having been in to meet you before this. It's lambing time—"

"And you are Angus Morrison," Sophia said, feeling foolish and struggling for poise. "Hugh has told me about you. And," she added quickly, "your wife. Mary, isn't it?"

"Mary, yes. And our bairns—Cameron and Molly."

"Yes, yes, Cameron and Molly. And you are all coming with us to Canada." Sophia was aware that she was speaking too quickly.

"We're going to Canada," Angus affirmed, "but independently. Our date of sailing and our ship will be the same."

"But you're going on to the prairies—"

"Not the prairies," Angus's gentle correction continued, respectfully. "The bush country."

"The bush! I'm very ignorant, I'm afraid. You mean northern Ontario?" The Galloways would be in Ontario.

"Not quite!" Angus's face lit with a smile. "Much farther north and west—northern Saskatchewan, actually."

"Saskatchewan—I've never even been quite sure how to pronounce it."

"Very primitive."

"Why . . . why have you chosen that area? Do you mind—"

"Not at all." After a long glance at Sophia's face, perhaps judging whether he might share his reasons, Angus said, "I don't know if anyone else understands, but how do the names Medicine Hat . . . Elbow . . . Overlook . . . Red Deer . . . Saskatoon sound to you?"

"I see," Sophia answered slowly.

"And, to be more specific—Bliss."

"Bliss . . . sounds too good to be true. That's the name of a place?"

"The place, specifically, to which I'm going. I've been in communication with someone there—an acquaintance—and have plans rather well worked out."

"I'd like to hear more about this . . . Bliss. Come to dinner tonight, Mr. Morrison—"

"Angus, please. Everyone calls me Angus. And thank you. I'll be happy to join you and Hugh tonight. We have many things to talk about, anyway, details to consider. It's a big step, at least for me and mine." The warm brown eyes were lit with the dream that would, after all, come true.

Somewhat numbly Sophia turned her mount and, followed by the faithful groom, wended her way toward the monstrous rock pile that was Heatherstone and could not stop the thought that crept, like a nibbling mouse, into her head: *An attractive man. A virile man. A virile man who has fathered children. . . .*

2

Dinner that evening in the cold and echoing hall at Heatherstone was filled with talk of Canada from beginning to end. Having heard a great deal about Toronto and Hugh's plans, Sophia now listened to Angus Morrison's expectations.

Early on, the Dominion of Canada had implemented a vigorous immigration policy. Agents were sent to Europe, and special fares were offered to immigrants. The provinces and the Canadian Pacific Railway offered inducements also. A revival of prosperity and the extending of the railway brought a brief rush to Manitoba, but settlement there and particularly beyond was slow.

The "beyond" beckoned Angus Morrison. Expressly the area around Prince Albert in the vast northern part of Saskatchewan and, specifically, a district by the name of Bliss.

"How enticing!" Sophia exclaimed. "Fancy living in a place called Bliss! The very name stimulates the imagination!"

Toronto suddenly seemed dull and uninteresting and lacking in adventure. Stricken by her disloyalty, she smiled guiltily on

Hugh; just as guiltily she stifled the thought that Hugh's cold aristocratic demeanor was almost a reflection of Heatherstone, while the challenges of the raw West were a perfect setting for the vibrant man across the table from her.

"The homestead system," Angus was explaining, "provides that a settler can have one hundred and sixty acres on condition of three years' residence and cultivation and a payment of ten dollars, which is a patent fee. You can imagine what that means to oppressed and downtrodden or simply poverty-stricken people."

"Angus," Hugh interjected with a smile, "you've never in your life been any of those."

"True . . . true," Angus conceded. "And most of it thanks to your father. But you, Hugh, are going. Could I stay behind?"

"All this, of course," and Hugh indicated the heap of rock around them that was Heatherstone, "belongs to my brother." Ian Galloway and his family were presently in residence at the family home in Edinburgh, where Wallace, the son, was studying. "Much as I love it," Hugh continued, "there's nothing here for me . . . or," with a small smile in Sophia's direction, "for my offspring."

To all, rich and poor alike, the new land beckoned, with promise of opportunity. The dedicated and devoted and desperate would survive; the weak and wavering would be eliminated by the very challenges they sought.

⁂

Eventually Sophia was to meet Mary and the Morrison "bairns," Cameron and Molly. Wee Molly was the image of her father, with his black, curly hair, but with the blue eyes of her mother and grandmother. Cammie was, himself, fair and golden.

Mary, far more than Angus, demonstrated an awareness of their station in life and, though not servile, was self-effacing. Perhaps it was natural, when one knew one's position to be inferior.

Barriers dividing the classes were strong, almost unassailable, as they had been for centuries. To Mary, Sophia was "Mum. Yes, Mum, no, Mum, thank you, Mum," or "Mrs. Hugh," while to Sophia, Mary was simply "Mary."

Here, at home, it was expected. Canada, Sophia understood, would be different. There would be a great leveling of stations, every man no better or worse than his neighbor. Perhaps it was part of the appeal for Angus and Mary, as for many others weary unto death of oppression.

But now it made a difference, and Sophia and Mary, though cordial, were not friends. Mary in her small "cot" and Sophia in the colossus that was Heatherstone were miles apart.

Moreover . . . there was Angus. And Angus was Mary's husband. Mary lived in a cot, Mary would travel steerage, Mary would endure the rigors of pioneer life, but she would do it all with Angus.

Like a sickness she couldn't shake, Sophia's fascination with Angus Morrison plagued her thoughts in the daytime and her dreams at night. It became almost an obsession with her to test his seeming devotion to duty. Was it real or a cloak to be donned when he approached the family? Was it surface only, the deference he displayed? What would it take for him to break over the boundaries? Could she . . . command his attention?

To reach beyond the overseer to the man himself became a passion with Sophia. Because of it she asked his attendance at countless dinners, to private planning sessions, for advice concerning packing, anything for intimate time with him. Finally, there were long rides together over the estate, picnics in the woods, trips in the carriage together to town.

Never considered beautiful, though always smartly dressed and graciously mannered, Sophia, as the weeks came and went, bloomed.

There came a day when her brilliant color and sparkling eyes prompted her one and only compliment from her husband.

"The estate of marriage is very becoming to you, my dear," he said, and it may have been the dry tone of his voice, but Sophia tensed and only relaxed when Hugh returned to his papers.

Perhaps Sophia was alarmed, and warned. Perhaps . . . who knows . . . she had satisfied her hungry fixation on a man other than her husband. At any rate, there came a day when Angus's presence was not demanded, and Sophia settled into becoming Mrs. Hugh Galloway of Heatherstone, soon to be transported to Toronto, Canada.

Soon, to her delirious happiness, she was able to inform Hugh that she was to present him with a child. Now contentment wrapped her in a beauty that even ungainliness and a swelling waistline couldn't dim.

Mary, too, was pregnant. The two pregnancies brought about the happy decision to take Kezzie along to Canada.

Kezia Skye, Mary's mother, had been with the Galloway family since her marriage to their gamekeeper. Though he was dead, Kezia, or Kezzie as she was fondly known, maintained her position as nurse and nanny to any and all Galloway offspring. Finally, with Wallace, Hugh's nephew, growing out from under her care, Kezzie became seamstress or whatever other household position could be found for her. "We'd no more turn her out than our own aunt," Hugh maintained.

It was Hugh who came up with the plan to take Kezzie along to Canada. "She'll be indispensable," he said. "She's been like a mother to me, and she'll be like that to our son. I don't know what kind of help along that line we'll be able to come up with in Canada. How comfortable to have our Kezzie, someone we can trust absolutely."

Kezzie herself was ecstatic. Mary was her only living child; it hadn't been easy to face old age without her daughter and her grandchildren.

"Of course," Hugh explained to Sophia when this was mentioned, "Cameron isn't Mary's child."

Sophia raised her eyebrows.

"Nor Angus's," Hugh added quickly.

"Not Angus's? You mean—Angus hasn't . . . ah, fathered a son?"

"A strange way to put it," Hugh said, and Sophia flushed.

"But Cammie is a true Morrison," Hugh continued. "It so happens that the boy is a relative—the child of Angus's cousin, or maybe it's a second or third cousin. The young man was lost at sea, I believe, hastening the delivery of the baby, and the mother didn't survive. Angus and Mary were newly married and took the wee'un in as their own."

"Does he—Cameron—know?"

"Oh, I expect he does, in a casual way. It won't sink in for a while. But it doesn't matter. His name is Morrison; he'll be a son of the family. And he'll go with them to the new land."

Kezzie's devotion, however, reached beyond her own flesh and blood. She was bonded to "Mr. Hugh" by duty and years of service and felt her life was inextricably bound up with the Galloways. To serve as nurse to another of the clan—Kezzie knew no greater fulfillment.

"Kezzie," Hugh warned when they talked about it, "Mary is to have another child, and she'll be far from you. You'll be staying in Ontario with us, you know."

"No matter," Kezzie maintained stoutly and loyally. "At least there won't be all that water atween us. We'll be on the same continent." This and more she said, with a mighty rolling of r's. In Kezzie the Scots burr was very strong; in Angus, as in Hugh, much of it had been—if not lost, then greatly muted, and an English accent substituted. Lowland Scots, after all, was but a northern form of English, being directly descended from the old Anglian speech. Originally, the northern English dialect spread into Scotland from Northumbria and steadily ousted the various Celtic dialects as it pushed northward. This Anglian speech developed into the distinctively "Scots" form of the English language that was so richly obvious in Kezzie.

And so it was settled: Kezzie was to accompany them.

18

But delay after delay put off their sailing date. Sophia, dreading a shipboard confinement and an unknown ship's doctor, consulted her own physician.

It was then old Dr. McGee pronounced heartily: "No need to worry! I've calculated very carefully, and there's plenty of time to make landfall. Never fear, yon child will be a Canadian! No, my dear, this baby won't be born aboard ship."

Unchurched for the most part but certainly not a heathen, Sophia had some knowledge of the Bible. She hadn't been on board ship long before she equated the immigrants' move with that of the Israelites. Most of the people, particularly below decks, were escaping bondage of one sort or another, and the routes to the Promised Land, whether across arid desert or over the bounding main, were equally miserable and unendurable.

Unlike those earlier trekkers, these had an abundance of water. Water, water, everywhere, and not a drop to drink was more truth than fiction according to Kezzie, who was back and forth between the two families. Only limited amounts were supplied the horde of people in steerage. The ration of drinking water tasted of the oily barrels, and strange and awful items were fished from it. As for washing clothes—only the skimpiest attempt could be made. The Morrisons were faring poorly.

Sophia and Hugh traveled first class and were much more comfortable, though crowded. Numerous remittance men were their companions, men with funds from home who were being urged or forced to locate far from home, having been involved in some ruckus or indiscretion and considered an embarrassment to their family. They were a jolly group, used to frivolity. The bar was well patronized, with champagne corks popping all day and far into the night. Here Saloon and Intermediate passengers mingled freely, and if Sophia had not been so obviously *enceinte* she could have joined the festivities; her "condition" forbade the indelicacy of displaying herself publicly. Hugh was thoughtful and attentive but escaped the confines of their small, cheerless quarters as often as he could.

The *Vega,* an old, slow boat, was built to carry seven hundred passengers but was crammed to the gunnels with over two thousand. The hold was stuffed with their goods, much of it laughable when the frontier was considered. Many immigrants, particularly those of the remittance men class, in their innocence imagined Canadians wore a sort of shooting costume with the usual jodphurs and shining riding boots but adding a belt and holster with revolver and a hunting knife. Advised to bring warm clothes, they substituted soft collars for hard and flannel for linen. They brought treasures such as boxing gloves, smoking humidors, stereoscopic cameras, the finest in fishing equipment—tackle boxes, patent folding canvas creels, braided waterproof landing nets and, in one instance, a frog spear—for braving the northern lakes and doing it in the style to which they were accustomed.

That their belongings might have to be transported on a creaking Red River cart or a dragging travois, none of them suspected. Babes in the woods, their fun and games would all too soon be changed to desperate reality if they dared the backwoods and to an ineffectual passage of days if they chose civilization; bustling energy was transforming hamlets to towns and towns to smoky cities with amazing speed. It was a land for the industrious and for those with a will to endure no matter what the hardship.

Sophia first realized just how bad things were below deck when, about three days after sailing, Kezzie climbed, white-faced, from the bowels of the ship, quite obviously on the verge of retching.

Sophia, reclining on a bunk that was none too steady, braced herself, sniffed in an indelicate fashion, and wrinkled her nose.

"Kezzie, what's that terrible stench?"

"Sorry, Mum." Kezzie, in spite of all training to the contrary, dropped onto the side of the bed, closed her eyes, and swayed alarmingly.

Sophia's eyes widened, as well as her nostrils. "What is it, Kezzie? Are you ill?" So far Kezzie had avoided any sign of sea-sickness.

"It's down there, Mum," and Kezzie's eyes, a bright blue, dropped in the direction of below deck.

"What, down there?" Sophia was a little impatient.

"It . . . it stinks, Mum!"

The back part of the ship, someone had explained, was all holds, and here the single men lived . . . existed. "I haven't been in there, Mum," Kezzie, fanning herself, explained, "but I'm told the whitewash is fallin' off and underneath is manure. This ship transported cattle or horses at one time. There are nearly six hundred men in there, some of them smoke, makin' the air worse than ever. Those poor men *smell!* One wants to hold one's nose when they are around."

"Is it as crowded where Mary and Angus and the children are?"

"The middle is for married people, and they at least have bunks. I was down there, tendin' to Mary—she's getting terrible weak, Mum, and looks dreadful—and someone in the upper bunk just leaned over and vomited. It splashed all over Mary and Molly who was lyin' beside her . . . missed me, but I guess I walked in it—"

Sophia shuddered. "How terrible. Please feel free to spend as much time with Mary and the children as is needed, Kezzie. I'll manage somehow. And now I think you should change your shoes . . . perhaps wipe the floor where you've walked . . ."

"Aye, Mrs. Hugh. Do you know they're fed mostly herring and potatoes down there and some soup? Fish makes Mary bilious. . . ."

"Can you take them something from our allotment, Kezzie?"

"I will, Mum, though it's hard, with all those other big-eyed, hungry people watchin'." Kezzie looked at the floor. "See this, Mum? It's sawdust. That's what they have atween the rows of beds—six inches of sawdust. When someone gets sick, it gets shovelled up."

"Enough, Kezzie," Sophia said faintly, the ship wallowing alarmingly and her own face paling.

<hr />

That evening there was some commotion below decks, enough so that the sound of it was heard in the Galloway cabin. Sophia sent Kezzie to check on it.

Kezzie came back shaking her head. "As near as I can make out, the men in the hold are beatin' their tables with their fists or whatever and hollerin' 'We want no trotters!'"

"Trotters?"

"They've been served pigs' feet once again, Mum, and they're in rebellion. I understand from Mary that they feel they are often given leftovers from the tables up here; once you get over the humiliation of it and get hungry enough, it's rather entertainin' to find a bit of sausage or some such delicacy in your bowl."

Sophia sighed, sorry she'd asked. Kezzie, who occupied a small space, almost closetlike for size, was comfortable enough near her Mr. Hugh and his lady. But that she was anxious over her daughter's condition became clear as the days came and went.

One day, at Sophia's urging, Hugh went below decks to check on Angus and Mary and the children. He returned shaken.

"It's desperate down there," he said, more angry than sympathetic. "It's hard to believe humans can live like that. Kezzie, see that they get some of our oranges and lemons. I'm going to have a talk with the captain."

Some improvements were noted, briefly, when Hugh Galloway raised his aristocratic voice on behalf of the steerage and hold occupants. A tub of hard-boiled eggs was transferred below and soon disappeared with insufficient to go around. Once cheese and ship's biscuits were distributed, the biscuits being about six inches in diameter and an inch thick and hard as cement. If one could avoid breaking a rotting tooth, one could chew away for a considerable length of time, a change from the quickly and easily swallowed, half-cold mess that usually comprised their meals.

More than once Kezzie, at Sophia's instructions, brought Cammie and Molly upstairs to be bathed and fed, with an opportunity to run around a little and breathe some fresh air. But it was painful to watch their small, pinched faces disappearing down the ladder again.

Angus spent most of his time at Mary's side and with the children. Seeing him on deck one day, leaning on the rail and gazing with unseeing eyes to the horizon, Sophia covered her bulk with a cloak and slipped out and to his side. The breeze ruffled the black curls whose luster had dimmed from lack of enough water to keep them clean. Even Angus's dark skin showed signs of the confinement in the sunless area below decks where he and his family were billeted.

Nevertheless, his smile was reminiscent of that first day when he had raised his face to hers, and Sophia's heart skipped a beat.

"I'm so sorry, Angus," she managed. "What can we do to help?"

"Just pray, Sophia."

Whatever intimacies had been between them, to call her Mum or even Mrs. Hugh seemed absurd. And were they not all embarking on a life of freedom from the old system of class and patronage? Angus, already his own man, stood a little taller under the new realization of his worth.

Pray? It was not unheard of, though ordinarily engaged in only in the direst of circumstances. For Angus to request it made the situation serious indeed.

How long since she'd prayed? Sophia realized guiltily that all her prayers had been answered when she found herself carrying a child. Hugh—and his money—took care of all her other needs.

Far removed from the zealous John Knox, under whose leadership the Church of Scotland separated itself from the papacy,

Sophia was a member of the Established Church, and as such, she believed, as privileged to pray as anyone.

"I will," she now assured Angus, asking delicately, "Is Mary . . . are there indications that all is not well?"

Somberly Angus nodded. More blunt than Sophia's fastidiousness allowed her to be, he said frankly, "She's cramping badly. The sack of waters broke yesterday, and the baby should have come but hasn't. Mary is struggling mightily, but there seems to be some obstruction . . . some problem—"

"The doctor—is he with her?" Sophia was horrified, not having known the situation from Kezzie's hesitant reports, no doubt because Mrs. Hugh herself was soon to go through the same experience.

"From time to time. Kezzie is with her or I am. I just came up to get a little fresh air and to pray." Again Angus's eyes sought the horizon. "There doesn't seem to be any hope of making land and getting her to a hospital, so I just pray for a safe delivery."

Sophia crept back to her cabin, to utter her own request in words that were unfamiliar to her, to a God who was all but unknown. It was a very tentative effort and left the petitioner no more comforted than before. In spite of good intentions, her fear centered upon herself and her own unborn babe. "Oh, God," she breathed with some desperation, "don't let it happen to me! Let my baby be born, healthy . . . perfect. But not here, God, not here!"

Two more days passed. It was clear now, to everyone, that Mary could endure no more. She lay—Kezzie reported from time to time, her blue eyes dull in her weary face—as one dead, all labor seemingly at a standstill after days of sweat and strain. An occasional movement indicated the baby still lived.

"The doctor," Sophia insisted, "can't he do something?"

"The doctor!" Kezzie half spat. "He's worse than nothin'! He thrusts that dirty paw of his into her from time to time—with the entire bunch of people leaning over their bunks and watchin'. He sort of clucks, and shakes his head, and growls aboot the unwashed masses that breed like flies. He's always drunk, Mum! There's an auld grandmither down there, and she's the main help we've got. She and I bathe Mary's face, wipe up the . . . the blood—" Kezzie cast an apologetic glance at Sophia, "and try and force a little soup doon her whenever we can. Oh, Mum—" Kezzie's iron nature crumbled, and her small frame shook with sobs.

Though Kezzie's apron was soiled, and though there was a strong unpleasant odor emanating from her, Sophia put her arms around her serving woman. "We'll have to move her up here, Kezzie. Now dry your tears and—"

"Oh, Mrs. Hugh, Mum, the doctor won't allow it. He thinks steerage people aren't human, somehow. He'll forbid it, I know he will."

"We'll see about that," Sophia said firmly. "He'll have to deal with me."

Sophia was reaching for her capacious cloak, fastening it around her swollen figure.

"Oh, Mum—you mustn't!"

"Nonsense, Kezzie. I'm going down there immediately."

"But Mum! Mr. Hugh—hasna he forbidden you to go down below?"

"This is an emergency, Kezzie. He couldn't possibly object if he knew just how serious matters are down there. Now you get my bed ready, and we'll have Mary up here right away."

Still Kezzie hesitated, though a ray of hope lit her tired face.

"Those steps, Mum—you'll be careful?"

"Of course. Now get prepared for Mary."

Sophia hesitated only fractionally at the gaping companion-way, more from the stench that rose from its dark depths than anything else. Then, gathering up the folds of her cloak with one hand, she reached for the railing with the other and began a careful descent.

It was the stench that was her undoing. Feeling as if she were about to gag, Sophia loosed her hand from the rail and put it over her nose. And then it was a combination of things—coming from bright sunlight into darkness, a fold of her cloak tangling itself in her feet, and, lastly, the slickness of the steps.

With a host of white faces staring up at her out of the dark, her two hands automatically flung out before her, and with her dark cloak billowing out behind, Sophia resembled nothing so much as a huge bat as for a split second she seemed to hang suspended between the light and the dark. With a crash she landed, face down and spread-eagled much like a diver doing a belly flop, all breath gone and nothing but one massive bolt of agony spiraling her off into darkness and silence.

Sophia awoke in her own bed and in more pain than she could have imagined. If she could have blinked out into unconsciousness again, she would have gladly. How odd it was to listen to a piercing shriek and know it to be yours, yet have the sensation it was a thing apart, with a mind of its own.

Hugh's face with its thin nose, high forehead, and deepset eyes, hung over the bed with an expression that frightened her. Grim, that's what it was. Was she in that much danger? Or—heaven forbid—was Hugh angry?

"Hush now," he was saying firmly. "If you cooperate, it will soon be over and you'll have our son in your arms."

Cooperate? How could she even listen when searing pain was tearing at her loins and gouging at her back? Hazily she felt Kezzie's hand on her forehead but had no time to wonder about Mary and her condition except to think *Is this what it's all been about?* and to dimly regret she hadn't been concerned for poor Mary from the beginning of her labor.

Across her vision floated the bulbous nose and ruddy complexioned face of the ship's doctor. Was it . . . could it be . . . or was it distortion of the light . . . but was that a *drop* on the end of the vein-marked nose? Surely this was a nightmare from which she would soon awaken!

"When is the child due?" the gravelly voice was asking.

"We were told we had plenty of time to make land," Hugh explained shortly, obviously as repelled as was Sophia and yet caught in their need of his services. "But, as you know, we're considerably overdue on that. I'd say it's her time or near it."

Hugh swung his inquiring gaze to Kezzie, who nodded her affirmation.

"What was she going down there for, anyway?" the doctor growled.

"On an errand of mercy, I believe," Hugh spoke sharply. "She was concerned—we're all concerned—for Mary Morrison. What seems to be the trouble down there, Doctor?"

"No trouble," the man reported quickly. "Woman just keeps going to sleep, won't work at the job properly. If she'd only cooperate—"

Kezzie's quivering, indrawn breath was enough for her Mr. Hugh. "When we're done here, Doctor, I want you to get back down there and take care of that situation. Understood?"

Sophia, weary of the talk, thought wildly, *Let the wretch get on down there and keep his hands off me and my child.*

Unspoken in words, the thought was expressed by a wild shriek that was half despair, half fury. Fury for Hugh, for Mary, for herself, and especially for the bumbling man of medicine whose bloated face hung over her and whose hot hands fumbled at her body.

"Get him out of here!" she hissed, threshing her arms and legs and remembering Kezzie's report of the man's intimate examination of the inert Mary.

"Hush now," Hugh said again, soothingly.

"I'll not!" And Sophia's voiced objections grew in vigor and clarity. "Kezzie shall care for me! Get that creature away from me!"

"Sophia," Hugh said, his lips only inches from her ear, "Kezzie has the responsibility of Mary—"

"Well, let this idiot get below to Mary! I want none of him. Kezzie—"

"I'm here, Missy," Kezzie's instant response brought the first quiet to Sophia's wild eyes and arching back. "It'll go better, Mrs. Hugh, and faster, if you'll just not fight it. Now—that's it . . . relax between times. . . ."

Hugh was handing the doctor his bag and turning him toward the door, speaking to him in a low voice, nodding toward the bed, taking out his watch and looking at it, and eventually turning back to the bed.

"This is no place for you, Mr. Hugh," Kezzie said. "We'll get along fine, now."

"But Mary," Hugh said with concern. "You'll need to be with Mary."

"She has Angus, and he'll send for me if I'm wanted. If you'll step in here occasionally, Mr. Hugh, I'll take a run doon there. Now ge' along wi' ye!" Kezzie was in charge of her Mr. Hugh, as she had been when he was a small child. That it brought relief to him seemed obvious; Hugh took a deep breath, smiled at his old nurse gratefully, and made his way to the bar and the slow passing of time throughout a long evening and into the night.

Kezzie battled as fiercely as did Sophia. Having heard her beloved Mr. Hugh's muttered words to his wife and knowing how much having a child of his own meant to him, she gave herself, as always, to fulfilling his wishes. *He should have his child, even at the cost of her own daughter's pain and suffering, if need be.* It was a wrenching thought, but not arguable; her years of service and accountability to the Galloway family were part of her very fiber.

But hasty trip after hasty trip to the dark hold below brought Kezzie, white-faced and trembling, back to her mistress's side. Sophia was resting more comfortably between pains, due to the laudanum Hugh had asked of the doctor.

"Take some of it to Mary," Hugh urged on one occasion when he had been with Sophia while Kezzie was absent, and noting the old attendant's anguished face when she returned.

"'Twouldn't do any good, Mr. Hugh," Kezzie said, sighing. "She couldn't swallow it. She just lies there like she's dead, except she breathes slowly and lightly. Looks like the baby is not going to be born at all. Looks like," Kezzie's eyes filled with tears, "we'll lose them both."

"Kezzie," Hugh exclaimed, "we can't just sit by and let that happen! That doctor will just have to do something!"

"He looks in once in a while, that's all."

"I'll see to it," Hugh Galloway said, and when Hugh Galloway spoke with that imperious tone of authority, lesser beings could but obey. Kezzie had no doubt the doctor would descend to the side of her daughter. But would he be sober, and would he, could he, at this juncture, be of any help?

When an urgent knock came on the cabin door, Kezzie opened it to find a shaken Angus.

"Can you come?" he asked simply.

"Go find Mr. Hugh," Kezzie responded immediately. "As soon as he gets here, I'll come."

Angus disappeared on the run.

Kezzie reached her daughter's side to find the doctor rolling up his sleeves, wiping his sweaty face with his hands, and drying his palms on his soiled breeches. He threw back the blanket and bent to his task. Kezzie knelt and cradled the head of the unconscious woman in her arms. Unconscious or already dead, for Mary's head lolled with the doctor's savaging of her body, and her hand remained limp in Angus's grip.

Like a rag doll she was tossed about as the doctor struggled by sheer muscle power to wrench the living child from the dead or dying womb. Torn free at last, the bloody scrap was all but tossed Kezzie's way.

Sympathetic hands held out a blanket, and Kezzie wrapped the baby in it even as the doctor was pulling a blanket up over the face of Mary, wiping his hands on the corner of it before he let it go.

The baby clutched to her, Kezzie fled the scene. Inside the Galloway cabin, leaning for a moment, white of face, on the door at her back, it was to find herself thrust into another birth scene, for Sophia was groaning and pushing, obviously swept into the bearing-down contractions from which there was no escape. Mr. Hugh's face lifted to Kezzie with relief, only to blanch at the spectacle: Kezzie in disarray and blood-spattered, a stained bundle in her arms.

Somewhat dazedly, Kezzie laid the newborn aside and turned her attention to the woman on the bed. Sophia's face was red, her eyes were screwed shut, and from her twisted mouth issued animal-like sounds as her body made its decision to expel its temporary inhabitant.

"I'll take over from here," Kezzie said briefly, and Mr. Hugh made a hasty and obviously glad escape.

So busy was Kezzie for the next half hour that she had no time to give to the grief that waited, just outside the door of her heart, ready to rip and rend, as the invading fingers of the brutal doctor had ripped and torn at the flesh of her only child. Nor was there time for her grandchild, except to take a rag and wipe mucous and blood from the tiny face.

Though to Kezzie it seemed but a few minutes, enough time elapsed for Hugh Galloway to make another check on the situation. He could see immediately that the birth was imminent. But his attention was caught by the small, blanket-wrapped figure on top of the goods in an open steamer trunk where Kezzie had laid it. Struck, perhaps, by the coincidence of two births, he leaned over the baby, and before hurrying to the head of the bed, Hugh touched the thatch of black hair that even as it dried, showed evidence of a curl, and caressed the soft cheek.

Sophia, caught in the desperate toils of nature's relentlessness, could no more have stemmed the forces at work in her body than to hold back the tide itself, and knew not, or cared, that Hugh was present. The indignity of the moment was beyond concern. Like an animal caught in a trap, she fought to be free.

Kezzie watched the crowning, the emergence of the narrow shoulders, and with the slippery rush of expulsion, reached, and caught her Mr. Hugh's own child. Another Galloway. Another favored and blessed human for whom life would be generous in a world of deprivation and cruel want; gentle, when to the masses it was harsh and uncaring. Blessed, favored baby.

Gasping, sobbing with a sound between relief and joy, Sophia fell back in Hugh's arms, only dimly aware that Kezzie was giving the baby rigorous spanks, eventually clearing its breathing passages, wiping it, wrapping it in a blanket.

"Oh," Sophia was crying with relief. "It's over . . . it's over, and my baby . . . give me my baby!"

"It'll be a moment, Mum," Kezzie spoke from the other side of the cabin.

"What is it, Hugh?" Sophia asked, turning her splotched face up to her husband.

"Why—a boy," Hugh responded, tenderly smoothing the tumbled hair. "Am I right, Kezzie?"

Kezzie was a moment in answering. In a daze of weariness and tears she looked down, down on two faces wrinkled and red, two heads misshapen from difficult births, two heads covered with black hair, bloody and matted. Gently she touched a small hand of each.

"Kezzie?"

Drawing a deep and quavering breath, "Girl, Mr. Hugh," Kezzie said. "It's a girl."

"Oh, Hugh!" Sophia said. "It doesn't matter!"

Hugh cradled his wife, eyes on his old nurse. "Did you say girl, Kezzie?" he asked over Sophia's head.

Kezzie turned and faced him, her eyes ablaze in the half light. "It's a girl, Mr. Hugh."

With a soft touch of her lips to the forehead of each child, Kezzie took up the softly mewing baby, walked to the bed and the man she adored and served, and laid the small bundle in his arms.

Blinded with tears, Kezzie watched as her Mr. Hugh studied the small face, then, turning his attention to the expectant face of his wife, transferred the child into her waiting arms.

"Here, my dear," Hugh said gently, "is your child."

5

From weakness or happiness, perhaps a bit of both, Sophia's tears ran down her face, spotting the clean gown Kezzie had put on her after sponging her weary, wracked body. Kezzie had also bathed the baby and dressed her in clothes dredged from the depths of the trunk, clothes they had been assured would not be needed "aboard ship."

But now it was over. Her child was here, *safely* here, she added, giving a thought to poor Mary. A euphoria never known in all her life flooded Sophia's heart. Turning back the blanket she let her hungry eyes feast on the tiny face and dark patch of hair, and she caressed the perfect wee hands that tended to wave aimlessly in their first taste of freedom.

Hugh stood silently looking down on the wrapped baby still in the steamer trunk. Too still, it was. Too silent.

"Dead." Hugh's eyes misted; his gaze went from the dead infant to the live one, safe and loved in Sophia's arms.

"Did it live at all, Kezzie?" he asked softly.

"Never took a breath, Mr. Hugh." Kezzie stood by her Mr. Hugh, also weeping. In an unexpected gesture Hugh Galloway put his arm around his loved nurse, and together they mourned the passing of one they had not known, would never know.

"Both gone," Kezzie said in a thick voice. "Mother and babe. It's just as well, Mr. Hugh. If Mary had to go, it's just as well the wee'un went with her."

"Poor Angus," Hugh said feelingly, glancing again at the contented scene just a few feet away where Sophia was crooning words of love to the child snuggled against her breast.

"He has Molly and Cammie," Kezzie answered quickly. "Dinna forget that. And that's all and more he'll be able to manage."

"Kezzie, I release you to go with him to the frontier. You'll be needed there even more than with us."

"Never, Mr. Hugh!" Kezzie said with such passion that Hugh blinked. "My place is here—with Mrs. Hugh and the bairn."

"Think about it," Hugh urged kindly. "Now, what will we do about this little man?" And he indicated the dead babe.

"It's . . . it's a girl, sir."

"A girl, Kezzie?"

"My Mary," Kezzie said steadily, "gave birth to a girl."

"Ah, yes, and Angus helped deliver it." And Mr. Hugh turned from the small body, adding, with a sigh, "You take care of it, won't you? Take him . . . her into your room, perhaps, and prepare it for burial."

"With Mary."

"Yes, with Mary. That way," Hugh finished with a broken note in the usually brisk voice, "it won't have the journey alone."

Sophia was dozing, and Hugh was wondering if he could escape the cramped quarters when Kezzie returned, the dead child sweet and clean in some of the Galloway selection of infant clothes and wrapped in a white blanket.

"You feel free to go, Mr. Hugh," she said, interpreting Hugh's indecision and knowing him well. "Mrs. Hugh will be fine for a while. I think," her eyes dropped to the waxy face in her arms, "this wee bairn should be in its mother's arms. I'll go now and prepare my Mary for . . . for burial." The wrinkled face sagged suddenly, and the eyes, blue beyond believing and no whit faded by age, filled with tears. Kezzie's last few incredible hours told on her at last.

"I'll go with you, Kezzie," Hugh said. "Let me carry the bairn. I need to have a few minutes with Angus, puir mon."

The transfer was made; Hugh and Kezzie closed the door behind them and turned toward the tragedy below, expecting to double it by the addition of the dead infant.

The Morrison bunk had been shut from public view by kindly loaned and hung blankets. Pulling them aside, Hugh and Kezzie were unprepared for the face Angus lifted to them from the bedside. It was ablaze with hope.

Angus on one side and an elderly woman on the other, Mary's wasted limbs were being massaged. Though her eyes were closed, there was a faint tinge of color in the sunken cheeks.

"Mary—" Kezzie stammered. "But I thought—"

"We all did," Angus almost sang. "I know the doctor thought her gone. It was while I was clasping her in my arms . . . speaking her name. . . ." Angus broke down. The strong face, ravaged by the last few days' despair, was run with rivulets of tears, which he let flow freely, unashamed of his sorrow or his blessed relief.

He turned momentarily from his ministrations, which were apparently meant to stimulate blood flow and were possibly all he knew to do.

"Mrs. Simms," and Angus indicated the woman still working over the prostrate form, "cleaned her up, and we've changed the blankets—"

"We know she's no' dead," the old midwife said. "An' that's a' we need to keep us workin'. More warm oil, Libby."

"The bleeding has stopped, all thanks to God. And none to the doctor," Angus said, and who could blame him for sounding bitter, even outraged.

Cameron and Molly crept from the shadows where they had been restrained by kind hands, and Angus gathered them into his arms.

Peering at his mother, Cameron asked, "What's wrong, Da? Why is Mum so still?"

"She's tired, Cammie, very tired. Just be patient; be a good boy a little longer. She'll be fine; you'll see."

Angus spoke with an assurance he could not have felt, but it satisfied the children. Holding them over Mary, Angus allowed them each a kiss to the white cheeks.

"That'll be just the medicine she needs," he said and set them on their feet and sent them off into the shadows again to the caring family who tended them.

"We're going up, Da," Cameron called back, excitement in his voice. It had been a nightmare, in the ship's bowels, that none of them would forget, even the young. A breath of fresh air on deck was a rare and treasured happening.

All this while Kezzie seemed as one in a daze, standing beside Hugh with the baby in his arms.

"Kezzie," Angus said now, with concern. "You look ill . . . very ill. But," his voice lifted, "isn't it marvelous? Our Mary—" His voice broke.

"It's wonderful!" Kezzie whispered through trembling lips. "If I'd only known! Oh, Angus," Kezzie's eyes were tragic in her white face, "her baby . . . oh, Angus—"

"What about the baby, Kezzie?" Angus turned eyes clouding with apprehension on Hugh and the blanket in his arms.

"The baby . . . oh, Angus, the baby is dead!"

At the brief committal that consigned the Morrison baby to the ocean depths, Hugh stood shoulder to shoulder with Angus, longtime friend and faithful retainer. Heatherstone, Scotland, would be the poorer without Angus's services; Heatherstone, Canada, would be the poorer for never having had them.

Here, in this inbetween place aboard ship, in the middle of the ocean, between countries, Hugh fancied he had already glimpsed the equality that was to mark their relationship from this time on. Angus continued his polite deference to his former master, but his innate politeness and good manners would dictate that. There was no obsequiousness, but then, there had never been the rank-and-file lick-spittle service from Angus as from others of his rank; from the beginning Angus had been different. It was that difference that Hugh's father had noticed, and being a kindly man as well as a wise one, had turned it to the advantage of Heatherstone, as well as to Angus himself.

Angus was an educated man. In him was the mix of the master and the menial, the liege lord and the laborer. And in him the one would not have to be sacrificed to the other. Angus would suffer hardship and hard work, but in it he would be in control and maintain a quiet air of confidence. As a first-generation Canadian Angus would be the perfect model, for in him would be the blend of the gentle, fine ways of culture and the daring, grit, and stamina of the pioneer.

In a way, Hugh envied Angus. But Hugh knew his place, and it was not on the frontier of the northwest. Even so, the new land and the new ways gave him the liberty he needed, and he was, in his own way, as liberated as Angus.

Kezzie, standing with her arms around Cameron and Molly, was straight-backed and dry-eyed. Hugh watched her and felt an admiration for his old nurse. Whatever grieving she had done, she had put it behind her. Nevertheless, to Hugh she appeared shrunken, and her eyes, though dry, were full of pain. The children, huddled against her side, were swept up in the final stages of a drama that left them uneasy and wondering.

Angus, having faced his loss and found it not as heavy as thought at first, was comforted by the fact that, with care and patience, his wife would survive. In her bunk below, Mary hardly understood the day's significance and dozed fitfully under the laudanum Hugh had insisted the doctor make available to her.

Sophia, of course, was bedfast, murmuring over her little Margaret Lorena, a name she had promptly produced and which Hugh surmised she had chosen long, long ago, perhaps in dreams of just such a time as this. Her joy, as well as her recovery, could not be compromised by a trip out on deck, with its accompanying heartrending sight of the canvas bundle slid so mercilessly into the sea. As a star is lost in the endless expanse of the sky, so the tiny body was swallowed up in the vast reaches of the sea. But the One who counted the stars and called them each by name was the One who also measured the waters in the hollow of His hand, and He knew the resting place of the small nameless one and would call her forth on that great reunion morning.

This Hugh understood only dimly from his stiff, limited, formal religious training. But now it served to comfort him. That it might comfort Angus, who had always been what was called a "God-fearing" man, he was quite sure.

When the rites were completed, Angus stepped to the side of his wife's mother and murmured, "You've overdone yourself. Come, Mam, leave the bairns to these good ladies, and ge' yoursel' back to your bed and hae a guid rest." Angus's tender words, spoken in the old familiar fashion, turned Kezzie from her study of the empty waves. For once Kezzie listened and followed her Mr. Hugh without argument.

Someone had Molly by the hand, and Angus put his hand on Cameron's shoulder, turning toward the companionway that led to their quarters below.

Cameron, an outdoor boy and losing color from the molelike existence of the past weeks, momentarily resisted Angus's urging away from the sunshine and fresh air to the dismal hole. Angus, though preoccupied with Mary's need of him, recognized the brief hesitation in the boy's stride.

Lifting the boy in his arms, Angus turned to the rail, and together they watched the waves rise and fall, noting the white wake that indicated that they were, at last, making time toward land, and sanity.

Finally, with the child's arms around his neck and the soft cheek pressing his own rough one, Angus hugged Cameron and turned to the ladderlike stairway where Sophia had fallen and which was still just as sticky and hazardous.

Cameron's brief resistance had ended. Young as he was he seemed to know the uselessness of it. Angus recognized the submission that marked the oppressed—those who had few if any rights and were considered inferior in all ways to their "betters"— and ground his teeth, hating the subservience in the boy even as he had always hated and fought against the same trait in himself.

Downtrodden people the world around were catching a glimpse of a better way and, no matter the cost, were following that glimpse. If there was a gleam, for Angus, it was no other than northern lights. To some, their eerie display was equated with the supernatural, somehow, and was unsettling in their strange beauty. To Angus they served as a beacon which, never having seen, he followed.

"Just a little longer, laddie," he murmured into Cameron's ear as, carefully, he made his descent. Fiercely, silently, he promised the boy that he should grow up free. Free to be an equal, to lift his head and look all men in the eye; to say "no" when "yes, sir" was expected; to arrive at his destination in life, be it success or failure, by his own choice. He, Angus, would suffer the present indignities gladly, to pass this on to his children. Angus could see the light, and it was sweet. For himself, and for Cameron, he would do what was necessary. It was enough to keep him putting one foot ahead of the other, down, down . . .

From the dark depths he looked up, up to the patch of blue sky, the light, and breathed out his promise and his prayer.

"Tomorrow, please, God—Bliss!"

Canada—1878

Early reports hadn't been favorable to the settling of the Canadian northwest. The "Emigrant's Guide" featured a sketch of Jack Frost bundled in furs and wearing snowshoes, nipping the nose of a nattily dressed man wearing a top hat and bearing a backpack marked "silk stockings, kid gloves." A bird flew overhead quacking "Who's a goose now?" while a wolf snapped at the man's slipper-clad heels. Stuck in heaped snowbanks were signs reading "Travelers taken and done for," "Fine land for turnips if you can plough it," and "Fine grassland 3000 feet below the surface of the snow."

No matter. Men, whether fools or heroes, persisted in daring the elements and the unknown and made their way west. From them word trickled out and around the world. The sound of their footsteps—whispering through prairie grasses and muted by dense forests—would swell, over time, to the tramp of hundreds of thousands of determined homesteaders who would tune their ears, and eventually their hearts, and rise up and follow.

And, for those with the listening ear and the brave heart, there was excitement and music and breathtaking beauty.

One's blood stirred at the pounding thunder of buffalo hoofs; wild geese calling in a vast blue sky was music set to beauty; a lark's song, high and piercing at dawn, was the sweetest of sounds. Endless vistas of prairie grass bending in the wind was an awesome sight. One could grow heady with breathing deeply of the unique fragrances of a land untainted by anything more than the smoke of a campfire. Sunsets were glorious beyond capturing on canvas.

The sight of cowbirds riding the rumps of horses, picking off gadflies, was enough to keep one entertained through a day's travel; the crack of a rifle on the still air and the bounty it assured were sources of satisfaction. The chickadee's cheerfulness touched the coldest day with charm, and the grinding of ice as it broke in the rivers in spring was as welcome as a royal parade.

Wrap a man in an unbelievably light, warm robe made of two hundred or so unsplit rabbit skins fastened head to tail, lay him beside a fire of poplar wood with a bowlful of stars tipped overhead, and you had one supremely contented and cozy individual.

Indians, when encountered, were sociable. They gathered wherever men congregated, along with the whiskey-jack looking for food. True, the Métis, people of mixed blood, were showing signs of discontent, which caused some unease but which was largely overlooked by the land-hungry immigrant. Trouble, brewing off and on for some years, was downplayed, and immigrants, like Angus Morrison, were assured that the area was under firm control. There was no hesitation in his decision to head for Prince Albert and Bliss.

George Bliss, Angus had been informed, was an early settler in an outlying district, and as the homesteads adjacent to his were under consideration, the area was referred to as, simply, Bliss. Many had reason to find it otherwise, for it was as plagued with problems, as say, Pile of Bones, which for obvious reasons was eventually named Regina. But Bliss had its allurements, being in the bush country, which appealed to Angus as to others who shuddered at the endless blankness of the lonesome plains.

Mary had regained her health before the Morrisons made the decision to push on; the season for travel was short, and they would need to locate and build a shelter before winter made many things impossible.

The farewell with Kezzie was hard.

"Are you sure you don't want to come, Mam?" Angus asked one last time, knowing the trip would be difficult, yet letting Mary's mother know she was welcome in his home and in his plans.

"Na, na," Kezzie said firmly. "My place is here with Mr. Hugh . . . and the bairn."

"It won't be long until the railway will extend up that way, I'm sure," Hugh consoled them both. "And then you can visit back and forth."

So Angus and Mary contented themselves, said farewell, and went by Grand Trunk Railway and Morgan Central to Milwaukee, and from there to St. Boniface, Manitoba. Here they crossed the Red River by ferry, reaching Fort Garry and the jumping off place for the long haul to Prince Albert.

Prince Albert was a community of growing importance for the homesteaders slowly filtering north. Here, beyond the vast, stretching plains of the south they came to settle in the park belt and on the fringe of the forest belt. Norwegians and Finns, Orkneymen and Highlanders, Europeans and a few Asians—adventurers all, settling here and to the south. New Stockholm came into being, and the Icelandic settlement Thingvalla; Romanians came and built the first Romanian Orthodox Church in North America. Hungarians, under Count d'Esterhazy, settled at Kaposvar . . . the Austrians named their new home Ebenezer . . . and on and on it went across the Northwest Territories.

The usual mode of travel was the Red River cart. Before its raucous *skreek-skrawk* faded forever from the northwest, it would have been in use one hundred years. While the buffalo were plentiful, the Métis formed trains of hundreds of carts, trailing their trading goods across the prairie, carts screeching to high heaven and raising a veritable storm of dust. Immigrants had been quick to see the cart's advantages. It was light and strong, could carry up to a ton of goods and, with wheels removed, it floated like a raft. And repairs were as available as the nearest tree—it was made entirely of wood.

Mary was appalled by the shriek of the cart, and Cammie and Molly always covered their ears.

"Why does it make such a horrendous noise?" Mary asked one day. "It sounds like a lost soul wandering through—well, it does!"

Angus laughed. "Think of it as prairie music," he said, and he pointed out the cart's advantages to her and the children, who approached the man-made monster as though it were a being ready to leap on them at any moment.

"For one thing, repairs are possible. If we have a breakdown, let's hope it's near a tree. Then all we need are a few tools, like an axe, a knife, and maybe a drill."

"Still, why the racket?"

"The axles are wood, of course, and so are the wheels. Dust gets in the wheels, and if they were greased they'd just gum up, so the hubs are left dry."

"And we put up with that."

"'Fraid so. But look—the two-wheel design reduces chances of bogging down . . . it can be drawn by one animal . . . and oh, there are numerous advantages to it. You'll see."

"I'm afraid so," Mary said doubtfully and studied less critically the general all-purpose vehicle of transportation on which Cammie, all hesitation dispelled, was clambering, with Molly not far behind.

When Angus said wood, he meant all of it. Their entire rig was joined by wooden pegs; some others, Angus reported, were joined with rawhide or shaganappi thongs.

"Then, if we broke down," Mary said with a twinkle, "we'd have to hope we were near a cow."

Angus gave her a hug, partly affection, partly relief. Mary would adjust—she was as dedicated to the idea of becoming a homesteader as he was.

"These wheels," Angus pointed out, "are six feet high, and deeply dished. See, they have twelve spokes fixed into holes in the rim—"

"Which is all wood, has no grease, and is never going to let us forget it."

"It won't be a silent passage, that's for sure," Angus admitted. "Especially if we are fortunate enough to get in with a caravan."

"Oh, I do hope so," Mary said fervently, reluctant to cross the wilderness alone.

While travel by oxen was slower, it was Angus's decision to purchase them for their transport; Angus was informed that, though slow and difficult, they could live off the land while horses required grain to supplement the grass that was bountiful but not enough, by itself, to maintain vigor and health.

Rates by water were high—freight was fourteen and a half cents a pound. Angus figured carefully, shipping only the basic farm equipment and packing on the carts their household goods as well as the smaller tools and enough food to see them to Prince Albert. At the last he invested in a buggy and a horse. Without them Mary and the children would walk most of the way, and Mary, though gaining, should not be tested so cavalierly.

Three carts, three oxen, a buggy and mare, and a cow tied behind—that was the array that joined the group ready to start up the trail, scorning the prairies and setting their sights and their hopes on the fertile belt that was known as "the bush."

That first evening on the trail, by the campfire, sore, dusty, but well-fed and safe, Mary wrote her mother.

Dear Mam:

We started rather early this morning with the children excited, the animals much less so, and Angus in great good humor. Thirty carts travel with us. The sky, though big, is not big enough to contain the sound of these greaseless wheels. I suppose I shall get used to it.

I'm so grateful for the buggy. Of course I had to hold the horse in, even stopping at times to allow for the slower progress of the oxen, which everyone in this caravan uses. We were on the trail about three hours when one cart broke an axle. The owner, a Mr. Parkey (although it could be Parki, or Parkee, or!), sent his son back to Fort Carlton for a new one. This slowed us considerably, but the boy joined us just a few minutes ago, the axle tied to the back of the riding horse they fortunately had brought along. The Parkey children took turns riding it, until, that is, the breakdown. Then, turn by turn, I tried to give the littlest ones a ride. One woman, I believe her name is Mrs. Swart, is far along in her time, and I only hope we make it to civilization before the child is born. Nightmares of those days on board ship often haunt me. She, as most others, walks rather than endure the rigors of the carts. The noise of these contraptions makes one's blood run cold, and the severe jolting one endures in them shakes one's very bones. In spite of it all we made 12 miles today and should do better many days.

We did not have to dismantle the carts and float them over water today; all our lakes and rivers were shallow. I expect when we do and I see my little Molly afloat, I shall struggle with the images I cannot help but conjure up occasionally of my precious baby, set adrift and so alone in the waters of the Atlantic.

8

Sophia turned herself critically before the handsome gold and white French mirror that had been hung in her boudoir and could find no fault with it, and very little with herself.

Hugh had been mistaken when he implied that Toronto styles would be out of date. Eaton, that estimable merchant, did his overseas buying personally and from the best European manufacturers. His goods, readily available in the Toronto store, were thoroughly up-to-date.

Little Margaret Lorena was just a few months old, and already Sophia's waist could be cinched in to the required eighteen inches. In attendance that morning, Kezzie frowned and pursed her lips even as she laid out the new corset.

"Oh, come, Kezzie," Sophia said, noting the disapproval, "it isn't all that painful, you know."

"It isna natural," Kezzie maintained, adding darkly, "and you willna be able to eat a bite."

The corset's iron grip molded Sophia's figure into an hourglass shape, the approved look of the day. Always previously fortified with whalebone, corset stays made of plant fiber had been substituted by a Dr. Warner. "A reward of ten dollars will be made," the good doctor promised, "for every strip of Coraline that breaks with four months' ordinary wear." With more pleasure than usual, Sophia reached for the "Fancy Four-Hook Summer Corset" with heliotrope bands (blue and pink had also been available), which supposedly not only added elegance but strengthened the corset as well. Surely this garment would be less constricting.

There was a rising tide of alarm, among some parents, that motherhood for the next generation was in jeopardy due to the corset. If a girl survived croup, which was treated by a poultice of mashed and roasted onions and hot skunk or goose oil, if she survived acne treated by acid nitrate, if applied spiderwebs successfully stopped bleeding from childhood injuries, and if the boiling of toads with tincture of arnica and butter had cured her of any rheumatism or sprains, she might still succumb to the grip of a corset that crushed her lungs and other internal, important, if unnamed, organs.

Sophia sighed; there were so many things to worry about! She wanted to give Hugh the son he longed for, and in spite of the necessity to be a slave to fashion, wondered about the corset and its effects.

Today Sophia chose cashmere stockings rather than balbriggan, and when they were on, reached for the first of the four petticoats that were the prescribed proper wear.

Wondering if she would ever become used to the luxury of dressing elegantly, Sophia ran her hand appreciatively over the taffeta silk waist Kezzie held out to her. Of royal blue, its inlaid front was of white silk and intricately tucked and trimmed with fancy embroidered gimp. The sleeves were tucked ten times, and the French back had five rows of tucking.

"You've heard the criticism, Mum," Kezzie reminded Sophia as she helped her into her skirt, "about all these clothes slung from the waist rather than the shoulders." Kezzie's decent white underslip hung from the shoulders, as did her white uniform.

Only her umbrella drawers hung from the waist, and only she knew that these featured a cluster of three tucks above the two-inch hem and that they were a great satisfaction to her.

"All this constriction about the waist, Mum," Kezzie continued, "isna natural. Hopeful mothers—"

"Well, everyone's doing it," Sophia answered, "and I don't see the population declining."

Nevertheless, all this worrisome consideration about such a simple and natural matter as having a baby threatened to dim the day, one of very few spent with Hugh, and Sophia turned her attention firmly to finishing her toilette. "Crepons have been all the go for the past season and they are the same again this year," had been the fashion note that persuaded her into the purchase of the royal blue skirt of crepon cloth. A little over three yards wide, lined with percaline and interlined with crinoline and bound with velvet around the bottom, it had double seams in front and featured the new bulge in the back. From the narrow waist it blossomed out like a bell from the force of the four petticoats beneath.

Seated at last before the mirror, Sophia allowed Kezzie to settle on her piled hair a modish black velvetta hat. Its straight brim was raised jauntily on one side over a bandeau of purple violets; two long jetted coques in plume fashion were set in a low, broad effect around the crown and finished with a knot formed of blue taffeta silk and velvetta. A long, jet stickpin was used, finally, to pass through the knot and secure the entire structure firmly in place.

Completely covered from head to toe, Sophia epitomized the woman of the seventies. Only an appearance on the beach allowed for the baring of the arm. So far Sophia had bypassed the out-and-out wearing of the bustle; to date her clothes simply reflected its emergence. To be properly proper, she admitted now, with another sigh, she would have to conform, and soon. Hopefully Hugh, waiting below, would not frown when she appeared. Though he said little in the way of criticism, his frown was enough to give Sophia the guidance she needed to fit into the lifestyle of Heatherstone.

Taking up her gloves—no lady of any consequence would appear on the street without them—Sophia perused her reflection in the mirror. Her eyes sparkled; she was a vision of elegance with no expense spared. She laid aside her trifling troubles and counted her blessings: a beautiful child asleep upstairs; a house of magnificent proportions and detail; a distinguished husband awaiting her.

"Will you and Tessie be taking Margaret out today?" she asked Kezzie before putting her anxieties completely out of mind.

"No, Mum, not today; Tessie will be goin' out. 'Tis the day of her husband's company picnic," Kezzie said. "The brass finishers, Mum, and the plumbers and the steamfitters, all havin' one grand day of it."

"Do you wish you could go, Kezzie?" Sophia asked, although it was a little late to do so.

"No, Mum. I'm happy as a lark here with the bairn."

Sophia knew it was true. Kezzie, she admitted, had more time with Margaret than she did. After all her yearning and longing, the never-ending tasks associated with a child were more than Sophia had bargained for. And so she was contented, perhaps even relieved, when Hugh had insisted that Kezzie be given responsibility for the baby. "After all," he had pointed out, "she's had lots of practice. I turned out all right, didn't I? I guess she can look after the child without any difficulty."

Though it was a time of great wickedness, most people still held firmly to fixed doctrines (or biases) that had been well established long ago and were not about to be relinquished here in the new land. It was a strongly religious time, with the day of rest strictly observed. Camp meetings ran for weeks; religion took on the form of recreation. Canadians were gripped with the need for revival, and churches flourished.

Circuit riders abounded, and the pleasures of sin were exposed mercilessly. But it was an era of drunkenness; whiskey was sold by the dipperful at the cost of a few cents, and saloons and taverns did a landslide business. Men made shameful displays of themselves as they staggered from bar to bar; often they ended up in the gutter for all passersby to see, perhaps stumble over. To think of her precious child surrounded by such debauchery gave Sophia's heart a twinge. It was a strong argument in favor of adopting the wearing of the blue ribbon that distinguished the abstainer.

And she should think about joining the small, concerned groups beginning to do something about the high infant mortality rate—everyone knew that half of the dead were children. Was it possible that the milk delivered to the door daily was the cause of it? Often it had the taste of wild turnips or stinkweed. Montreal's water, when it was analyzed, showed "animal and vegetable refuse, manure, fish spawn, straw, hayseed, and a small cistoid worm." Could Toronto's be any better?

To suffer what she did aboard ship to bring her child into the world and then to lose her to one of the many ailments that picked children off so quickly—the thought was unendurable. The Galloway cupboard bulged with hyped patent medicines that promised cures for everything from scrofula to cancer. Expectorants, balsams, and bitters—Sophia bought most of them. But to actually swallow them was another thing.

Ayer's Cherry Pectoral, the persuasive vendor had claimed, would cure colds, coughs, and all diseases of the throat and lungs, and was cherry-flavored. That it smelled like alcohol and made her head spin when she tried it caused Sophia to put it at the back of the cupboard for the time being. But when one was desperate to save one's child's life—to what lengths would one go? Very far indeed, she admitted, and she invested in McKenzie's Dead Shot Worm Candy against the possibility of such a problem, common among all children. "Your child will ask for it," the purveyor assured, "because the taste is so pleasant." Could something taste good and be potent at the same time? Or was it just colored water, or almost pure alcohol? Sophia stared at the bottles with their colorful labels and was none the wiser.

Uncertain as she was, just this morning she had bought a bottle of Mrs. Winslow's Soothing Syrup, called by some "gripe water," against the day small Margaret would begin teething. Doing the very best she could, still it felt like groping in the dark. What in the world had people done in the old days, before marvels of modern science such as Hostetter's Stomach Bitters came on the market? Or Warner's Safe Kidney and Liver Cure, Sage's Catarrh Cure, Piso's Consumption Cure? If one suffered from la grippe, malaria, blood poison, rheumatism, or sour stomach, wouldn't one try, from pure desperation, a bottle of Dr. Plew's Microbe Killer?

Having done the best she knew in regard to proper medical care for her child and knowing Margaret would be safe at home with Kezzie, Sophia felt free to go on her outing with a clear conscience.

And so it was without undue guilt she slipped into the nursery, ran her fingers lightly through the silky black tuft of hair on her sleeping daughter's head, and turned toward the graciously appointed room where her husband waited.

In the new land as in the old, Victorian rules and regulations reigned, and one was expected to follow specific guidelines for accepted behavior. Etiquette books advised against "undue emotions whether of laughter, anger, mortification, disappointment, or selfishness." Therefore Hugh, a gentleman through and through, was calmly reading the paper as he waited. No gentleman ever stared at his pocket watch in polite society unless invited to do so, a rule, Sophia felt now, that kept Hugh from such uncouth behavior. And since conversing in loud tones was the mark of an oaf, his tones were mild when he looked up and asked, "Ready, my dear?"

With one quickly stifled thought for the more earthy and virile but gentlemanly (and absent) Angus, it was no effort at all for

Sophia to return her husband's smile. And why not? Dressed in frock coat, double-breasted waistcoat, wing-collared shirt, and striped trousers of excellent cut and material, Hugh was an escort to be proud of. Thank heavens he had no need of a corset!

What a glorious round of entertainment was available! It was a time of beginnings, or "firsts," for the nation: the first organized hockey game, world champion oarsmen, golf club, bicycle club, and intercollegiate football games. Archery, croquet, baseball, yachting—all were available for participation or for spectating.

Lacrosse was billed by some as "Canada's national game," and it was to a special match the Galloways intended going. Pitted against the Canadian team were the famous "Twelve Iroquois Indians" who had played a command performance game before Queen Victoria. Their captain was listed as Tier Karoniare; Sophia found the player's names unpronounceable as well as incomprehensible and much preferred their aliases: Pick the Feather, Hole in the Sky, and more.

Hugh placed Sophia's mantelet of English covert cloth around her shoulders, took his silk hat in hand, and turned toward the door where Casper hovered ready to usher them out to the hansom cab awaiting them. Settling herself comfortably, Sophia wasted a brief moment's thought on her brother—*is Preston as satisfied with his end of the bargain as I?*—and cared not a whit for his satisfaction or lack of it.

With her master and mistress gone and the house quiet around her, Kezzie hastened to the nursery, dismissed the impatient Tessie, picked up her precious charge, changed her napkin, settled in a rocking chair and put in the pink mouth the rubber nipple that, with its sediment of stale, caked milk—and with sterilization unknown—was an almost certain death trap.

Dear Mam: July 5, 1878

Of course there is no place to mail a letter (unless we meet a traveler going back to Fort Garry, and these are few and far between), but I will keep working away as I get a chance, jotting things down to help you understand what this migration is all about. How I wish that, like the children of Israel, our shoes would not wear out! Angus walks most of the way. It would be wonderful, too, if quail (or the local partridge) would rain down upon us every day. Game is plentiful, however, though Angus grieves to see the waste of buffalo. Often they are slain and just the tongue removed. It's counted a great delicacy. The hump, also, provides very fine eating.

One learns to try new things. For instance, Mrs. Varnisch, having stripped the large bone of a hind leg free of all flesh, buried it in the fire, and in about one hour served us a taste of baked marrow. Truly delicious, and a change from rabbit, which seems to be our main bill of fare. That is because the boys of the group love to hunt and often enliven their days with some kind of contest to see who can bring in the most. Cammie begs to go with them, but I cannot allow it. He is much too young, and I fear some terrible accident, or being lost in the grass, or being stolen by an Indian. The very thoughts make me shudder!

July 8—We have barely begun, and already we have had a death. It is Mrs. Swart. All night we could hear the sounds of her suffering, and I suffered with her, you may be sure, with the memory so near of my own recent loss and the terrible agony of that time. They say time makes you forget—pray God I will. To go through so much and have no baby! I yet grieve.

We buried Mrs. Swart and the infant with her. We women washed them both and wrapped them snugly in what Mr. Swart called her "marryin' quilt." Well, it has become her "buryin' quilt." We could hardly bear to watch that poor man, with his two little girls clinging to his trousers, and him shaking and trembling so. The only thing that helped was that we have a man in our group who is a sort of lay preacher. We've never acknowledged his religion any more than to ask him to say grace whenever he is around when we eat—a sort of politeness on our parts, I guess. Well, this Carlton Voss took out his Bible and we all expected the usual ashes to ashes and dust to dust. We'd sung "Nearer My God to Thee," when Mr. Voss read something I've never heard before—all about King

David and his little baby that died, back in the Old Testament. King David said, "I shall go to him, but he shall not return to me." And then Mr. Voss talked about how that babies, being innocent, go straight to be with the Lord, which I guess I knew all along but never got much comfort out of because I never expected to see my dead baby again, me being unfit for heaven and all.

Well, Mr. Voss, right there at that hole we dug in the prairie, said plain as day that we are sorrowful but not as sorrowful as we would be if we had no hope. Hope? I said to myself through my tears—that's what I need. I dug out our old Bible, Mam, and looked up that Scripture, which is First Thess. (too hard to spell, and even harder to find!), chapter 4 verse 13. I'm puzzling on this. Perhaps there will come a day when I can talk to Mr. Voss and get him to explain this hope to me. I need it, Mam, I need it bad.

July 9—Started early today because of the short day yesterday. We ate bannock for breakfast, made quick over the fire, and not exactly as bannock is made in Scotland. Here, if you have baking powder, you add it to the flour along with some lard or grease and a little salt. If you don't have B.P. you go ahead anyway and it turns out flat, but when fried good it tastes well enough. I like it best just to leave the shortening out of the dough and fry it in butter about half an inch thick. It is delicious! Of course I can't see you making it there at Heatherstone.

We are all weary tonight, made about fifteen miles. The two little Swart girls rode with me; they seem so bewildered at leaving their mother back "in the dirt in her blanket." I guess there are worse things than leaving your loved one in the deep, cold depths of the sea. It will always grieve me that I

wasn't there to say farewell to my baby. Did I tell you I
named her? In my heart I call her Angel.

July 12—Had a miserable day. Had to cross creeks twice.
Angus waded in water up to his knees, and, before he had a
chance to dry off, it rained. These trails soon became gumbo
mud! The feet of the oxen and all the stock were soon great
gobs of mud and the wheels of the carts—well! We stopped
early, but could find no dry grass for a fire and were far far
from trees. Angus put up a tarp, and we crowded under it,
tried to change into dry clothes, and ate a cold supper—
leftover bannock again, not nearly so good as it was this
morning when it was hot.

July 15—Before we went on, after the rain, we took time
to dry out our things and let the children run and stretch their
legs. But not too far. You can't imagine what a sea of grass this
is, Mam. It is endless. Once in a while we come across a
settler, and I must say their shelters, which they call soddies,
are pathetic sights, so lonely and small on the big stretches of
land around them. One man charged us a dollar to cross his
land! We made about eight miles today, Angus figures. The
trip, God willing, will take close to fifty-five days or
thereabouts. The more I see of this prairie, the happier I am
that Angus has chosen to go on to the bush country. Trees!
How I long to be among them again.

July 19—Yesterday an old Indian came alongside from
somewhere or other. He seemed to be starving, and so we fed
him. The Indians are pathetic. The Métis, on the other hand,
are proud people but are very restless and discontented. They
see their land being divided and taken from them, and I can
hardly blame them for their unrest. No one wants to be
governed by faraway Ottawa. They have found a leader in a

young half-breed by the name of Louis Riel. Watch for his name, Mam; you will hear of him, I'm sure. The people of the Red River give him much resistance, and there is bitterness and fear in many places. Still, this old Indian was peaceful enough and trudged off across the prairie wrapped in his blanket and bothered us not at all.

Although I haven't had my talk with Carlton Voss (the preacher I told you about), I heard him give a sermon last Sunday. We stop on Sundays, Mam, for most of these people are good, God-fearing folk. Well, Mr. Voss kept using a term I certainly never heard in the kirk back home. It was "born again." You must be born again, he said. Some people were nodding their heads, some said "amen," like they knew what he was talking about. Some people were sort of uneasy. Me—I confess there was something stirring around on my insides like I never had happen before. When the time is right, I'll talk to Angus and see what he makes of it all.

July 21—Days slipping by before I know it, though it seems each one is very long indeed. Today we got a slow start because some of the oxen had strayed away and the boys searched until they found them about four miles away. We passed Portage la Prairie yesterday; saw some wonderful farms near there. We camped near one of them, and they let us have water—good cold water—and we bought fresh milk, our cow barely giving any milk now, probably due to all this walking. Tonight I am baking bread, and the next time we have a stop of any length, if we're near water, some of us ladies are going to have to do washing. We are a dusty and, I'm afraid, smelly bunch!

July 25—Making slow time, they say. Rigs keep breaking down. Red River carts are supposed to be easy to fix, but one has to have material (wood) available. We camped last night at Rat Tail Creek. A great many freighters passed us today. An old squaw came by selling pemmican. The children picked strawberries and we had them with pancakes for supper.

July 28—My heart is very heavy today. The Carney baby fell out of the cart and the huge heavy wheels ran over him and crushed him to death. Once again I heard Mr. Voss standing beside an open grave, giving comfort from the Bible. I came straight back to the cart and searched out my Bible again and looked up the words he said before I forgot them. They are found in John (much easier to find and to say than Thess.) 11:25. Jesus is saying that He is the resurrection and the life. "He that believeth in me," He says, "though he were dead, yet shall he live: and whosoever liveth and believeth in me shall never die." He ends by asking "Believest thou this?" and it seemed he was talking right at me. Do I believe all this? I must, for I have such a yearning in me to understand it, like as if someone (Someone?) is calling me on the inside. Martha (that's who Jesus was talking to) answered Him right back and said, "Yea, Lord, I believe that thou art the Christ, the Son of God," and I have a sort of swelling up in my heart, like as if I feel the same thing. Now here I am, preaching to my Mam! The gospel really is good news, like they say. More later, I think.

Days later—I know we're into August, but I've lost track. So much has happened. One day we met a man coming out of the sea of grass shoving a wheelbarrow. In it, on top of their gear, sat his wife. "Stop, Henry," she said, and he seemed glad to do so. She reached out a gloved hand and he helped her out. "Good day," she said to all us watching (probably with our mouths open). We all chorused "Good day" in a sort of ragged chorus. "Is there coffee?" she asked as graciously as if she were Queen of England, and someone hastened to the campfire and poured her a cup. We saw to it that her poor husband had one, too, and that they had a good meal. (It was noontime and we were grazing the animals and resting a bit ourselves.) Their story, which is too long to repeat here, is that Madam Queen is sick and tired of "living like this," and she swept her hand over the prairie's vastness, and that their animals died somewhere back there and they were on their way "out." We think she has gone straight out of her mind, poor thing. She finally climbed back in that barrow and the last we saw of them, Henry was trudging her on down the road. We passed three more graves today, which didn't lift our spirits any.

August 7?—Travel is slow due to lame oxen. And lame people! I think we could have walked to the moon by now. Passed freighters again today. Had many sloughs to go through or around. We are in hill country, having passed Fort Ellice, where many Indians were gathered. They stole, we believe, two oxen and ate them. When we passed their tents later, they laughed at us. Well, it's better than scalping! The Indians' dogs were a big nuisance, and you couldn't blame Frank Grimm for shooting at them. But we were uneasy after that and glad to be on our way again. We are nearing the bush, and it is very pleasant. Bought some milk today from a settler and some cream, as raspberries are ready.

August 18, I think. At least two hundred carts passed us today. We are in the Touchwood Hills, much cooler, and everyone is considerably cheered. You'd be surprised how often we meet people heading back! Of course some are going for supplies or some such reason, but some have had enough and want out. One man ate supper with us a couple of nights ago and gave Angus directions to Bliss, the place Angus has in mind. Said it was a good place, and his land is available. Maybe we'll settle on the Fairfax land. Though I wonder why we think we can make it if he can't. But, poor man, his wife died in childbed.

Speaking of which makes me remember. Two days ago Mr. Swart, whose wife and infant we buried soon after starting, married Rose Fennel. She is only fifteen. It was a sort of sad occasion, and while we gathered around and wished them well, it was with mixed emotions. Poor Rose; she deserved a happier wedding. But that's the way it is out here, they say. Mr. Swart had to turn his back on what's happened and go on. Certainly he couldn't make it without a wife, and his children need a mother.

August 26—Yesterday we reached the south branch of the Saskatchewan River. Thankfully there were Indians to ferry us across. (More than once we have had to remove the wheels on the carts and float them over. These were such tense and tiring times that I had no strength or will to write when evening came.) There is so much I have not had time to tell you about, Mam. Someday, hopefully, you'll come visit us (I doubt that we'll ever make it back out—we're here to stay), but when you do, we'll hope the railroad has come up this way. When it does, land will go much faster and soon all this wonderful farming country will be swelling with people.

Today we have camped at St. Laurent Mission, and that's how come I know the date; though this isn't civilization by any means, they at least know what time of the year it is.

They have a garden here, and we were able to buy potatoes. Ummm, good.

It's just a few days now until we reach Prince Albert. From there we'll make our way to this Bliss place, if Angus has his way. But time is growing short for talking to Rev. Voss if I am going to do so. I keep wondering if he'll turn off at some of the spots where others turn aside; two families, for instance, turned off for Nipawin, and another family turned back, even though we are so close to our destination. Rev. Voss is coming by our tent tonight, and oh, Mam, perhaps I'll find some answers to this cry in my heart.

Sept. 1—It's so simple, Mam. So simple and yet so profound. I'm a changed person. It's hard to understand that people looking at me probably can't see any difference. But inside, where the hunger was and the longing, it's like a candle is burning, and it's bright and light and full of joy. I want to tell everyone about it! Rev. Voss says the way to tell it is to live it (and that may be much harder). But I've begun, Mam, I've begun.

He explained, so simply, all about Jesus coming to earth to save sinners and that though He went back to heaven, His Spirit, whom He called a Comforter (and He surely is that) is with us, and He has been drawing my hungry heart to God. That's when the candle was lit, Mam, and I understood. Then it was so easy to pray, to say all those things that made the past forgiven, and I gave the future into His hands.

Oh, Mam, the peace! And the healing—it has finally begun. About my wee Angel, I mean, and (never mentioned before but hidden in my heart) a certain bitterness toward Angus for bringing me to this new life and that terrible *voyage. Last night, late, I confessed this to Angus and we had a very tender hour together, praying, loving, planning. I think we were a happier bride and groom than Mr. Swart and Rose, God bless'em!*

I tell you, Mam, this buggy ride is taking me to Bliss in more ways than one!

Breakfast was over, Hugh was enjoying a final cup of coffee, and Sophia, dawdling over her tea, stifled a yawn by smothering it delicately with her lace-edged handkerchief.

Even so, Hugh noticed. "Tired, my dear?" he asked, with a smile. Their previous day had been a long one; the lacrosse game had been just the beginning.

Not ordinarily given to the festivities that marked an age when the rich grew richer while the poor became poorer, but having committed himself to the game, Hugh had good-naturedly devoted the remainder of the day to his wife.

They had joined the rest of the "posh" crowd—a new word coined to fit the times—in the mindless sort of thing they did every afternoon between 3:00 and 6:00: parading up and down King Street with no other intention than to gossip and strut the latest fashions. Hugh despised it, and even Sophia admitted that, once indulged in and experienced, she could see no practical reason to continue.

Then there had been the dash for home and the changing of clothes for dinner at the Miltons' large and garish mansion. But it boasted the new tin bathtub and the hot water that was just now making its appearance in a few homes. Heatherstone, of course, had both, but neither its master or mistress was crass enough to make mention of it.

And what a dinner it had been, keeping them seated for three hours followed by coffee and a boring piano recital by one of the Milton daughters. Ten courses the Milton servants had served, if Hugh's memory served him correctly, peaking with a huge stuffed boar's head and concluding with rare and exotic fruit, imported cheese, and fancy glacés. Hugh's four-button cutaway, tailored to fit without a wrinkle to be seen, was snug and uncomfortable. Sophia, he was certain, was breathing with difficulty in the prized new corset with its Coraline stays.

Sunday stretched before the Galloways, an attractive alternative with the quiet peace and comfort of a home they enjoyed and a rather rare opportunity to be together.

"I noticed you were having quite a conversation with that scarlet-coated individual across the table from you," Sophia prompted.

"North West Mounted Police uniform; quite attractive, I'd say, certainly eye-catching. Their motto, by the way, is 'Maintain the Right.' Seems fitting."

"I do trust they are in evidence where Angus and Mary have gone."

"Well," Hugh said, half humorously, "mounted means horseback, and police means enforcer of the law, so I assume North West refers to the Alberta and Saskatchewan territories."

"I suppose so," Sophia said dubiously. "We'll just have to wait and hear what news comes from this . . . Bliss, is it? At any rate, this enforcer seemed to keep everyone at that end of the table spellbound."

"Fascinating, the account of their activities, like nothing we've ever heard of, that's certain. The force was formed in the first place to eliminate the whiskey forts in the territories. Indians, of course, can't abide whiskey but crave it. Unscrupulous men made and traded it to them at these forts through small openings or wickets. An Indian would hand over his buffalo robe and receive in return a cup of whiskey. A full quart would cost him his pony."

"Gracious!"

"Listen to the recipe for this firewater; if I remember what this man Dillard said, a bottle of Jamaica ginger, a quart of molasses, and a handful of red pepper were added to a quart of whiskey. When this was heated, it lived up to its name."

"Gracious!"

This interesting exchange of conversation was interrupted by the timid voice of Tessie, helper in the nursery.

"Mrs. Hugh—"

"Yes, what is it, Tessie?"

"It's the baby, Mum. Miss Margaret. She's—"

"What, Tessie? She's what?" Alarm had crept into Sophia's voice. Instinctively she stood to her feet. Hugh peered over the top of his paper.

"She's sick, Mum."

Something like panic rose in Sophia's motherly bosom. About to run unceremoniously from the room and her husband's presence, she caught Hugh's level look.

"Excuse me, Hugh," she said, pausing in flight.

"Of course, my dear," he said pleasantly.

Prince Albert

I t's beautiful!" Mary breathed, while Cameron and Molly frolicked in the abundant grass at her feet, happy to be released from the confines of the buggy and the cart. They had made a rush for the river flowing just a few feet away, but Mary had drawn them back from the tantalizing water.

She could understand the impression of the Rev. James Nisbet when he had stood in almost precisely the same place not too many years before and said, "I am satisfied with the excellence of the locality for a settlement."

Nisbet, too, had just completed the trek of five hundred miles in Red River carts drawn by oxen. He, too, had forded streams, battled mosquitoes, crossed flooded valleys on improvised scows. Here he had stood with his wife and daughter and recognized the promised land. "I have not seen any place with equal advantages," he had said.

Not far away stood the Mission House he had erected, and behind Mary were the scattered buildings of the town Nisbet had named Prince Albert in honor of the Queen's late consort.

The same things that had attracted Nisbet drew men today in increasing numbers—the fertility of the soil, the abundance of hay land, the clear, flowing waters, the myriad sloughs with their ducks and geese. The free land!

The trouble was—and Mary shut her eyes and shuddered, just thinking of it—the difficulty in getting here. One trail had to be abandoned because of the many creeks and valleys that must be rafted. Another trail, dry and level, was not used extensively due to the lack of wood, scarcity of water in dry seasons, and the fact that no one lived along it for great stretches.

Those trails that offered plenty of wood and water were heavily traveled, and large freighters, in wet weather, made what was a bad trail almost impossible. Over one of these the Morrison party bounced and shook, with dozens of breakdowns in the group, many delays, numerous sicknesses, and three deaths.

But Mary, and all other newcomers, recognized the Prince Albert Settlement as one of the most picturesque in the Dominion. Houses, mostly of logs, were scattered for six miles along the river. A windmill added to the unique ambiance, and over all stretched a sky as big and as blue as one's heart could desire and one's imagination conjure up. Wild fruit abounded in season—blueberries, saskatoons, raspberries, cranberries, incredibly sweet strawberries. And the trees! Mary basked in their lushness.

"We made it." Angus's voice, quiet yet filled with intense feeling, broke Mary's train of thought. She leaned back against him and couldn't help but wonder if she smelled. Certainly he did—of sweat, and oxen, and wood smoke. Locating water for bathing had not been the problem. But finding privacy to do it properly had been another matter. As for the family wash, an occasional day had been set aside for this purpose, near water naturally, but if the weather turned bad, the heavy garments failed to dry, were tossed into the carts or draped over the buggy seats, and grew dusty and muddy before drying.

Mary breathed a prayer of thanks to the heavenly Father who had brought them through. How often, jolting along behind a weary horse, she had lifted her voice in the hymns of praise taught to the group by Carlton Voss.

Even now, in spite of dirty clothes and sweaty body, hair too long unwashed, appetite over-gorged on rabbit, loved ones many miles away, and tomorrow's problems too mountainous to grasp, her heart—in its newfound peace and joy—lifted in praise.

"The lots are taken all along the river for many miles," Angus was saying.

"Why should that matter?" Mary asked. "Haven't we been headed for this Bliss place all along?"

"One of the locals back there predicts that Prince Albert will outstrip Winnipeg when the railroad reaches here. The area is hovering on the edge of a boom in growth right now. We got here in good time. Can't you just see—back there—" and Angus waved an arm in the direction of the settlement, "factories, machine shops, paper mills, all bringing people who love this clear sky and wonderful land, and gambling everything on a chance to have a piece of it for their very own. If they're not farmers, they'll fit in right here and offer goods the rest of us need."

"There's a sawmill and a flour mill in operation now."

"I'll probably have to do what many of the homesteaders do, Mary, and that is work the land in the summer months and when harvest is done, find work somewhere else—here, perhaps, or further north in the logging camps."

Still too unlearned concerning bitter winters within the confines of a small cabin, without seeing another woman for weeks or perhaps months, Mary nodded assent to this development in the new life. Already her heart clung to the knowledge that whatever the circumstances, she had a Friend who had promised He would never leave nor forsake her.

"I can do all things through Christ which strengtheneth me," she murmured. The long buggy ride had been enriched by Bible reading and memorization and acquainting herself with her new Companion, and the weary days had been brightened and the endless hours shortened, or so it seemed.

Angus's gaze softened as he watched his wife and heard her. Her new relationship, rather than making a wedge between them, had strengthened their marriage bonds. The One who was to her the rose of Sharon and the lily of the valley shed His sweet perfume through her life; to Angus it seemed that it should naturally be so, and it was a testimony to him and all who met her, in a manner beyond words. The One whom she acknowledged as the bright and morning star shone His light through her, and Angus warmed his own hungry heart at that flame. The Good Shepherd who had found Mary was, clearly, seeking another wandering lamb.

"We'll stay here a few days and rest," he said now. "We'll look over the available goods—everything, by the way, has had to come over the same trail we did, or by river. The Hudson's Bay steamer, the *Lily*, made six trips to Edmonton from here this year, I'm told, carrying flour and other goods as well as passengers. So," he said, more serious than teasing, "we're not really locked in here."

"It surely can't navigate in winter. And Edmonton, Angus—that's the wrong direction." She was, obviously, thinking of her Mam, back east.

"Knowing Kezzie," Angus said, and it was a comfort for the moment, "she'd make it if she had to snowshoe all the way."

"You've been looking over the store's goods," Mary judged. "Now, let's go see these snowshoes."

Mary rounded up the children, straightened their clothes, and herded them down the street toward the Hudson's Bay Trading Post.

While Mary browsed through an interesting assortment of goods, Angus was engaged in conversation with a couple of men.

To his surprise he learned that very little cash was available; his would be welcome, for sure.

"Good country for cattle," he was told. "Start a herd and it may bring you returns sooner than a crop, because you'll have to clear your land and so on. Cattle are bought by the government and the Bay for their posts throughout the territories."

"It's this first winter that concerns me most," Angus said, his Scots accent fresh and strong but not strange; the Scots were well represented in the area.

"You have a couple of months before it gets really bad. Though it could be sooner . . . never know. You won't want to let any grass grow under your feet."

This reference to the grass that burgeoned so thickly around them caused considerable hilarity in the listeners, and when Angus responded with, "Well, if it does, I'll cut it for hay," he was slapped on the back and told, "You'll do!"

A plump, rosy woman not much older than Mary entered the building, bustled over to the newcomer, held out her hand, and said, "You must be the lady from Scotland. Well, I'm Sadie LeGare—French name, of course, my husband is part French . . . we're a motley crew here, and I welcome you to our—" Here the flow of words faltered, and a sparkle of fun lit the kind eyes— "our city," she finished.

When Angus joined them and was introduced, the two were old friends, a mark of the camaraderie that flourished among the settlers, who needed each other so desperately. Unless he was mistaken, this Sadie LeGare was part Indian, a Métis, many of whom were being assimilated into the current society and way of life.

"The constant need for food three times a day will challenge your imagination," Sadie LeGare was saying, following Mary to the various sections of the store. "If you don't have it already, you'll need flour, of course, sugar, baking soda, salt—" Mary was pointing these items out to the clerk, and they were being assembled on the counter.

"Tea ... syrup ... oatmeal; oh yes, oatmeal—some poor bachelors, I understand, exist on oatmeal and rabbit," Sadie informed them. "Dried beans, rice, lard—though you can render your own from most any meat you butcher or hunt or trap. You do have a rifle, I guess?" And on and on the needs went. Mary was grateful, having felt dismayed at the prospect before her of being isolated for long periods of time, with travel impossible except, she supposed, on the aforementioned snowshoes. And did they need to buy snowshoes?

"Come over for supper," Sadie invited cordially, "and we'll get better acquainted. It won't be fancy," she explained but without apology. "Not much fanciness here, seein' as how everything has to be freighted in or handmade. You'd be surprised, though. There's a piano or two and some very fine silver and dainty china that managed to make it through. But not at our house."

The Morrisons were welcomed to the LeGare log house with cheerful kindness, and they thoroughly enjoyed the fresh bread, so often missing on the trip, and the roast beef with fresh vegetables.

The dessert was sweet strawberries with mounds of whipped cream. When Angus and Mary "mmmmmmed" their appreciation, Pierre LeGare, a short, dark man of undoubted Indian as well as French ancestry, quoted, "Doubtless God could have made a better berry, but doubtless God never did."

Pierre LeGare was a freighter, "gone a lot of the time," he admitted. He and Sadie were childless and took immediately to Cammie and Molly, sitting them down after supper to sorting through a box of arrowheads.

Sadie and Mary settled themselves with a last cup of tea, and the men went for a walk, where Pierre told Angus, "The plow is the most important investment you can make. And a grub hoe and of course an axe or two or three. ..."

When, finally, the Morrisons left for their own camp, they felt they had made real friends. And in spite of the almost overwhelming list of things to buy, things to do, they were not discouraged, and only a little daunted.

"Neighborliness goes beyond tolerance," Angus mused, "and it is so freely offered. Pierre tells me that dislikes and likes, religious affiliations and political persuasions, though not stifled or forgotten, do not interfere with neighborliness or being accountable to one another. A good feeling, that."

"Cooperation—it seems to be incorporated into the building of the frontier. Sadie says there are working bees—"

"As opposed to drones?" Angus asked, grinning through the late evening shadows.

Mary smiled. "Bees where people come and help each other with their work, like putting up their buildings."

"And we'll need to be quick to do our share."

"No locks on doors, Sadie says. Well, maybe on places of business but not on cabins out in the bush where someone might need to have shelter or food."

"It's a whole new way of life, that's for sure," Angus said as he scooped a weary Molly up into his arms. "Give us two or three days, and we'll be on our way."

"To Bliss."

L ike a bird on the wing Sophia flew up the stairs, the voluminous wrapper skirt drawn out of the way of her hurrying
feet.

For once she failed to take in and appreciate the charm of the
nursery she had so lovingly and carefully designed, decorated,
and furnished for her child. The walls were daintily papered, the
windows were adequate to allow plenty of light. There was a rosy
carpet on the floor, and cherub-figured lamps sat on cherry tables
and hung from the ceiling. In one corner stood an intricately
curled-iron bed. The sides were made to be let down; the pillars,
or corner posts, were topped with brass rods, or vases, and it was
fitted with a "superior wire-woven" mattress, covered now by
snowy linens and frothy, lace-edged "comforts."

In the center of the room a handsome cherry cradle moved
silently on its patented hangers, as promised by its builder. At its
side, her hand resting on the cradle, sat Kezzie in a rocker of the
finest curly birch, the seat upholstered in satin brocatell of a vivid
blue, its back panels ornamented with heavily scrolled carving
now clearly seen as the old nurse leaned forward, her eyes on the
child in the cradle.

Sophia's gaze was fixed on the cradle as she flew across the thick carpet.

Margaret was asleep, or at least the long lashes lay dark on her flushed cheeks. When Sophia touched her forehead, she found it startlingly hot, and she drew her hand back in alarm. Her eyes, frightened and questioning, turned to Kezzie.

"What's the matter with her?" she whispered.

"I dinna know, Mum. She didn't sleep well, first off, so I held her most of the night. She's only got so feverish this last couple of hours."

"Is she eating?"

"Keeps turnin' her head away from the bottle, Mrs. Hugh. Takes a sip or two and then throws up."

"Spits up, you mean?"

"No, it's more of a vomit, I'd say. I think we better get a doctor, Mrs. Hugh." And Kezzie's lips trembled with an unusual display of concern that served to frighten Sophia most of all.

"Tessie," Sophia said, turning to the girl who had followed her up the stairs and into the nursery, "go tell Mr. Galloway to send for a doctor. He'll know one, I'm sure."

Tessie ran to do her mistress's bidding. As Sophia watched, the small body jerked spasmodically, and Margaret woke with a wail. Kezzie reached for her, but Sophia was quicker.

"Oh, my darling," she crooned, lifting the babe and laying its hot cheek against her cool one. Almost immediately there was a convulsive move of the small body, and a dark, wet stain spread itself foully through the child's wrappings and ran onto Sophia's garments.

Horrified, Sophia's eyes flew to Kezzie, who reached for Margaret and hurried her toward a padded tabletop in the corner of the room.

Holding her stained gown pinched out away from her body, Sophia, momentarily, seemed unsure what was happening or what to do.

"Go change, Mrs. Hugh," Kezzie said practically.

"Has she been doing this . . . this . . . bowel thing, before now?"

"Nae, Mum." Kezzie was filling a china basin with water, unwrapping the child, and preparing to draw the soiled clothing out and away from her.

With one anguished glance toward the baby, Sophia turned toward her own room and a hasty discarding of the smeared morning gown. Washing herself thoroughly, still it seemed the sick, unnatural odor lingered in her nostrils. She dressed herself quickly and hurried downstairs to Hugh.

"Something's dreadfully wrong with Margaret—"

"I've sent for a doctor. Now sit down and have a cup of tea; you look sick yourself, and that won't help."

"I can't drink a drop," Sophia declared, then proceeded to do so, turning eagerly at any sound that might mean the doctor had arrived, her cup wavering in her hand.

Hugh rose politely when Casper showed the doctor into the room.

"Doctor Wiggins," the man said, holding out his hand.

"Thank you for coming, Doctor. Our daughter seems to be ailing. This is Mrs. Galloway—"

"Doctor—" Sophia began, wringing her hands.

Hugh interrupted smoothly, "Relax, my dear. All will be well now. Casper, please direct Dr. Wiggins upstairs. Doctor, if you will please stop in here on your way out—"

"Certainly, Mr. Galloway."

Sophia made as if to follow the doctor from the room. Quietly Hugh drew her back, seating her and saying kindly, "You can't be any help up there, my dear. Things will go better if you keep calm and in control."

For an instant a spark of rebellion at her husband's authority caused Sophia's lips to tighten. But, not really being emotionally ready to cope with a severe illness anyway, she allowed herself to be persuaded that Hugh, after all, knew best.

But after the doctor had made his examination, reporting in ungeneral terms a "flux" complicated with symptoms of colic and teething and saying he had left medicine with the child's nurse, Sophia, with an apologetic smile for her husband, made her way quickly upstairs. Kezzie, almost as flushed as the baby, was rocking Margaret. Her blue eyes smoldered.

"What does he know! I tell you, Mum, I don't have much confidence in this modern mumbo-jumbo. The old ways will do, I'll be bound. Teethin'? Not at her age! I know teethin' when I see it!"

Sophia picked up the dark bottle the doctor had left and read from its enscrolled label: "Useful and a sure cure for any form of diarrhea, cholera morbus, cholera infantum, sour stomach, etc."

Sophia blanched. The diagnosis was worse than she had thought. "This sounds worse by far than teething."

"Well, if it is, we're prepared," Kezzie said grimly, pointing to more bottles on the table beside her, which she had obviously set aside.

Picking one up, Sophia read, "'Cures toothache, faceache, neuralgia.' It seems," she said faintly, "that we are prepared for anything. Surely something will work."

The door opened, and Tessie slipped in with a pan of milky looking water in which a cloth soaked. She raised big eyes to Mrs. Hugh and Kezzie.

"What's all this about, Tessie?" Sophia asked.

"It's a disinfectant, Mum. Doctor's orders. We're to use it on everything. It will purify the air, remove all f . . . f . . . foul odors, and destroy pests of all kinds."

"Heavens, let me see the container, Tessie."

Tessie set the pan down and withdrew a pint can from the pocket of her voluminous apron.

Squinting, Sophia read, "'Can be used to disinfect drains, sinks, gullies, urinals, water closets, farmyards and buildings, chicken pens, rabbit hutches, birdcages, cattle trucks, slaughterhouses, ash barrels, garbage cans—'" As she read, Sophia's voice rose in pitch until it finally trailed off on a squeak.

"And," Tessie added with relish, obviously having read the instructions before readying the mixture, "it destroys fleas on dogs and other animals, lice on chickens, cures mange, and protects from the torment of flies, mosquitoes, gnats, and ..."Tessie's memory faltered.

"This concoction," Sophia said, astonished, "would make a million dollars, I should think, if the inventor took it to the Territories. Mary and Angus write of the terrible mosquitoes there ... worse than here, if such a thing could be."

"So thick," Kezzie said, nodding, "that a bay horse looks yellow all covered with them, Mary says."

"So," Sophia asked with a sigh, "what do you suggest, Kezzie?"

"I'll bathe the wee bairn in cool water, Mrs. Hugh. That will bring the fever doon. And I'll not gi' her any milk for twenty-four hours. We'll start there."

Sophia hung worriedly over the rocker and its occupants.

"I'll take care o' her just like she's my very own." Kezzie spoke with a quiet confidence that did more to allay Sophia's anxiety than anything the doctor had prescribed.

With relief and guilt mixed, Sophia left the nursery and the child snuffling into the old nurse's shoulder, not hearing Kezzie's muttered, "I'll no hae that doctor bleedin' this bairn if I can help it!"

Several of Kezzie's low-voiced comments were heard, however, in the following days when Sophia slipped unannounced into the nursery to bend over the sleeping child, to take her at times into her arms and rock her. But Margaret, perversely, seemed restless in her mother's arms and only settled down when the comfortable, known arms of Kezzie were around her. That, in itself, may have accounted for the small worm of jealousy that began to eat at Sophia.

Coming in quietly one afternoon Sophia heard the soft tones of the old nurse as she crooned a lullaby of her own making to the infant. "Whoosh, whoosh," she soothed. "Whoosh, wee angel, whoosh."

The intimacy of the scene and the sound quite took Sophia aback. With rather more roughness than courtesy she took the baby and, in spite of Margaret's squalled displeasure, rocked far too grimly for far too long.

Another time Sophia burst in on her husband's solitude with such emotion that Hugh's frown indicated it was uncalled for in civilized people.

"The child is improving, is she not?" he asked before Sophia had a chance to speak, and giving her the clue to get herself under suitable control.

Nevertheless she sputtered, impatient with protocol, as she reported. "Do you know what she's saying now, to Margaret?"

Sighing, Hugh turned from his desk. "Sit down, my dear, and tell me sensibly."

Sophia threw out her hands in a dramatic gesture. "When I went into the room, Kezzie was leaning over Margaret, about to pick her up, and she said . . . she said . . ."

"She said?"

"She said—and I'm certain of it, Hugh—'Come to Granny Kezzie, my angel.'"

"Nothing wrong with angel, is there?"

"Oh, Hugh! She called herself Granny to *our* child!"

Hugh's eyes sharpened. "I see," he said thoughtfully. "Well, there's still no harm done. Perhaps she feels like a granny. She's that age, you know."

"I don't like it," Sophia muttered. "Not at all. Just because her grandchildren are away is no reason to be calling herself Granny to someone else's child. Especially a child of a different . . . class."

Sophia had the grace to hesitate before saying the word and to look uncomfortable after it was out. She well knew Hugh's feeling for Kezzie and the equality he seemed to allow Angus Morrison.

Hugh's lips tightened. He turned to his work, saying tautly, "A child would be blessed indeed to have Kezzie as a grandmother. She'll never have another, now will she? Leave the situation alone, Sophia."

Fume as she might inwardly, Hugh's word was law. And the child, God be praised, was feeling better. But, for Sophia, some germ, a germ that no miracle concoction could touch, ate away at her from that time on.

I n spite of Hugh's assurance that Kezzie's relationship with
Margaret was no problem, Sophia was to watch, helplessly, as
bonds very like grandmother and grandchild were woven between
her servant and her child. But always, as during Margaret's illness, the nurse's service was such that Sophia didn't know how
she would manage without her. Somewhat detached from her
child, Sophia often fretted; it certainly was not the way she had
planned and dreamed that things would be. Life as the Galloways
lived it, however, called for Sophia to be mistress, and children,
as ever across the years in aristocratic households, to be seen and
not heard. But seen only occasionally.

Now, during Margaret's illness, was no time to reprimand
Kezzie or jeopardize the delicate situation in any way. And, truly,
Margaret was in the best hands possible. Sophia took comfort
from that fact and turned her attention to being the companion
and hostess her husband needed. Life, for Sophia Gowrie, had
indeed turned out remarkably well.

Margaret's ultimate restoration to health was due mostly to a
service about which the household knew nothing. A small

kitchen menial had been added to the staff, replacing a slovenly and undependable woman. Raised in a poverty-stricken but spotless home where dirt and grime were abhorred, Angie scrubbed and cleaned until her poor small hands were red and cracked. Caked nipples and milk rimmed bottles were put to soak in hot and sometimes boiling water, not because the girl had any knowledge of germs and infection, but because of her fetish to be clean. She took her few cents home at the end of each day, and no one ever knew the daughter of the home owed her health and very possibly her life to a simple country girl with a penchant for cleanliness.

Kezzie was eventually able to write, sitting near the bairn's bed, well within the sound of any faint cry or call.

Dear Mary:

We have just come through a very bad time. Wee Margo has been near death's door. Many a time I've wished for some of those prayers you write about.

As you can imagine, I looked on all the bottles the doctor left with little confidence. Modern medicine! There may come a day, but as of now, the old ways are best. Certainly they worked for wee Margo, and she is recovering nicely.

As for those bottles, I took one sniff and marched them downstairs to be destroyed. Cook uncorked one, gave the cork a lick, made a face, and agreed with my decision. Geordie, the handyman, was put in charge of getting rid of them and he promised to do so. Just how he did it is not really known, but cook and I thought he seemed unusually frisky for a day or so, and his breath smelled remarkably like alcohol. I will say this—he didn't show any symptoms of biliousness or colic!

Out of all of this has come the conviction that I have done the right thing by staying here with the wee bairn, though it means separation from my Mary and her babies. Often I am torn by the separation. But I know you are contented where you are, and I know Molly and Cameron are better off being raised free and proud, rather than in the bonds of service as our people have been across the centuries.

Let me tell you about Margo, so you can picture her. Her front teeth have come in; she has such a charming grin that it is hard to resist her. Her hair is as dark as ever and loses none of its curl. Her little face is rounding out again. Her paddies are dimpled now, just as Molly's were, and the little fingers on each wee paddie have that same inward curl to them as Molly's, making me think often of my darling girl so far away. If you could see her you would love her, Mary, I know you would. It seems a precious task to spend the rest of my life looking after her.

I t takes a real man to beat the bush," the hardware man told Angus as he helped him accumulate what he would need to get started, "and Bliss is in the bush. Not little bitty trees and willows, you know, but real trees, big trees. It'll be chop, chop forever to get your land cleared. First, a place for a cabin, then a barn, then a garden spot . . . a spot for the cattle . . . finally fields—"

Angus broke into the discouraging litany; obviously the man had come as a homesteader, been defeated by the work or the isolation or both, and settled for clerking in "civilization."

"And you know," the man continued grimly while Angus studied files, saws, spikes, and more, "you'll be a squatter. Ain't got no land office here."

"Yes, but it won't be for long," Angus answered cheerfully, knowing that the established settlers in the Prince Albert area and the Carrot River Valley were demanding such an office. "I think we'll be safe in our choice. There doesn't seem to be a big rush out Bliss way."

"Oh, there's one or two brave souls out there. Maybe you should find a place and settle down here in town over winter. Ever think of a winter in the bush, mister?"

"Yes, and that's why I'm asking you to help me purchase the things that we'll need to be under cover, and quickly. Now what can you tell me about these stoves?"

Thus appealed to, the clerk fell to with a will. "Well, now," he said, "all our stoves are Sunshines. Depends on how big your place will be—"

"One room, to start," Angus supplied.

"Well, then, you'll want one that will not only give the heat you need, but that you can cook on, too. So here you have your Merit Sunshine model, your Star Sunshine, your Northern Sunshine—though it's freighted in from the south—and your Glad Sunshine. All of them, of course, are for wood rather than coal."

"The prices—?"

"Well, now, take this Merit Sunshine. It has your cut top plates with heavy, deep edges; it has your heavy rim covers and centers. It has your heavy grate and firebox lining; your dumping and shaking grates are the finest. It has your nickel knobs and hinge pins; it has your tin-lined oven door, and your oven—" the salesman swung open the oven door, "is, as you see, nearly square, with your broad rack."

"And the price?" Angus asked patiently.

"Well, now, you're talking size here. This'n has a firebox seventeen by nineteen by eleven, as opposed to your nineteen by twenty-one by twelve. And you're talking weight: two hundred sixty-five pounds as opposed to two hundred ninety-five pounds."

"And the price of this seventeen by nineteen by eleven, two-hundred-sixty-five pound model?" Angus pursued.

"Forgot to mention the length of the firebox: sixteen inches, as opposed to the twenty-inch firebox in this here Star Sunshine. And that's the length you need for wood; t'other is more suitable for coal. Which, of course, we don't have here to speak of as yet. Course, you can get your True Sunshine here with a firebox of twenty-four inches. Take some time, though. Months, in fact."

"This Star Sunshine with the twenty-inch firebox looks fine. How much is it?"

"Well, now, with your top oven plate inlaid with non-conducting plaster composition, your nickel teapot stand, your towel rod, your portable outside oven shelf and your extended rear shelf—"

"Aren't those standard features?"

"—and your large capacity reservoir—"

"How much?"

The man looked grieved, as if he hadn't been allowed to do his job decently. With no one else in the store and business slow simply because of the limited demand, it was obviously a source of entertainment as well as a selling job.

With a sigh, "Twelve dollars and sixty cents," he said. "But," he added immediately, "that's with your twenty-inch firebox. Now with your twenty-four-inch—"

"I'll take it," Angus said, and couldn't help adding, "Wrap it up."

The man looked thoughtful, put a hand to his head and scratched it, "Well, now—"

Angus, hiding his grin, waved a hand, and said, "I'll take it, as is."

"Well, now," the clerk said, regaining his composure and moving ahead with renewed fervor, "along with this stove you can get your set of stove furnishings at a bargain price. See here, twenty-one items, or actually twenty-three if you consider there are two black dripping pans and two tin bread pans."

"We have numerous kitchen items with us, have been using them on the trail. What's this?" A curious Angus pointed toward the stack of twenty-one items, or twenty-three. . . .

"Well, now, that's your flat-handled skimmer. And this here's your cast iron spider—"

"I'll let my wife look at this selection, I think," Angus said firmly. "We have a teakettle, a coffeepot, bread pans—" Angus was pointing to recognizable items.

"But do you have a fire shovel? Tin dipper? And here's your Common Square Bread Tin, as opposed to your—"

"I think, if you don't mind, Mr.—"

"Bone. Marley Bone."

"Angus Morrison." And the two men, sparring partners in a pleasant half-hour conversation, shook hands.

"I certainly know where to come for good sound advice about equipment," Angus said feelingly, and Marley Bone looked properly modest.

"Well, now," he said, "about your equipment for your stove. You'll need your lid lifter, your poker, your asbestos stove mat. Then there's your damper at six cents, and your chimney thimble—"

"Chimney thimble?"

"Use it where your pipe goes through to the floor above, safeguards against fire from an overheated stove. You have your common thimble as opposed to your adjustable thimble, which has your lip here with openings to allow for the conducting of heat to the above floor."

"We'll be lucky to have one floor, let alone two," Angus reminded Marley Bone, who was in full spate again, and enjoying it.

Deflected but not discouraged, Mr. Bone said, "Right," and turned smoothly to copper boilers, butter churns, milk pails, milk skimmers, and more.

Just as smoothly, having caught on to the game and enjoying it as thoroughly as Marley Bone, Angus interjected, "I'll just leave all that to my wife, Mr. Bone," and reminded himself to warn Mary about the experience ahead of her. "Now if you'll just instruct me concerning hardware—"

It was all the encouragement Marley Bone needed. With the alacrity of a ballet dancer he turned—physically and mentally—toward hatchets, adze-eye bell-face nail hammers, froes, chisels, and much more.

At a question from Angus the man happily pointed out the nails, common nails as opposed to fence, shingle, and flooring nails; nails by the keg as opposed to nails by the pound. This led quite naturally, it seemed, to a carpenter's square, slide rule, plumb bob, level, planes—your bench plane or your bull-nose rabbet plane. . . .

———

"I think exhilaration drove him outright crazy," Angus reported to Mary later on, "when he got into the whiffletree section."

"Whiffletree?" Mary asked faintly.

"Whiffletree tongues, whiffletree hooks, whiffletree ferrules, whiffletree plates, whiffletree tips . . ."

"I hope you used good sense, Angus," Mary said anxiously. "Whiffletree tips?"

"The common," Angus reported solemnly, "as opposed to your silverplated or your closed end, core malleable."

"My goodness! How in the world do they get such items away back here?"

"Away *up* here. And by freighter, or by riverboat. Believe me, when you need a whiffletree tip you'll be glad you don't have to send clear to Fort Carlton, or back east or wherever for it."

"I suppose so. And here I was worrying about needles and thread and mousetraps. They say mice are a terrible scourge here, Angus!" Mary, faced with the prospects of a mouse in her future, was more intimidated than when informed that bears roamed the country occasionally.

"Don't worry," Angus reassured his wife. "Most of what he spouted was for his sake as much as mine. If I ever saw a man put heart and soul into his work, it's Marley Bone."

Later, over supper with the LeGares, Pierre broke into hearty laughter upon hearing of Angus's experience.

"I should have warned you," he said. "But perhaps it was more fun this way. Yes, he's a disgruntled homesteader, yet he's bent on stayin'. What's more, he's in the market for a wife. He keeps writin' letters—they go out with the freight, so I know—to any prospect he hears about. So far no one's showed up. But I wouldn't rule it out. We have more than one mail-order bride in the area."

Being between runs, or so he said, Pierre LeGare had offered to go with the Morrisons on their initial trip out to Bliss to locate a homestead. Angus was overwhelmed by such kindness and generosity in someone he scarcely knew but wasn't hard to persuade. His three carts he had managed more or less by himself on the trek across country. The oxen, obviously broken to it, had tucked their heads below the tail end of the cart just ahead and plodded stolidly on, with very little trouble, leaving Angus free to lead the front cart and Mary to drive the horse and buggy. Now, as planned, Angus sold off two of the oxen, much in demand, and retained the strongest and best for his own use, as well as the horse for riding and pulling the buggy.

While Cammie and Molly played quietly with a kitten (which Sadie—after hearing Mary's shuddering comments concerning mice—promised they could take with them), Pierre located an old envelope that had been opened and saved, and, with a nub of a pencil, settled Angus and Mary down to specific talk about their cabin.

"First off—what size?" he questioned, and answered, "one room, I suppose. Easiest to put up, easiest to heat."

Angus and Mary nodded agreement.

"We'll cut logs twenty-one feet long for the sides, and seventeen feet for the ends. How's that sound?"

Nods.

"That will give you a room measuring fourteen by eighteen feet inside. Still noddin'?" He raised his black eyes to his new friends, was reassured by their nods, and continued.

"I figure we'll need fifty logs. We'll cut 'em, trim 'em, and tote 'em on our shoulders to the site. We'll clear off a place, then fit and notch our base logs, and the foundation should be done in a day."

Mary and Angus looked amazed. And relieved. Obviously the task, which they knew was a big one, was shrinking, with Pierre's help, to manageable size.

"We'll only trim 'em enough so that they fit as snug as possible. Got to get this shack on up before freeze-up, for several reasons—shelter, of course, but also so's the ground won't freeze and buckle. Also, we want to take time, before ever startin', to dig a cellar. A cellar is a must, friend. Only way to keep your food stuff from freezin' solid; also gives you some space for storage. You'll be more cramped than you can imagine in that one room.

"Once the walls is up, Mary and the children can do the chinkin'—just mud or clay, dependin' on what we can find. Any moss around would be helpful. When it dries you should be as snug as a bug in a rug. But first—"

Pierre went on to explain about the gable ends. Unless, he said, they'd settle for a slant, or shed-type roof. At Mary's indecision, Sadie spoke up, quietly but firmly. "Give 'em a decent roof, Pierre. No mud fallin' through. It'll take longer, but the livin' will be so much better." And Mary looked relieved and grateful.

"Well, buy a faroe if you don't have one," Pierre instructed. "We'll have to make shingles. Slow us up some." When he saw Mary's worried face, he continued heartily, "No matter. I have a feelin' snow is goin' to hold off. Plenty time. One window be enough?"

"Two," Sadie said firmly, and at Mary's nod Pierre docilely pencilled in two windows.

"Better buy double panes—that is, storm windows—if you can afford 'em."

<hr />

A brisk fall morning saw the Morrison carts ready to roll. With reluctance Mary embraced her new friend but was able to mount the buggy with a rising feeling of excitement. With a slap of the reins she turned the horse to follow the carts. As arranged, Pierre would bring back the two extra oxen with the empty carts, and their new owners would take possession. "You'd do well to sell that last cart," he advised Angus, "and get you a wagon as soon as you can. With bobs in place of wheels you'll have transportation winter as well as summer."

With the children vying over the privilege of carrying the cat, which they had named Patches, and a basket of food at her feet that Sadie had prepared for the day's meals, Mary felt as if she were once again embarking on a tossing sea for some distant port. But this was a wilderness of living green and not a sea of water. Remembering the horrors of that other navigation, Mary breathed a prayer and set her sails—and her horse's ears—facing directly into the small opening that led to . . . what? For mice and misery she was prepared, for hard work and hardship, for lonely days, anxious hours, and wrenching homesickness. But there would be sunsets too glorious to describe, fulfillment too satisfying to be expressed, and freedom past anything known or experienced. And there was her newfound Friend to see her through both good and bad. Mary squared her shoulders, lifted her face into the wind's nip, called a strong "Giddap!" to the horse, and set her sights and her heart on Bliss.

15

With wee Margaret, often called Margo, fully recovered, life in the Galloway household returned to normal. Sophia, greatly relieved over her daughter's improved health, became a hostess of some note, constantly giving and attending "at homes" and joining several organizations devoted to doing good to the poor and downtrodden. Hugh's business enterprises prospered, and he was more and more involved with them and spent less and less time at home.

Margaret's world was small. There were daily visits to Sophia and Hugh—if his schedule permitted—but mostly her days and months and years were spent in the upstairs nursery in happy association with Kezzie . . . Nanny . . . Granny.

The Galloways made their first trip back to Scotland when Margo was five years old.

"Perhaps we shouldn't ask Kezzie to make the trip," Sophia ventured to Hugh as plans were being laid, still resisting the unseen bonds that existed between Kezzie and Margo and suspecting they were those of love rather than dependency alone.

"Are you prepared to take charge of the child yourself?" Hugh asked pointedly.

Sophia hesitated, reluctant to admit that she was not, and just as reluctantly, eventually advised Kezzie that her presence on the trip would be needed and to please prepare herself as well as Margaret for the voyage and a stay of three months or more.

"I thought she'd be more pleased about it," Sophia said to her husband in a somewhat injured tone.

"Well, think of it, my dear. Mary, her only child, isn't there, and all her own siblings are dead. Other than a few friends, there's little or no reason for her being happy about that long trip. Maybe," Hugh said so quietly that Sophia barely heard, "she has bad memories of the trip over."

"As we all do," Sophia agreed, adding, "but we, of course, have the blessing of our child, while Mary—"

"Yes—Mary," Hugh repeated simply. "Mary, and Angus."

"Do you ever think of making a trip to the Territories, Hugh?" Sophia asked. "Wouldn't you like to visit Angus someday . . . see how he's doing?"

"I'd like it very much," Hugh answered warmly, or as warmly as Hugh Galloway ever allowed himself to speak. "We've had a letter or two, of course, and Kezzie keeps us up-to-date on what's going on, and it all sounds as if they are prospering. After much hard work, of course. But go see them? No, not, at least, until the railroad goes through."

"Surely Kezzie will want to go then. Perhaps live with them. She's getting old and bent, Hugh—"

"Kezzie has a home with me as long as she wishes it," Hugh said firmly. Sophia sighed; Kezzie, to Sophia, was such a mixed blessing. A veritable tower of strength at all times, and totally dependable, yet there was something. . . . Never able to put her vague unrest about Kezzie into words that Hugh would accept or understand, Sophia sighed again.

Hugh, his face in his newspaper, heard, raised an enigmatic but unseen eyebrow, and said no more on the subject.

Margo's clearest memories of her early years were of that trip to the land of her parents' birth. Perhaps it was the general air of excitement and the hustle and bustle of disembarking on Scottish soil, being met by members of the staff of Heatherstone, the fawning over by one and all as they commented on her black and curly hair, her dark eyes, her impish smile, her lovely clothes. But more likely it was due to the encounters with her cousin Wallace, already in his teen years but childish to a marked degree, and spoiled. True, he was neglected in some ways, his mother being dead and his father absent most of the time. Wallace spent most of the year in school in Edinburgh but had come home for the special occasion of his uncle's visit from America. He showed little interest in most of the gifts Sophia had painstakingly selected for him but received with a chortle of satisfaction the bow and arrows that were fashioned, supposedly, in the manner of those of the American Indians. The small scar that was to remain on Margo's upper arm all of her life was forever a reminder of Heatherstone, Scotland, and Wallace's tormenting ways.

Margo was always to remember, too, the trip from the ship to Kirkcudbright. Though Scotland was no longer considered home by Kezzie—with Mary and Angus and the children and Mr. Hugh all in America—she obviously retained a deep love for her homeland and described it to Margo with feeling.

"Look now, lassie," she was to repeat time and again, especially as they approached familiar territory. And Margo would look and, often, remember.

"This is the River Dee," Kezzie said as the carriage left the ship behind and approached familiar territory. She seemed to feel it necessary to apologize because now, at low tide, it was all a sea of mud.

"The Dee empties into the sea here at Kirkcudbright. When the tide is in, Kirkcudbright is one of the best-looking burghs of the Stewartry, in my opinion," Kezzie continued.

"Birds!" Margo interrupted. "Canada geese."

"Greylag geese, lassie. Below the town is where you'll find birds—herons. Oot there," Kezzie nodded in the general direction of the sea, "on St. Mary's Isle, there's been a heronry for centuries. Perhaps we can go see it while we're here. We can visit the old priory ruins at the same time."

"Priory?" Margo questioned.

"A religious hoose," Kezzie explained, and Margo, none the wiser, blinked her dark eyes and nodded.

Hugh, listening idly—while Sophia leaned her head back, her eyes closed—added, "The old home of Lord Selkirk is there, too."

Making a connection between the history of the old home and the new, Sophia opened her eyes to ask, "Didn't Lord Selkirk help establish the Red River Colony?"

"That he did; made quite a name for himself overseas."

There followed a brief discussion, meaningless to small Margo, concerning certain Scots and their contributions to society beyond their homeland: Andrew Carnegie, of course, who started work as a bobbin boy, following the skill of the weaver father who took his family from Dunfermline to the new world to make a fresh start; Canada's first and second Prime Ministers were Scots—John Macdonald and Alexander Mackenzie; Canada's Fraser and Mackenzie rivers were named for Scotsmen; and of course there was John Paul Jones, founder of the United States Navy, who came from Solway's shores.

Scotland had, indeed, a superior educational system and was turning out "lads o' pairts," or lads of talents, but, with no appreciable place or way to use those talents at home, emigration was the answer for many. The 1800s were years of mass migrations, triggered by economic factors such as a fall in the price of kelp, one of the few Highland industries; a fall in the value of the small Highland beef cattle; and a failure of west coast fishing. Most hurtful of all were the infamous Clearances when large numbers of Highlanders were evicted from their long-held ancestral crofts—landlords had come to realize that mutton and wool brought better profits into their coffers and needed fewer workers than beef and dairy products.

As is so often the case, something good came from what was a terrible upheaval and misery. And Angus Morrison was a prime example; thrust, by necessity, from everything his people had known for untold generations, he would find a new challenge and future—not only for himself but for his children and his children's children—in a new land.

"A few miles east are the ruins of Dundrennan Abbey," Kezzie was murmuring quietly to a wide-eyed Margo as she peered from the carriage window. "Of course you dinna know aboot her yet, but you will—Mary Queen of Scots spent her last night in that Abbey—"

"Oh, look!" Margo pointed to the quaint town coming into sight: Kirkcudbright.

"Don't point, dear," Sophia said automatically, while Kezzie whispered, "Home!"

Accustomed to the noise and confusion of a vigorous city, Margo couldn't restrain her cries of pleasure at the color-washed houses with their blue slated roofs.

"The Tolbooth . . ." Kezzie breathed as they rolled past the ancient prison with its slender Mercat Cross dating from 1610. "Witches were tried here, lassie . . . as late as 1805. . . ."

"Enough, Kezzie," Sophia said sharply. History or not, her child should not be subjected to topics of witches or burning.

The shadow cast by this reference to witches was nothing compared to the fear that was to haunt Margo upon their arrival at Heatherstone.

It was pleasant enough pulling up to the courtyard of the massive house so like her own home in Canada with but subtle differences; the greetings by staff and Hugh's brother Ian were, as expected, cordial. Margo's eyes went automatically to the only other child present, her cousin Wallace, in his early teens.

Gangly, small-eyed, and already pimply faced, handsomely clothed over narrow shoulders and thin legs, Wallace watched his father kiss Sophia and stoop to kiss the cheek of the child, and he followed suit. Lifting her round cheek for his kiss, Margo jerked and barely restrained an unacceptable shriek when the boy pressed his lips further and took a quick nip at her ear.

Around her, everyone was busy—Kezzie helping with the unloading, the adults getting reacquainted, the staff turning back to the house, their arms and hands full. Margo clapped a hand to her stinging ear and stifled her outcry but was not quick enough to hold back the tears that filled her eyes. Wallace stepped back, keeping hooded eyes on Margo's face. As young as she was, she understood the satisfaction on his countenance and determined then and there that, come what may, she would never give him such satisfaction again. It was a vow that was tested repeatedly.

"Come, cousin," Wallace said calmly. "Let me show you around."

"Thank you," Margo managed in a shaking voice, "but I need to . . . to . . . go with Kezzie." And she fled into the wide hall of Heatherstone and up the stone stairs following closely at the heels of Kezzie, who seemed to know just where to go.

The children's supper was served in the nursery, with supervision by someone named Beadle, a sharp-eyed, needle-thin woman who apparently knew her charge well and kept a keen eye on Wallace. Nevertheless, his booted, swinging foot managed to cruelly crack against Margo's shin time and again, until she turned sideways in her chair, to Wallace's amusement and Beadle's disapproval. Beadle was even more grim of face when Wallace, watching for a time when the woman's face was turned, overturned Margo's glass, flinging its contents not only all across the table but onto Margo and—heavens!—Beadle as well. This fiasco came as near bringing the shaken Margo to tears as anything could have; not for her own sake, but for Beadle's. With tears burning her lids and her voice thin, Margo managed, "I'm sorry, Beadle," but she was rewarded by that lady's sigh and Wallace's smirk.

Too young to defend herself, too young, really, to understand, the child Margo suffered countless humiliations and numerous physical hurts during the next two months when, mercifully, the visit was shortened and the Hugh Galloways returned home.

Kezzie, who had cared for Wallace when he was small, was not blind to what went on; she was not always available, however, to protect her young charge. But she was as ready to leave as Margo, having visited the graves of her husband and three dead children, made a few visits to old acquaintances, and taken Margo, and often Wallace, on various expeditions around the area.

With the carriage at the door and farewells being said, Margo had come prepared. With care she had stood before the mirror after Kezzie had fastened her small hat on her head, and worried and worked a hat pin into it so that it thrust itself out over one ear but was concealed by her hair.

Sure enough, Wallace, with considerable delight that he had her at his mercy for the moment, and after he had dutifully kissed Sophia, backed Margo against the carriage wheel and brought his face down to hers. Turning her cheek toward him and quickly raising her hand as if to hold her hat, she waited the proper moment. Wallace kissed the proffered cheek and, with purpose, pressed his face toward her ear. Margo gave the pin a thrust with the hand already raised and in place. With a gasp Wallace jerked back his head, his hand going to a lip that had promptly showed a drop of blood.

Frightened and trembling, Margo turned and clambered into the carriage. The last she saw of Heatherstone, Scotland, was her cousin Wallace, handkerchief to his lower face, his eyes slitted with fury, one fist clenched at his side.

"Well done, lassie," Kezzie murmured as she made a show of rearranging her young charge's hat.

Through the passing of the next uneventful years, Margo was almost able to put Scotland and its bad memories from her mind. Heatherstone, Canada, was all and in all, and her world rarely extended beyond its borders.

When, at age thirteen, another visit to the "old country" was planned, Margo barely gave Wallace a thought, believing he would have outgrown his foolish childhood. Consequently she looked forward to the trip with some excitement; it would be a welcome change from the ordinary routine of her life.

Now in his early twenties, Wallace had lost most of his pimples, but his complexion was pallid, his mannerisms languid, his eyes too knowing, his hands too free.

Though the outright physical injuries ceased, Wallace's attentions were just as physical in another way. At five the child Margo had been shaken and appalled at actions she couldn't understand; at thirteen it was no different. Innocent as a Scottish bluebell, she was again shaken and appalled at actions she didn't understand: a hand run up and down her arm, a leg thrust against her own, kisses—no biting of the ear, but attempted nibbling of her lips—and glances that, not understood, sent shivers up and down her back. She left Scotland a much wiser girl.

Wallace's farewell kiss this time was proper enough, but his hand, on the side away from the family and servants, pinched Margo—not cruelly, but suggestively—and his face, when he drew back, was filled with that remembered, and hated, satisfaction.

That pale face with the light of victory in the narrow eyes was Margo's last glimpse of her cousin Wallace.

"I'll never, never come back," she vowed silently as the carriage whirled away from Heatherstone, Scotland.

But Wallace—would he come to Heatherstone, Canada?

16

Dear Mam: *Feb. 11, 1879*

One thing I will say about the life of a homesteader: the role of womanhood is greatly respected. Here, on the frontier, our worth is being recognized! While, of course, our physical strength remains inferior to our men's, our strengths in other areas are far superior. I think history must show it to be so.

Our special gifts, Mam, are not only shown in the old, recognized ways—housekeeping, child-bearing, and so on, but in nursing, teaching, and all the finer skills that are so often taken for granted. If there is no wife and mother in the pioneer homestead it is a sorry place indeed.

Pity the poor bachelor! And we have several in Bliss and the surrounding areas. Sometimes they are unmarried, other times the wife cannot or will not submit to the stringent requirements to prove up their place. I figure, Mam, that what Angus must endure, I must also. As for the children, they will remember these days, I think, as sweet in many ways. Certainly the family is close in all ways, for we need each other so. Company is always enriching in one way or another, and every little gain, in any way, is a source of satisfaction.

Winter is upon us, and it is severe. Hidden away here in our wee 'hoosie,' we're not much different than the rabbits when they burrow away, or the beavers hidden in their lodges. For us all, survival is basic.

But for us humans there has to be more than food to make us feel fulfilled, and this is where a mother is so important (never have I blessed my role so fervently as I do these days, nor appreciated how important it is).

It was a great moment when we unloaded our carts and emptied our tent and moved into our cabin. Of this I've written before, and trust my letters have reached you. We must go to Prince Albert for our mail and, during this winter weather, that is not often, so we hear from you seldom. I must say, when Angus makes the trip, I am overcome with dread that he will not return, or that he will be greatly delayed somewhere, and we will be left alone here, with wood for the stove running out, food getting low, and the animals in the little barn needing attention. I know this is wrong of me and that I am showing little faith in the love and care of my heavenly Father. I do need help along this line so much, Mam! I feel like I am holding on to a very slender thread, having been taught so little and being so ignorant of spiritual things. All I know is, the slender thread has been enough. I know God won't let go, and I daren't. But oh, I need discipling so badly! I read my Bible and pray.

"Mummie!" Cameron called from the window. Having heard a sound other than the scratching of his mother's pen, the popping of the fire, and the stirring of his small sister in her sleep, he had hurried to the window, breathed on its ice-furred glass, rubbed and scraped a hole, and discovered the source of the sound, now the jingle of harness, and turned to call over his shoulder excitedly, "Comp'ny! Somebody's coming!"

Hastily gathering up her writing material, Mary thrust it aside, gave a hasty glance down at her apron, found it spotted and removed it, and joined Cameron at the window. Sure enough, a horse and cutter had stopped at a hearty "Whoa!" As Mary and Cammie watched, the lap robe was pushed back, and someone reached a foot toward the snow-packed patch of yard just outside the cabin door.

So bunglesome were the newcomer's wraps that Mary had the door open and had called a greeting before she determined if it was man or woman (or bear!) that approached. But the voice echoing cheerily through the scarf wound around the head was clearly feminine. Behind her, another figure had gone to the horse's head, and called, "Is there room in the barn?"

"Yes, yes, of course!" Mary called back. "Angus—my husband—is there—"

"I'll find him," came the response, and the man led the horse and rig toward the small log barn. The nearer rotund figure had reached the door, stamping at the sill to remove whatever snow had been picked up on the way from the cutter, gray eyes sparkling and the mouth, as soon as the scarf was unwound, smiling.

There they stood—two strangers—smiling so happily at each other that they might have been bosom friends for many years. And indeed, if it hadn't been for the bulky, snow-flecked wraps, Mary might very well have drawn this new acquaintance into a warm, welcoming embrace. As it was, her voice rang with the sincerity of her feelings.

"Oh, do come in. I can't begin to tell you how happy I am to see you. I'm Mary Morrison—"

"I know," the voice emerging from the scarf said. "Sadie LeGare told me."

God bless dear Sadie!

"We were in town last week. Sadie saw me in the store and told me about the new family in Bliss." Removing her gloves, stuffing them in her pockets, and beginning to unbutton the fur coat that made her almost as round as the beavers it had originally graced, the woman added, "We're the Raabs. I'm Cee, short for Celia, and Bela, my husband. No children—yet." And the removal of the coat revealed the reason for the rolling gait and the round form: Cee Raab was very much "with child."

"Due—soon?" Mary asked, though it was not too difficult to assume as Cee seated herself to better remove the overshoes on her feet and even then, with a laugh, needed to submit to Mary's help.

"Very soon. And that's one of the reasons I'm here. Though I'd have come anyway—to get acquainted."

"I'm so glad you did," Mary said fervently, setting the overshoes by the stove and hanging up the coat and scarf on the nails beside the door where her own family's wraps hung.

"This is Cameron, our son," Mary said, turning to the boy standing expectantly at her side. Like a man, Cammie extended his hand, his warm, small one going into the icy-cold one, in proper fashion.

"And this," Mary added, having caught sight of Molly's black, tousled curls peeping around the curtain that had been strung to partition off part of the cabin in an effort for privacy for sleeping and dressing, "is Molly." In a flash Molly was across the floor and to her mother, burying her head in her mother's skirt; it had been a while since the Morrisons had had "comp'ny."

Mary moved her guest to the comfort of a rocker and the warmth of the spot at the side of the stove. While Cee spoke to the children, Mary stuffed fresh wood in the range and pulled the kettle toward the front where it would quickly boil. Tea— good, hot tea—that was the next step in protocol, whether in croft in Scotland or cabin in Canada. Tea—it would bond the two new friends as they sipped together, equally as important as the warmth and comfort it would minister to the traveler.

While the water heated and the teapot warmed, Mary turned to the newcomer, seating herself and saying, "Now, tell me about yourself, Celia Raab."

"Well, for one thing, we live about four miles from you. We're closer to town, near enough to the road so you could stop and see us whenever you go." Cee Raab looked hopeful as she said this. She was, obviously, as lonely as Mary, but without the company of children and the attention and time they consumed in a long, isolated day.

"I'll get my story over quickly," Celia Raab said, adding, "I'm interested to hear yours."

And the two friends settled down while the kettle came to the boil, to begin a friendship, knowing they had all the time they needed to share whatever they wanted. If time ran out today, all the better; there would be another trip and another visit to look forward to, a small glimmer in a dark winter.

"I may as well tell it first as last," Cee said. "If I don't, someone else will. It's not unheard of, but unusual enough to cause considerable interest. You see, I'm a mail-order bride, I guess you'd call it."

Mary's eyes widened. "Hold it," she said, "while I get the tea things. I must hear all about this."

Mary made the tea and, as it brewed, set out the remains of a gingerbread cake she had made the day before. Flushing with satisfaction, she drew her few dainty cups and saucers down from the shelf where they were on display, brought from her trunk four crisp serviettes, and served up the treat.

"You'll stay for supper, of course," she said, thinking ahead.

" 'Fraid not," Cee Raab said with regret. "It gets dark far too soon these days, and we've a distance to go. And if you haven't learned it yet, you will—there are the everlasting chores to take care of. Feeding, milking, egg gathering, not to mention straining the milk and washing the pans and all those things. I guess," she said thoughtfully, "I'm grateful for them, keeps me from going crazy, I suppose."

But Cee spoke with such a good humor and the by-now-familiar sparkle in her eyes that Mary wasn't alarmed. Rather, she was encouraged. Cee Raab had an outlook that was healthy, and Mary was the better for having had a glimpse of it.

"The mail-order bride part—" Mary prodded.

"I guess you know the plight of bachelors here and across the prairies. Truly pathetic, and many of them don't make it, just fold up and quit. Or almost starve to death." Again the twinkle. "Well, Bela was one of them. He'd come from the old country—Hungary—five years ago. Worked in the east for a while until he got enough money . . . and nerve . . . to tackle the wild west. And, of course, here in the bush it's about as wild as you can get. He'd been alone here a couple of years when he met a neighbor of ours from Iowa who gave him my name and suggested he write."

"So you started a correspondence—"

"Not really. His very first letter was a proposal. It was startling, to say the least. But I looked around me—my first husband had died, I was living with my brother and his wife and not too happy about it, and I had no future as far as I could see. The person courting me was a miserable excuse for a man, but my brother was pressing me to get married again. I saw Bela's letter as an avenue of escape—not a very good reason for marriage, I suppose. But having decided to accept his proposal, I made up my mind to make a go of it and be a good wife, regardless of the price I had to pay." Cee's laughter trilled out, happy and free. "Oh, what a price! I gave up nothing, really, and gained so much. And on top of all the blessings Bela brought into my poor, lonely life, there's this—" And Cee's hand was placed gently on her rounded waistline.

Mary couldn't help it; her eyes misted. "Someday," she murmured quickly, for she could hear the men approaching, "I want to hear the details of this remarkable love story."

"And I want to hear yours," Cee said, confident that her new acquaintance, so simple and honest and direct, had a love story of her own.

After Angus and Bela Raab laid aside their wraps, there were the necessary introductions and the seating around the stove— the designated spot for fellowship in any snow-wrapped, bush-bound home—and the subsequent enjoyment of tea and talk.

The following two hours fled by far too rapidly, a wintry oasis in a long dry spell of meaningful relationships.

Finally, when Bela's sigh and glimpse of his pocket watch indicated the time had come to leave, Cee said, with a rush, "Oh, I've forgotten my most important part. Is it possible . . . do you think?"

"Yes?" Mary prompted.

"When it's time . . . for the baby . . . would you come, Mary?"

Mary's eyes grew wide; perhaps the shadows in them were discerned by the expectant mother, for she said, with a rush, "Am I asking too much? Please . . . feel free to tell me if I should look for someone else. But I thought . . . having two of your own—"

"Yes," Mary said slowly, "I've had two of my own. But not these two," and she indicated Cammie and Molly playing quietly nearby. "There was another. . . ."

Angus's hand reached for his wife's as Mary's tale faltered. "We lost our second child on the trip over. I'm not sure Mary has gotten over the experience. Cameron is ours by love, not birth."

"It's time," Mary said into the silence that fell with only the popping of the poplar wood to interject sound, "it's time . . . for healing. I don't know how much good I'll be, Cee, but I'll come and do what I can, and gladly."

Obvious relief struggled with uncertainty on Celia Raab's round face.

Angus's words sealed the bargain. "Good girl," he said quietly to his wife. To his new friends he said, "Get word to us, and I'll see that Mary gets there. Now, if you are sure you can't stay for supper—"

But Bela Raab was rising and turning toward his coat and overshoes; Cee took Mary's hand in a quick grasp and, smiling, said through tears, "Thank you, my friend."

With the cutter once again at the door and Bela waiting, Cee, bundled and swathed, gave the children bearlike hugs and said her good-byes. With her hand on the doorknob, she turned, drew the enveloping scarf away from her mouth, and said: "I almost forgot the best part . . . the best part of my story. It's about my heritage. You see," the gray eyes shone, "I'm the child of a King."

"A . . . a king?" Mary questioned, clearly surprised, and clearly puzzled by such an amazing confession.

"By birth," Celia Raab explained happily. "New birth, actually. I've been born again."

"Why then . . . why then . . ." Mary whispered, beginning to grasp the implications of what this new acquaintance was saying, "why then, we're sisters."

"Oh, Mary! Have you . . . are you—?"

"Yes! Yes!" Mary was singing, her joy in her friend more than she had known it would be. "I'm part of the family!"

In spite of Cee's girth, the two women wrapped their arms around each other; in spite of Cee's awkwardness, the two women performed a small jig of pure delight before they stepped apart, Mary's tears mopped by a corner of the clean apron she had donned and Cee's tears disappearing into the wool of her scarf.

"And Bela?" Mary finally asked.

"Bela, too," Cee said. "It's what finally caused me to write and tell him I'd come. He ended his letter, you see, by telling me he was a Christian and had prayed over the whole plan and hoped I was the same, and praying, too. How could I have come, otherwise?"

After the cutter disappeared, with Mary and Angus and the children waving a shivering farewell from the snowy step, the small house seemed a bright haven to the little family who shut the door on snow and ice that went out across their known world, over the bush, over the silent and frozen lakes and the frozen tundra, to the north pole, and beyond. Here they were safe, here they were content. Here, in this wee spot, their dreams were incubating and, with spring and sun and showers, would blossom into reality.

Mary chattered on about her new friend, telling as much of Cee's story as she knew "To have a friend and not too far away, Angus," she said, "means so much. And then to know she, too, is part of the family . . ." Starry-eyed with the wonder of it, Mary's voice trailed off.

Bela, it seemed, as overflowing in his witness as his wife, had left a small but clear testimony with Angus. On top of all that Mary had shared across the past months, it was all that was needed.

"Do you think," Angus asked quietly after the children were snug in bed for the night, "there's room for one more son in the family?"

Bowing his head over the oak table, the icicles around Angus's heart melted in a God-sent chinook that warmed and melted all resistance, and tears—first of repentance and then of pure joy— ran down his craggy Scottish face to be absorbed eventually by that long-suffering apron as Mary wrapped her arms around her husband and welcomed him to the family of God. Now, truly, her heart told her, they would be a close-knit unit. Now they could be the parents they ought to be; now they would be the influence and blessing this new land needed. *Yea . . . yes, yes, yes . . . happy is that people, whose God is the Lord.*

<hr>

Mary's letter, long unmailed because of many interruptions including storms and birth, was finally to be completed.

Dear Mam:

I hope you don't think we're dead or, at the best, snowed in. We have been that—snowed in. Thank God for a good woodpile and a fairly well-filled cellar. As I told you, we

*did a lot of preparing, or as much as time allowed, before
winter hit.*

*We're so blessed, Mam. Since my last attempt at writing,
more than one significant thing has happened to add to those
already considerable blessings. First, Angus found the Lord!
That does seem like a ridiculous way to put it, as if the Lord
were lost or something. It's more like the Lord found Angus,
for he's the one who was lost, and the Lord, the Good
Shepherd, was the one doing the seeking. It all came about
this way.*

It being a long day, with no interruptions, Mary filled the time
with writing the details of the Raabs' introduction into their lives,
of learning that Celia was a Christian and her husband, also, of
how Bela had quietly dropped a word in Angus's ear as they visited in the barn and how the Holy Spirit had used it to fan the
small flames already ignited and smoldering into a bright flame
in Angus's heart.

My joy is complete, Mary wrote, trying to express the happiness.

*It seems to me that both husband and wife should believe,
truly making them one, and that a father and mother should
be of one mind in what they tell their children and how they
live before them.*

*As for the Raabs, they have become dear and trusted
friends. And how we do need one another on the frontier. One
never knows when an emergency will arise. Cee Raab is what
is known as a mail-order bride, a fascinating story and one
that turned out well. Others, in like situations, find
themselves not only married to a stranger but one for whom
they have little or no liking, and with whom they have to live*

in the most close, even most intimate, association. I shudder to think of it, shut in for long months with some unwashed, uncouth, unlearned—Oh, I could go on and on as I conjure up the dreadful picture of such marriages.

Though I dreaded it much, I promised Celia that I would be with her at the time of the birth of her expected bairn. Some stranger came for me, since Bela would not leave Cee in her fears and anxieties. Believe me, it took a lot of pluck on my part, and more on Angus's part, to climb into the sleigh of a complete stranger and head out into the whiteout with no sure destination in sight. But people are honorable and helpful, and women are much respected, and I was perfectly safe, being delivered to the Raabs' door.

Of the birth I will write but little, Mam. It brought back memories, few of them good. I tried to think about Molly's birth and the joy, but horrible memories of my wee Angel's arrival and death threatened me every moment. Oh, how I prayed (and Angus has told me he did the same, here with the children), and somehow I got through. And I was able to be happy for my friends in the safe arrival of wee Howard, who was almost immediately called Howie, whether or not due to his howls I can't say!

I stayed another day with the Raabs, and Cee and I had many a good talk. We long to spend more time together. Homesteads, though isolated from each other, are not so, extremely, and it is possible to visit from time to time. Prince Albert, I understand, has its Merrie Minglers Sewing Club, about which Cee and I are somewhat dubious, not being the greatest seamstresses. But we will surely set up some system just as soon as we can find out what other women may have settled in our district.

You know, of course, that we have no school as yet, and that I am teaching Cammie and will teach Molly. Usually, in these homesteading areas, the community is quick to build itself a school, and this will come along in due time. Right now our children are too scattered. But with spring and better weather, the available land will be taken up, it is believed. And when a school is erected, Mam, can church services be far behind? This thought occupies our thoughts and prayers very much. Many such church services carry on without a minister, with the women (I must admit, sadly) usually carrying the responsibility. Cee and I are willing to do this but feel blessed that in our case we have menfolk who are as eager for spiritual things as we are.

"I'm hungry, Mummie," a small voice said at Mary's knee, and she looked into the eyes—so like her own—of her own dear Molly.

"Why, of course you are, lassie! It's time for tea and Da will be in soon. Give me a moment to finish my letter to Grandmam—"

The birth of wee Howie, Mary wrote lastly, *has made me long for another bairn for Angus and me. Seeing Bela Raab with his son made me yearn to place a son of his very own in Angus's arms. And then, I suppose every woman feels a sort of sadness when she thinks she may have given birth to her last child. The Lord (and Angus) willing, I shall experience that wonderful blessing once again.*

Yr. loving daughter, Mary

Accustomed to the world of good breeding, impeccable manners, and refined conversation, Sophia felt at times as though she were living on the edge of chaos, where all she had known was challenged by the untamed, the vigorous, the brash.

Accustomed to the aristocratic life with its contempt for unbridled emotions, she sensed the ebullience and turbulence that throbbed and pulsed with explosive possibilities, to the very gates of Heatherstone.

Accustomed to an accepted pattern dividing the genteel from the vulgar, and where the line was not crossed, this new intermingling of classes and crossing of standards seemed, to Sophia, to threaten her personally.

Far, far removed from Sophia the cabins where mothers raised their children on dirt floors, with low doors, no windows, and rain seeping through sod roofs. Beyond her understanding the home where chairs were tree stumps and a feather bed was considered a luxury. Her dreariest imagination never conjured up a home with a water bucket and dipper and, on a shelf, some coffee, dried beans, flour, salt, and baking powder if you were lucky. Never had she seen an iron pot, frying pan, and coffeepot as the only utensils available to prepare her meals. Canvas or bed sheets never separated her sleeping quarters from those of her children.

All her life she had known that among crofters impoverished conditions existed, but it was so accepted, so much a part of their way of life, never challenged and rarely complained about, that her personal feelings had never been affronted. Now, though she had not experienced the rawness of life on the frontier, its very existence in thousands of rude dwellings seemed a thing alive, pulsating, pressing, not to be endured unendingly. There was a restlessness in their world, and even behind the massive doors and over the quiet carpets of Heatherstone it made its presence known. Legions of men and women came, like caterpillars creeping, moving, pressing into all the valleys and over all the hills and down all the rivers of the west, and their silence was loud.

Drinking her tea and planning her next garden party, just out of mind but not out of sense, countless women—no less wise, just as lovely, no better suited—washed on a scrub board beside a soddy, cooked over buffalo chips, swept wooden floors and sprinkled dirt ones, churned their own butter from cows they had milked, spun their own wool from sheep they had sheared, bathed their children in washtubs with soap they had made.

Of their gardening, canning, slaughtering, curing, and spinning, Sophia knew nothing but sensed much. Their activities, though removed in space, stirred the strong bastions of tradition in some unknown way, and Sophia felt herself to live on the edge of change. And didn't like it.

Thank goodness for Hugh and his unchanging observance of all things solid and familiar. Well-bred, well-educated, well-mannered, well-behaved, well-spoken, a gentleman in all respects,

Hugh would do nothing more rash than raise a proper eyebrow should the world cave in.

And so, with grim disregard of the changing times, Sophia took extra care to raise her daughter within the boundaries of decorum and the traditions set by good Queen Victoria. Margaret ... "Margo" ... sewed daintily on nothing whatsoever useful, had music lessons and voice lessons, memorized Bible verses (within reason), and had supervised play. There were tea parties, croquet, skits and amateur plays, and, in the winter, sleigh rides and skating.

Margo took care that all her friends wrote in her autograph book and she in theirs, such things as:

> Be good, my dear, and let who will be clever;
> Do noble things, not dream them all day long;
> And so make life, death, and the vast hereafter
> One grand, sweet song.

At times she called with her mother and made brief appearances in the drawing room when guests were received. Tessie or some other qualified member of the staff took her for walks and occasionally picnics with friends.

With money no object and Margo's training of vast importance, private tutors were hired for her education. Of course the spacious house offered a library of impressive proportion, and Margo had free rein (within reason) to all her father's historical and scientific material. All instruction, all learning, was laced liberally with moral and cultural lessons so that, to all intents and purposes, Margo might as well have been raised and educated with her mother and father a generation earlier. Well educated in certain ways, she was ignorant of life, especially life in the new land, and peculiarly unsuited to be anything other than a lady of leisure.

Not unhappy, Margo was never truly happy except in the presence of Nanny Kezzie. Here the outside was forgotten as though it didn't exist. Here, no matter her state of mind, no matter her age, she found acceptance and love, a love that didn't have to be earned, a love that was never questioned or doubted. Kezzie soothed her angel child in times of distress, doctored her every illness, and, through it all, dispensed honest, down-to-earth wisdom that was to offer the only balance Margo was to know to her pointless lifestyle.

The greatest misery of her young life was suffered with the appearance of a letter from Angus, Kezzie's son-in-law in the savage and untamed territories (for so Margo supposed them to be).

Dear Mam, a shaken Kezzie eventually read to her Mr. Hugh, to Sophia, and, later, to Margo. It was the only way she knew to make the child understand why her Granny/Nanny would forsake her.

After all these years, Mam, Mary is to have another child. While it has always been the longing of her heart, and mine, too, still I am near distracted with concern. As you know, though it has been almost a dozen years since we lost our wee bairn at sea and came close to losing our Mary, the memory has faded but little, and this new pregnancy has brought it all back. Especially since Mary is no longer young. My heart is very sore over the thought of the suffering she must endure.

You've talked often of coming to see us. And yet it has never come to pass; one thing or another has hindered. Now that the railroad is within two hundred miles of us, the trip is easier, and, except for the winter months, it is not the endurance experience it once was.

I'm asking, Mam, if you will come. Mary will not ask, and yet her anxieties are plain to me. Your presence is needed, Mam. Too, you haven't seen our Molly and Cammie in all these years. Cam is almost a man, and Molly is budding into a sweet young woman.

117

Will you come? We all join in our pleas and prayers that you will do so.

Margo could not imagine life without Kezzie. And yet she was mature enough to understand the reason for her going. White-faced and silent she watched Kezzie, almost equally white-faced, make preparations to go.

Finally, whispering from quivering lips, Margo asked, "Kezzie . . . Granny . . . can I go, too?"

With an outright sob Kezzie turned from her packing to take the thirteen-year-old in her arms. Wordless, weeping together, Margo understood the futility of her request.

Sophia did her best. Gratified in some ways that the association had been broken between her child and her servant, she felt it was time to move on. Margaret, as she always called her daughter, would soon forget, and she hoped earnestly that Kezzie's move would be a permanent one.

"After all," she told Hugh, "it isn't as if there is anything . . . constructive she can do anymore. . . ." Her voice trailed away when Hugh's head, bent over his paper, stiffened, and his cheek tightened.

"I'll never understand," he said at last, quietly, "your attitude toward Kezzie. You're not in some sort of competition with her, you know, Sophia—"

Now it was Sophia who stiffened.

"The Galloways are indebted to her in ways. . . ." Hugh was shaking his head back and forth, back and forth, in a way that was more speaking than the voice that trailed off into silence.

"Hugh," Sophia began, helplessly, never quite able to express the uneasiness she experienced regarding Kezzie's relationship to Margaret. Perhaps it stemmed from the fact that the elderly woman had been present at the child's birth; perhaps she had bonded in the age-old way. At any rate, Sophia knew relief that the call had come for Kezzie's help, so far away.

"We shall have to let her go," Hugh said simply, adding, "but I believe she'd stay . . . if I asked her to do so. I'll not, of course.

It's Cameron and Molly's turn. And Mary's due." With that he turned back to his paper.

Sophia did her best to step into the gap left by Kezzie's absence, and there was a sweet summer of getting to know her own daughter better than ever before. Bordering on womanhood, Margo was showing signs of the dark beauty she would become. But a beauty she did not know she possessed, with no pride or arrogance because of it. If Margaret Galloway had any pride, it was in the Galloway name and the Galloway position. Understated in all ways, still it existed, a powerful force if necessary; a silent force, held in abeyance, at other times. It gave Margo a dignity, an assurance, the air and manner of an aristocrat taking all advantages for granted.

How much of this was based on the Galloway name and prestige, and how much on the love and security of fiercely loving and loyal Kezia Skye, was hard to say. But the first shifting of Margo's confidence, not to mention her satisfaction with life, came with Kezzie's letter in the fall of that year.

This is a very difficult letter to write. My heart, as always, is with my Mr. Hugh and his family. Such service, it seems, is born and bred into us, and, after a lifetime devoted to it, cannot be easily turned from.

My Mary has had a most difficult time of it, almost as bad as she went through on the crossing thirteen years ago. The bairn did not survive, and Mary barely.

This is the busy time of year, what with threshing, canning, reaping the bounty of a year's hard labor and God's free provision through the bush. One's very existence during the coming year depends on the harvest. While my own strength has faded with the years, still I can do many things, and with dear Molly's help (she's almost sixteen now), we

*manage. Most of all, I can keep Mary quiet and resting,
whereas she'd be wild with worry otherwise because of the
work.*

*Thankfully there is a school in Bliss now, and Mary has
not had to teach the children for several years. Cameron
attends Emmanuel College in Prince Albert; in bad weather
he stays in town all week, with old friends Sadie and Pierre
LeGare. There are numerous advantages here, and we are by
no means an uncultured people. The "Penny Readings
Society," for instance (so called because of the admission
charged), is uplifting as well as entertaining—when one can
get to town. Sports are vigorous and exciting; Cameron excels
at a game called "shinny," which is played on ice. Baseball and
cricket flourish but have been passed in enthusiasm by curling.
Yes, Prince Albert possesses many natural advantages, and
intelligent people are at work turning it into an even more
attractive place than before.*

*In spite of all of that, winter is desperate, with many dark
and dreary days. In Mary's frame of mind it is important that
I be here, especially with the children gone so much. I know I
am rambling on, but it is so difficult to just come out and say I
am not coming "home" at this time. Perhaps by spring.*

Margo's tears, when she was allowed to read her parents' letter, ran like rain, in the privacy of her own room. And they
increased, if that were possible, when she opened the small, sealed
note included for her.

Dear Margo:

*By now you've read the letter trying to explain why I
cannot come back at this time. You cannot understand how
torn my heart is, wanting to be with you and needing to be*

here. Somehow we'll both—you and I—get through this long, hard winter; and spring, God willing, will find my darling girl in my arms again.

Spring, with its promise of so much, didn't live up to expectations where Kezzie was concerned. The next letter was from Angus.

I regret to inform you that Mam (Kezzie) had a very bad fall on the ice shortly after the new year and has not healed well. Perhaps it is rheumatism that has set in, or perhaps the hip was more severely damaged than we knew and has not healed right. At any rate, she is in no condition to travel, though the train has made it to our area at last and is a great boon to industry and trade as well as travel.

I believe she was about fifteen years old when you were born, Hugh, and she became your nanny and nurse, and you became her life. So you know how old she is now (seventy-five, I believe), and for all of that time you, and eventually little Margaret, have been the center of her life. Now she needs care herself, and we are able to offer it. Her care will be our chief concern; you may count on it.

Kezzie cannot bring herself to write at this time and has a hard time reconciling herself to her present weakness of body. Her heart is as game as ever. She sends her love to all, particularly Margaret for whom she cares a great deal.

Sophia read the letter to her daughter and was uneasy at the girl's reaction. Other than paling a trifle, there was little or no indication that the news had affected her. Perhaps Margo turned away more abruptly than she might have otherwise, and perhaps she was more quiet than usual from that time on, but Sophia was gay enough and talkative enough to cover any and all such awkward moments.

By fall even Sophia had to admit that Margaret was drooping. "Her blood is thinning," she told her husband and plied Margo with more of the nostrums she had continued to put her trust in. "She's on the verge of becoming a . . . becoming . . . well, she's leaving the girlhood stage, and her—" Sophia, a true Victorian, couldn't bring herself to say "body." "Her *system* is, er, maturing. It's all perfectly natural. You'll see."

Nevertheless, Sophia worried. She could establish no warm comradeship with her daughter, being turned aside with politeness, casualness, and silence on Margo's part.

Finally, with impatience, Sophia suggested boarding school. To her surprise Margo offered no objection and was trundled off to Ontario's best. Christmases and holidays brought consolation to Sophia's heart; Margo seemed natural and at ease, though more quiet than she had thought a daughter of hers would be. They had some good times together, Hugh usually occupied elsewhere, but both Sophia and Margo seemed relieved when it was time for school to take up again.'

And so the next blow, when it came, may not have had the impact it would have had if Margo and her mother had developed and maintained the relationship they both needed and longed for but were never to know.

⌐——∘

Margo was summoned to the head sister's sitting room. She went with some trepidation since her decorum and obedience had never made such a bidding necessary before.

"Sit down, my dear," Sister Grace said kindly. "I'm afraid the news isn't good. Your mother is very ill, and your father has asked that you come home immediately."

"What . . . what is wrong?" Margo managed, stunned. One's mother—so much younger than one's father—was the vigorous, healthy person upon whose long life one could depend.

"Something to do with the lungs, I believe," Sister Grace supplied, but she could add no more information. "Someone—your father's groom, I understand—has come for you."

More lonely than she had been since Kezzie's absence, Margo's only sign of affection had come from her mother. And had not been recognized. And was only dimly recognized now. Margo, in fact, felt hardly more lonely after Sophia was declared dead than she had before. Hardly more lonely but infinitely more alone.

Sophia, who had always been there, a bond between the girl and the man, was gone, and Margo had no inroad to her father's heart or life.

Heatherstone—1897

I'll be bringing several business associates for dinner tonight," Hugh Galloway informed his daughter over their morning coffee. "Will you take care of it?"

"Of course, Papa. I'll talk to Dauphine immediately when we're done here. There shouldn't be any problem. Will there be women in the group?"

"No, just men. You can count on eight, I believe. It's a business affair, actually." Hugh often substituted the dinner table for the conference room.

Margo sighed, half relieved, half disappointed. Hostess to these affairs of her father's, she found them to be both a trial and a pleasure. She accompanied Hugh on occasional dinner engagements and to various social functions, and these were enjoyable enough but rarely included people her age. As for entertaining at Heatherstone, she occasionally gleaned—and enjoyed—small glimpses into her father's business affairs. If only he allowed her to be a part of them! She would find her interest rising, only to be snuffed out by ignorance. For usually, when dinner was over and coffee served, Hugh excused her, and she spent the evening in the library or in her room.

Hugh's shutting her out of all things connected with his business puzzled her. She understood, though she couldn't recall how she knew, that he had wanted a son. But all men do, she reasoned, and, not having one, surely they should settle for the daughter the Lord gave them and make the best of it!

Hugh was sixty. Though in fairly good health, time was running out for training someone to be in a place of responsibility with the eventuality of his sickness or death. She, Margo, was the logical person. Moreover, she had reasonably good intelligence, knew how to conduct herself around people of importance and, most of all, had little or nothing to do. Dauphine ran the house very well; cook had been with the family ever since Heatherstone was built; and Hugh's personal needs were attended to by his attendant, Bailey. Margo felt ready, and frustrated, in all respects.

Now, planning another business dinner, a surge of rebellion at her uselessness and Hugh's lack of interest in her life caused her to say, daringly, "I'd like to stay in, Papa. I'd like to be in on what goes on. I'd like to—"

Margo's words faltered. Hugh's face was not scornful, it was not angry. It was not bored—the reaction she dreaded most. The face her father lifted toward her was simply blank. Blank, as if what she had said was incomprehensible to him.

"I'll tell you what," he said. "After we've adjourned to the drawing room, you be prepared to join us. Perhaps you could bring in fresh coffee at that point. A little feminine company would go well about then. There will be," he added thoughtfully, "several young men present tonight. How does that sound, my dear?"

Hot color surged into Margo's cheeks. Had her father deliberately misunderstood? Or was he showing a father's natural interest in his daughter's future, which, of course, could only include marriage?

It was neither of those, Margo thought instinctively. After almost twenty years under his roof, she knew her father well. Here again, as across the years from her first memory, she had come face up with supreme indifference. And again, as countless times across the years, she was at a loss to understand why.

Never cruel, never anything but mannerly, Hugh had a reserve that did not allow Margo's entrance. When she spoke, he listened politely, almost as a stranger might listen. Her every need was cared for. But he lived behind closed doors—where Margo was concerned. As a child she knew him as an idol to be worshipped but from afar. Entering her young womanhood, she realized that to his wife Hugh showed a degree of warmth and an interest that Margo was not privileged to share. The hurt increased, but the understanding did not.

Now, with her mother gone and doing all she could to be not only daughter but companion to him, she failed again, and finally, battled resentment, despair, even anger.

Now, with yet another demonstration of her father's complete lack of understanding, Margo rose to her feet, her breath ragged and her lips, in spite of everything, trembling so that natural speech was difficult. She spoke from behind her serviette before laying it aside: "As you wish, Papa."

As it turned out, three of the eight gentlemen were young, unmarried, eligible, and obviously attracted to the young daughter of magnate Hugh Galloway. Myron Dalton, Chester Fleer, and Winfield Craven all made themselves agreeable, even entertaining, and when Margo withdrew from the table, stood and bowed, expressing a desire that she join them later.

It would have taken a very indifferent female, indeed, not to enjoy, even enjoy greatly, the attention. When at last she opened the great double doors to the drawing room and, accompanied by Casper, the butler, with a cart of after-dinner refreshers, carried in the silver service, the three young men were on their feet, quick to take the tray, to assist Margo in serving and, at last, to settle at her feet and side with warm glances and earnest, sometimes arch, conversation.

Margaret had the good sense to know that, with her dark beauty (though she never thought of it as that) and her vivid coloring, it would be easy to look overblown and gaudy, and so tonight, as always, though dressed expensively, her costume was simple to the point of plainness. Fitting snugly at the waist and flaring above at the shoulders and below over the hips, its chief attraction was its variegated color. Walking through the park and entranced with the autumn hues, she had whimsically gathered a bouquet of leaves touched with the muted fading colors, and had taken them to a French dyeing establishment to be copied. When delivered, the proprietor, Lewando, had cunningly added his personal verse, thus proving again his rare gift for pleasing his customers and bringing a smile to Margo's lips:

> What loveliness! Whose art is this?
> It leaves naught to desire!
> Lewando's name upon the box
> Proclaims the Champion Dyer.

Her dark hair, so excessively curly that certain hairstyles were out of the question, was pulled back loosely and gathered at the nape of the neck with a large, pomegranate-colored bow. Slippers of the same shade peeped from below her hem line, and their French heel and satin strap buttoning across the instep proclaimed them handsome as well as expensive.

Margo's natural vivid coloring was enhanced by the attention she was receiving as the men vied for her glance and smile. Before long, the expertise of Winfield Craven became clear. When Chester Fleer turned to direct a comment toward Hugh and the other gentlemen, Winfield skillfully engaged Margo in a conversation that kept her gaze turned his way; only with rudeness could she have interrupted the flow of the account he was telling not only verbally but with flashing hands and expressive face. Then, when Myron Dalton rose to replenish his drink, Winfield slipped from his position on the hassock at Margo's feet to the coveted spot at her side, where the fascinating story continued. Nor did he move when Myron returned, to stand, fiddling with his drink, shifting from foot to foot and finally turning to engage someone else in conversation.

When the men rose to take their departure and Casper had brought their hats, canes, and coats—ankle-length, with or without velvet collars but macintoshes without exception, and all, without exception, including a detachable cape and made of the finest wool or cashmere—Winfield Craven managed to insert himself with his back to the men, facing Margo.

"Thank you for a most enjoyable evening," he said, making it sound her personal accomplishment and taking her hand and holding it.

As Margo was responding to the usual banalities of the others, Casper opened the door. It was clear that the snow, which had begun earlier in the evening, was still falling and falling thickly.

"Miss Galloway," Winfield Craven said, "it seems too golden an opportunity to miss the first sleigh ride of the year. Unless we have a thaw, would you do me the honor of accompanying me on a sleigh ride this coming Sunday afternoon?"

Seeing no reason not to . . . rather dreading the beginning of the long, quiet winter . . . and rather amused at the persistence of the man, Margo assented.

Parting to go to their separate quarters, Margo turned to her father and mentioned the invitation. "I don't suppose you mind, Papa," she added, and would have found her pulse leaping if he had so much as voiced an opinion—approval or disapproval, it mattered not.

But Hugh Galloway turned toward the stairs, to shut himself away until coffee time the next morning, with a murmured "fine, fine" that said, clearly, nothing at all.

Margo removed the autumn-tinted gown, prepared herself for bed, and gazed into a future that was as dark as the night itself.

Having nothing better to do, she turned her thoughts to the handsome face and polished manners of Winfield Craven. Drifting off to sleep, she fancied the darkness showed the faintest glow of light.

19

In an era that was to have the distinction of being known as the "Gay Nineties," life within the silent walls of Heatherstone proceeded much the same as always. Never having suffered want, the young woman Margaret Galloway hardly knew that with the passing of the mid-nineties, a painful depression lifted, and the dream of countless men reasserted itself: Every man could be a success. Birth no longer controlled one's destiny; anyone with sufficient gumption could go from rags to riches.

Such confidence made for snobbish women and brazen young men. Margo, in her stone prison, had no reason to feel superior, never having known anything else. But young men such as Winfield Craven often were brash seekers of the status and wealth that could be had for the grabbing. Legitimate fortunes, on the other hand, were being made; a country founded on fur, fish, and timber was benefiting from the raw energy that immigrants and the sons of immigrants were exhibiting.

Ostentation abounded, especially among the newly rich. The overall effect in home décor was pompous, and clutter was adored. To most people the simple richness of Heatherstone smacked of "old fashioned." To Hugh it was an oasis after an exhausting day in a world gone wild.

Everything was huge; Chicago builders were erecting a skyscraper ten stories high! Doors were massive; stairways were wide; hotel styles were medieval castles; department stores, churches, city halls towered on new-paved boulevards.

People were huge; extra weight was looked upon as proof that health and affluence were being fully enjoyed.

Though men's clothing was sober and conservative, and bushy sideburns and beards were out of fashion, the nineties change was apparent in women's fashions.

The bustle was finally gone, but its bulk, which had been concentrated on the lower rear, was shifted to the sleeve and the bosom. The wasp waist was in, with the tight-laced corset responsible for the new look. Tight at the waist, skirts flared to a bell shape below, and waists puffed out over cummerbunds and sleeves ballooning to leg-of-mutton proportions and larger. Below the dress skirts a haircloth lining extended to the knees in order that female thighs would not reveal shape or movement. But women were lifting their hemlines a shocking eight inches and in many other ways giving more than subtle hints of the liberties they were to strive for and, eventually, to gain.

At home, in the dark-paneled library, the clock ticking away her life minute by slow minute, Margo spread out each day's newspaper and read how women were entering into arts colleges; women (the naughtier ones!) were on the stage; women novelists abounded; factories and offices bulged with women.

Not everyone approved. When some two hundred women had taken jobs in one Ontario city, a subscriber complained "only cupidity, selfishness and pride" were behind it, and added that soon only housework would be left for menfolk to do.

Hugh didn't approve. Such organizations as the Women's Temperance Union, as devoted to fighting for women's right to vote as they were against booze, darkened his aristocratic brow. Margo, yearning to gain his approval, couldn't muster the courage to suggest that she do something constructive with her life. She saw her father's business enterprises as perfect outlets for her energies but got nowhere with her hesitant suggestions.

With Kezzie moved away and her mother dead, Margo's education along some lines was almost totally nonexistent. She had understood, when puberty came, that it was proper to lower her hemlines; she knew she could go nowhere alone; she knew that even engaged couples didn't appear in public without a chaperone and, on those rare occasions when a young man came to call, some member of her father's staff was required to be in the room. She knew, somehow, that flirting was dangerous and, if indulged in, might lead to the downfall of some young man; her very conversation could refine him and drive from his bosom ignoble and impure thoughts.

Hugh probably never knew that his library contained a plain brown-wrapped book titled *Light on Dark Corners* that was to puzzle his daughter as much as enlighten her. Old wives' tales, sermonettes, Victorian morals left Margo no wiser than before she read them. "Strive for mental excellence," the book urged, "and you will never be found in the sinks of pollution. . . . Beauty is shallow, dangerous, deceitful, reigning only to ruin. . . . No sensible young man with a future will marry a flirt. . . . Any improper liberties will change love to sensuality and affections will become obnoxious if not repellent."

One bit of advice caused her to have second thoughts regarding Winfield and how very little she knew of him: "Never marry a man that does not make his mother a Christmas present." How, she wondered, does one determine such matters, without prying—certainly an undesirable trait in a female.

On one point only was she reassured: "Red-whiskered men," the treatise on Advice to Maiden, Wife, and Mother—Love,

Courtship, and Marriage propounded, "should not marry brunettes." Winfield was not a redhead! On this one fragile point Margo cautiously moved into a relationship with Winfield Craven.

With change sweeping around her, Margo was almost as cloistered as a nun. But with less, much less, to do. And without the satisfaction of one devoted to her chosen lifestyle.

While Margo had little more to worry about than giving an "at-home"—those designated hours when the other ladies of the city were free to call—with its strict rules of etiquette, railways were spilling settlers by the thousands into the void that was the West. Towns mushroomed, springing up around schools and churches and police posts. Raw railway stations became centers for squalid, pathetic Indians hoping to sell feather work or buffalo horns, their garments tattered and almost as disreputable as those of the former buffalo hunters who wandered aimlessly across the land, their future uncertain and their livelihood gone.

While Margo and others entertained themselves with Mr. Edison's amazing talking machine, out west families still huddled in huts of sod or tar paper; roads were rutted nightmares; ornate cast-iron stoves blazed summer and winter, and porridges, soups, beans, and rabbit stews simmered endlessly on the back lid. Here men struggled out in temperatures of fifty degrees below zero to do chores morning and evening; here women washed clothes and hung them on lines to freeze into bizarre shapes. Here injuries were treated at home, and the dead were packed away in granaries to await the spring thaw and burial.

Tested and tried beyond their eastern sisters' ability to understand, pioneer women overcame—if they were a tough breed and most were—or broke under the strain and died. In such instances their place was filled without delay if that were possible. Often the distant family, hearing of the need, sent another sister, or cousin, or some willing female, to marry the bereaved husband and to raise his children.

In the deep bush, in a district named Bliss but just as often known for despair, Mary Morrison was one of the survivors. Always, through sickness, deprivation, loneliness, and weariness, the grace and beauty of her Lord was evident. Mary's life was a shining light, a bright example of her Savior's purpose as set forth in John 12:46: "I am come a light into the world, that whosoever believeth on me should not abide in darkness."

Mary barely pulled through the birth and death of the child that had brought Kezzie from the east to be with her. Kezzie's joy in being with her daughter and grandchildren, dear as they were, could not make up for the emptiness and grief she felt upon leaving her Mr. Hugh and beloved Margo.

Mary recovered, but her physical strength was limited. Her spirit, however, glowed its strength without flickering and beckoned many a hungry-hearted neighbor to its warmth and fulfillment. Many a neighbor and visitor—but never Kezzie.

Kezzie saw, and Kezzie listened. At times it seemed that the need lurking deep in her fading eyes would break the silence of her lips. She warmed her heart at Mary's joy; she bowed her head when Mary prayed, but never a prayer passed her lips.

Angus, Cameron, and Molly had found Mary's witness irresistible, and each, in time, confessed a need for "something," prayed a sincere prayer of repentance, and found satisfaction in Christ Jesus.

It was not often that Kezzie accompanied her family to the church services held in the small Bliss schoolhouse. One time, however, when she was present, the minister, speaking of death and urging his listeners to be ready, mentioned the "Grim Reaper." Mary's eyes turned to Kezzie's face, watching it whiten and her jaw tighten. Kezzie's eyes, the blue of the wide Saskatchewan sky, took on a sick expression; still she did not move out and forward when invited to do so.

Soon, in her devotional time at home, Mary shared, casually it seemed, the story of Lazarus and the rich man, reading aloud for Kezzie, who mended nearby, the last half of the sixteenth chapter of Luke.

"Did you catch that, Mam?" she asked, repeating "the beggar died, and was carried by the angels into Abraham's bosom."

"Abraham's bosom?" a puzzled Kezzie questioned.

"Before Christ and the New Testament," Mary explained, "the best hope of the Hebrew people was to be welcomed by Abraham into a place of supreme happiness. Abraham was called the father of the faithful, you know. And he welcomed into paradise the godly person. Now we know—through the New Testament—that when believers die they depart to be with Christ, which is far better."

"Ah."

"But the part that makes me so happy . . . so blessed, Mam, is this part about the convoy of angels waiting there, ready to just fly away with this poor beggar."

"Ah-huh." Kezzie's response was guarded.

"Think of it—angels, Mam. No grim reaper for God's people!"

Kezzie started. "No grim reaper," she whispered.

Mary was quick to follow up her point. "That takes all the fear out of dying for me. With my final breath I can expect angels to take me right away into Christ's presence!" Mary's voice thrilled with the thought.

"And for you, too, Mam, and all who accept Him as their personal Savior."

The shutters came down over the eyes again, and though the lips quivered, they remained sealed.

Mary saw, and the light on her face quenched. "It's so simple, Mam, so simple. Anyone can do it, pray a sincere prayer of confession, receive forgiveness—and God never fails to forgive—and accept Christ. Old things pass away, all things become new—"

But Kezzie's head was bent over her mending. Mary's voice trailed away . . . she had explained it so many times. And always, as now, it seemed she ran head-on into a brick wall.

"I can't understand it," Mary said later to Angus as they prepared for bed. "I know God is working—I've prayed so much, He just has to be! And I can see the hunger in her eyes and on her face. But it's as if she's bound. Much as I want to," Mary's voice broke, "I can't do it for her."

Angus, dear faithful Angus, knelt at the bedside with his wife, and together they lifted the dear one up to the throne of grace—again.

Margo's first realization that something was ailing her father came at the breakfast table. Hugh refused his coffee in favor to tea. At Margo's raised eyebrows he explained, "Just a little stomach upset, my dear. Tea—if you remember Kezzie's firm conviction—is a great healer." Hugh's smile did much to allay Margo's small concern.

And after several days of tea and toast, Hugh did appear to be feeling better. Enough so that when Margo raised the question of the sleigh ride, he waved a thin hand, shrugged, and went back to his newspaper with, "Young Craven, you say? As good as any, I suppose."

Because there was such a cavalcade of cutters making the Sunday afternoon jaunt, personal chaperones were unnecessary. Winfield at the reins, Margo bundled under a fur rug beside him, swung into a line that extended a mile or more across town, heading for the country.

It was winter at its best. The sun shone on a silver world glinting from every bough, bush, fence rail, and housetop. Better yet was the fact that the jingle of sleigh bells, the creak of harness and runners, along with the merry shouts and happy laughter floating back from dozens of merrymakers, made intimate conversation impossible. Margo relaxed and enjoyed the experience—in the company of a handsome man, warm and comfortable, and more at ease with a masculine escort than at any other time.

Conversation consisted mainly of "Comfortable?" "Just look at that!" "Hungry yet?" shouted from a man intent on handling the reins of a lively horse, keeping the proper distance from the rigs ahead and behind.

Later—warming themselves before an open fire in the drawing room at Heatherstone, drinking hot cocoa and indulging in an array of delicacies from a tray Lorna the maid had brought in, to withdraw into a corner of the room, seat herself, and lower her head into a book—Margo and Winfield forsook Mr. and Miss in favor of first names. As if this intimacy were not enough, Winfield, with his back turned to Lorna and hiding his face and actions, took the cup from Margo's hand, set it aside, and regained her hand. Surprised, Margo raised her eyes to his while he tightened his hold against her tentative move to free herself.

"Allow me this small favor," he said tenderly, and he looked into Margo's eyes so deeply and so steadily that she found herself flushing.

"Tell me you don't mind," Winfield said, and his half-whispered words throbbed with unspoken feelings.

Uncomfortable, Margo considered her answer. "I don't *mind,*" she began. Her honest "But I can't say I really care for it" was cut off by Winfield's instinctive tightening of his grip, with suggestive manipulation, that, to Margo's surprise, sent little ripples of pleasure up her arm.

Pressing his advantage, Winfield murmured such things as Margo had never heard before, and she found herself half mesmerized by the hearing.

"Has anyone ever told you," Winfield murmured, "that your eyes are like"—Margo expected "olives," the term she herself had used critically when studying those dark features in the mirror—"pools," he said, showing no imagination at all, but fresh and flattering to Margo.

"And your hair," he said, fleetingly touching a straying strand, "is like"—*a tangle of brambles,* Margo immediately came up with silently—"midnight," Winfield supplied. He seemed to surprise even himself with the additional "misty midnight."

With a quick glance at Lorna, finding her head nodding and her eyes closed, Winfield slipped from the hassock on which he was perched to a seat beside Margo, his arm going neatly around her shoulders but in a tender, gentle manner more fraught with meaning than if he had "pressed his suit" more vigorously. Margo found the man's dark eyes, under dark brows, saying things not spoken aloud. The uniqueness of it so gripped her that there was no telling where the evening might have gone if the couple's fascination in each other had not been rudely interrupted when Casper opened the door, stepped inside, hesitated momentarily, then approached.

Margo, flustered and annoyed at the flustering, said, more sharply than usual, "Yes, what is it?"

"It's Mr. Galloway, Miss."

Guiltily imagining her father had somehow discerned his daughter's indiscretion, Margo halted between a haughty response, coolness in front of the butler, or embarrassment.

"He's ill, Miss Margaret." Casper's starchiness had quite hidden what apparently was serious, for he allowed a faint tone of concern to touch the simple explanation.

Casting foolishness aside, Margo said immediately, "I'll go right up. Have you called the doctor?"

"Yes, Miss. It's not the first time." A muscle moved in the man's stern jaw, the only emotion he allowed himself.

"Not the first! Why haven't I been told?"

"Mr. Galloway's orders, Miss." Casper's eyes flickered toward Winfield Craven, and his mouth tightened disapprovingly. Obviously he wasn't going to say more with Winfield present.

"Winfield . . . Mr. Craven," Margo began, turning toward her erstwhile wooer. Only later was she to try to puzzle through the expression on his face. So recently flushed with fervor, it was alert, the eyes thoughtful. Certainly it showed no surprise, a surprise in itself. Had Winfield observed something about Hugh's condition that she, Margo, had not seen? Seeing Hugh only occasionally while Margo saw him daily, was Hugh's deteriorating health quite obvious to Winfield? Noting this only dimly, it made no great impression at the time.

"You must excuse me, Mr. Craven," she said, giving Winfield her hand briefly.

"Of course. I'll come by tomorrow—to see how things are. . . ." Even now Winfield's tones spoke of something other than the present topic of conversation. But Margo, free from the spell that had gripped her, spoke crisply to Casper, requesting that he bring Mr. Craven's coat and hat, saying to Winfield only, "It was a delightful day, Mr. Craven. Thank you, and good night."

Margo flew to her father's room, to find him in bed and his manservant, Bailey, in attendance. Elbowing Bailey aside, she leaned over Hugh, her eyes widening in alarm. Even in the dim light Hugh's color seemed dreadful, but what was worse—the evidence of stark pain that twisted his patrician features.

"Papa, Papa—what's wrong? Oh, what's wrong?" Margo managed and thought she didn't have his attention through his suffering.

Eyes shut, mouth twisted, Hugh spoke. Not to Margo but to Bailey.

"Remove her. I—don't—want—the—girl—here."

With an apologetic glance Bailey replaced Margo at Hugh's side. "I think you ought to go, Miss," he murmured. "The doctor will be here soon, and things will be better."

Consequently, Margo was waiting in the drawing room when the doctor, a man unknown to her, appeared before the room's open door, where Casper waited with his cloak.

"Doctor," Margo said from the drawing room's dimness, and the man turned his head. "Please come in for a moment. I'm Margaret Galloway," she added when the doctor had joined her. "Can you tell me what's wrong?"

"I'm afraid not, Miss Galloway. Mr. Galloway's strict orders. I feel bound to honor them. If I don't he'll simply replace me with someone else who will have the same instructions."

"But—but, I'm his daughter, for heaven's sake! Don't I have a right to know what's wrong with my own father? This suffering—I don't understand it. Will it happen again? Has it happened before?"

"Sorry, Miss Galloway."

Margo attempted to speak calmly. "Doctor, my mother is dead. There is no one, no one else at all but me. I want to be a help—"

With a slight shake of his head, the doctor turned, received his hat and bag from the waiting Casper, bowed to Margo, and left the house.

Casper, who had been with the Heatherstone menage since the Galloways had come to Canada, looked with pity at the girl's face. Usually so free of care of any kind, pleasant, even lovely, it was now twisted with concern. He saw the dark eyes fill with tears, understood the utter bewilderment on the flushed face.

"Casper," she whispered, "why?" Knowing she shouldn't, to a servant, still she did, allowing the very proper staff member a glimpse into her personal feelings.

It was more than Casper could stand. Having already broken faith by advising her that Hugh was ill, Casper went a step further.

"Missy." He had called her that when she was a very tiny girl of two and three, many years ago, and it came naturally now. "Missy—I've felt for a long time that you should know. Your— that is, Mr. Hugh—is ill. Very seriously ill, I'm afraid. In fact, Miss Margaret . . . he's not going to get well, and I think you ought to know. Ought to be able to plan. Ought to be able to—"

141

Casper's voice trailed off before the anguish in the two dark eyes before him.

Putting a fatherly arm around the shaking shoulders, Casper helped Margo to her room.

"Try to put it aside—get some sleep," he said. "I assure you, your father will be asleep, too. The doctor gives him morphine. The medicine ran out tonight; that's what the trouble was."

"Morphine! Oh, Casper, what's wrong with him?"

"It's a cancer, Miss. Somewhere—in his stomach, maybe in his lungs." Not knowing whether he felt better or worse for having told her, Casper turned away, confident only that here was a woman, not a girl, and one who was left entirely too much in ignorance of life as most people knew it.

"Thank you, Casper," Margo managed. "I needed to know. I truly needed to know. And," she added wisely, "I'll not let on. But, from now on, I can act more like a daughter to him."

And though it was difficult to accomplish, Margo spent more time with her father. His visits to his office and other interests grew less and less and finally ceased altogether. His meals at the table were discontinued and, eventually, Hugh was bedfast. Margo read the paper to him and attempted to bathe his forehead if he seemed to be in pain, a personal touch that he resisted more often than not. There were three months of misery, for Margo as for Hugh, though in a different way. Her pain was an inner one, and morphine wouldn't touch it. To her, it seemed her father was slipping away, and she didn't know him, had never known him.

Hugh's business partners and associates, at first, visited frequently. His lawyer was often in evidence. Hugh displayed the characteristics that had made him a rare businessman and was just as careful in his dying as in his living.

"Papa," Margo asked, more than once, "shouldn't I be in while Fletcher Wren is talking to you? Can't I help . . . shouldn't I—"

"No, no," Hugh would answer impatiently. "There's no need, no need."

Two things made her turn toward the waiting arms of Winfield Craven. First of all was the need to talk about her father's affairs; Winfield, to a small extent at least, was privy to some of the estate's vast tentacles. Connected in a minor way with the construction business under the Galloway name, Winfield was in a position to understand, Margo felt, her helplessness and her concern about her ignorance.

To Winfield she was able to say, "Ralph Greeley was in today; he and Father talked a long time. Surely it was greatly important and yet—"

"The railroad," Winfield supplied. "Greeley is vice president. They're talking about the extension into the Territories, back of beyond, I guess you'd say."

"But shouldn't I know?" Margo would ask anxiously, twisting her hands.

Winfield would take those tense hands in his, smile gently, and assure her that everything could quite reasonably be put under one person's leadership at her father's ... passing. And he, personally, would be dedicated to helping her find that man.

"I'm sure," he said, more than once, "your father has it all down in writing. He has confidence in his associates and knows you will be able to depend on them. And, if you wish, I'll stand by to help interpret, explain, perhaps relay some of your desires and wishes concerning, well, all kinds of things."

All kinds of things, Margo knew, would be overwhelming alone. Winfield, at least, knew enough to calm her fears and more—to actually take on the work that would, undoubtedly, fall upon her at her father's death. It was a source of comfort to Margo, and she clung to it rather desperately. Certainly, without Winfield, she would be absolutely alone.

The other reason that made Winfield indispensable was more personal—Margo simply had no one on whom to lavish the love that hungered for an outlet. Like a pent-up dam that finds a small leak, lets a droplet through, then another, to find all energy eventually pouring through the small opening, so Margo's emotions, so long pent up and so denied any outlet at all, catapulted through the opening that was Winfield Craven.

There came a time when, after her father's oft-recurring battle with pain, Margo had left his room, shaken, tearful, desperately alone, to find Winfield's arms open and his shoulder available. More and more often this happened, until it seemed a natural haven.

One day, leading her to a comfortable seat in the drawing room, Winfield seated himself by her, drawing her head to his shoulder and patting her, as he had often done before. This time, however, he tipped back her head, dried her eyes with his own handkerchief, and kissed her lips. So tender was it, so natural after the many embraces, that Margo could not object. Nor was she sure she wanted to. After all, she was twenty years old, mistress of Heatherstone, heir to millions, and able to make up her own mind concerning her future. And she was alone, terribly alone.

Moreover, she was healthy and had a young woman's normal physical response. In spite of herself Margo felt her breath quicken, felt the pound of her heart, felt, in fact, quite dizzy with her response. So ignorant, so unpracticed, still her lips responded with a warmth and urgency that surprised her and, apparently, surprised Winfield. Surprised and pleased Winfield. Recognizing that he had an advantage, he was not slow in following it up. Three kisses he allowed, no more. Then, gently, wisely, he looked into Margo's bemused face and murmured, "Darling Margaret, may this sweet privilege always be mine! Tell me I may look after you always . . . keep you in my arms always. Marry me, Margaret."

What was there to say, to do? Having thus committed herself, Margo could not withdraw from his embrace declaring it was all an act on her part or something she indulged in without meaning. It was easier to offer him her lips, again, in capitulation and assent.

"You've made me the happiest man on earth!" Winfield said fervently. "When may we marry, my dearest?"

"Why," Margo stammered, drawing back, "not for a long time, I'm sure. Not while Papa is sick. Not after . . ."

"But, my dearest," Winfield said, brushing the hair back from her brow, drawing her near, and giving her another lingering kiss, "that may be too long to wait. Don't you think?"

"No, no . . . not at all . . . not at all. . . ." It was hard for Margo to sound positive with his lips so insistent on hers and hers so absurdly responding.

Winfield bided his time. A beautiful ring appeared, an announcement of the betrothal was made, and Winfield's unrelenting plans for the marriage made it all more real day by day.

One place Winfield was no help—in the sickroom. Though he seemed to suffer Margo's presence at times, the one time Winfield entered, to stand supporting her at the bedside, Hugh had roused with an agitation that brought the nurse swiftly to his side.

"What's he doing here?" the invalid's voice demanded. "Get that pecksniffian weakling out of here!"

Ugly red surged up into the handsome face at Margo's shoulder, while her own face turned pale. "I think you should go," she urged, and with a dark glance at the man in the bed, Winfield left the room.

"Whatever did he mean?" Margo asked Winfield later. "Pecksniffian—I never heard the term."

Neither had Winfield, but "weakling" he well understood. "Remember, my dear," he said with an effort at rationality, "the man is not responsible for what he says. He's clearly raving."

"Papa is a great lover of Dickens," Margo said thoughtfully. "He often read his works aloud to Mama . . . sometimes to me. There was a Pecksniff in *Martin Chuzzlewit* as I remember. Not a savory character . . . selfish and corrupt behind a seeming display of benevolence. Whatever could have possessed Papa—"

"As I said, clearly out of his mind. He's back in Dickens' days, living them out in his imagination."

"I suppose so," Margo said rather doubtfully and, at the first opportunity, when Hugh had a good day and was lifted into a chair by the window to watch the snow as it fell and the chickadees as they fed, she sat beside him and hesitantly brought up the subject of Winfield and her proposed nuptials.

"Papa, you know I'm engaged . . . you remember I told you about that?"

"Of course I remember. I haven't got cancer of the brain." Hugh spoke more harshly in his sickness than ever in health.

"What do you think of it?"

"Every woman should be married, I suppose." Hugh was supremely indifferent.

"To Winfield Craven, Papa."

"As good as any, I suppose. I imagine you have your full wits about you. He certainly has."

"Why do I get the impression, Papa—" Margo's voice was smothered as she dared ask the question, "that you don't like him? You do like him, don't you, Papa?"

"Like him? Like him? Is it necessary that I like him?" Hugh watched the scene outside the window for a moment, then, with a return to his usual politeness, said, "Marry him, my dear. Yes, yes, you must go ahead and marry. I think," he swung his sunken eyes toward her, "if your mother were here, she would urge you toward marriage. Believe me, I'm thinking of your best interests. If Winfield Craven is your choice, so be it—marry."

Margo sighed. Everything, it seemed, herded her toward Winfield and marriage. The alternative—life alone, with no family, and with the burden of the Galloway estate to care for by herself as unready as she was—was too dreadful to contemplate.

⌐══════⌐

Margo's helplessness and aloneness were emphasized when Hugh slipped away in his sleep, in the middle of the night. Margo was not even at his bedside. Casper woke her and broke the news to her, but aside from his sympathetic face there was no one to whom to turn, no one to put an arm around her, no one to advise her. When, later in the day, Winfield arrived, Margo threw all reserve and training to the wind and flung herself into his arms.

It was now, when she was at her lowest ebb, when his presence and help were so desperately needed, that Winfield pressed his advantage and urged an immediate marriage.

"Oh, no!" Margo whispered, horrified at the thought of the impropriety of it.

"My dearest, who is to care? Let us please ourselves rather than society at this time. I can't bear to leave you—tonight or any night hereafter. I can't bear to let you out of my arms, when you need them so." And Winfield held her tenderly, wiping her tears away, soothing her fears, assuaging her loneliness.

In Margo's weakness and need, Winfield did indeed appear as a tower of strength, and it wasn't difficult for her to be persuaded. Especially when Winfield loved her so and pledged such devotion and faithful attention to her needs.

With Margo's tearful acquiescence, Winfield stepped in to take charge of the countless details in regard to the funeral, any business problems, and the running of the Heatherstone staff. "With your permission, my dearest," he had said, and Margo had gladly turned all such matters over to him. How desperately, after all, she needed him!

"One week, Margaret," Winfield eventually persuaded. "One week after the burial. That's enough time, isn't it, my dear, to be ready? After all, it will just be us, the staff, and a couple of close friends. Then—oh, then, my love," and Winfield's voice deepened with the thrill of "then."

Margo was persuaded.

21

Dear Margo, my angel child, Margo read. In a miasma of bewilderment, sorrow, and depression, her old nurse's love, coming clearly through the pages of the letter, stole like balm into Margo's battered heart. Oh, if only those loving arms were here now, what comfort they would bring. Even after all these years, Margo felt a rush of warmth toward the distant Kezzie and a very great yearning to lay her head on the withered bosom and feel the tender pats of consolation on her shoulder. With Kezzie, one never wondered about one's acceptance, never had to deserve that acceptance, never doubted its steadfastness.

But Kezzie, growing old and infirm, was thousands of miles away, wrapped in the vastness that was the Northwest Territory, in one small district called, strangely, Bliss.

I could do with a little Bliss, Margo thought a trifle grimly, not certain that even the coming wedding would supply it. Perhaps it was just because Kezzie was there, perhaps it was her strange desire to flee the present circumstances, but Margo picked up the letter with a sigh, and, shaking her head as if to rid it of the impossible dream of Bliss, a dream that had often gripped her heart ever since Kezzie's arrival there, read on.

For me, shut in with my aches and pains, time seems to stand still. At times, now that my Mary is well, I wonder what I am doing here. But, of course, I know there is no need for me any-more at Heatherstone. No need! Now, more than ever, there was a need for Kezzie at Heatherstone. Tears splashed the pencilled pages, tears for Kezzie and her feeling of uselessness, tears for herself, Margo, and her feeling of helplessness. Two great needs—so far apart, with no chance of fulfillment.

Yes, my Mary, to the uninformed, is well. Those of us who know her, however, know that she is not strong. And that is hard for me, when I can do so little anymore to help. Dear Molly is such a blessing. As you know, she is about two years older than you and has been raised here on the frontier. I guess you could call it the frontier, but we have come a long way. The railroad has made a great difference. Unfortunately it does not come through Bliss but bypasses us for another route to Prince Albert. That growing little city is about twelve miles from us, too far to run in often but close enough to be available for many things not stocked here in our small Bliss store.

The letter drooped in Margo's hand; she pictured again, as across the years of Kezzie's letters, the area called Bliss, in the heart of the bush. Margo had watched, in imagination, as Angus had cleared land, planted, harvested; Margo had lived through the exhaustion of threshing day vicariously and the long, lonely winter days of isolation. She had thrilled to the occasion of the chinook and its warming breeze; she had knelt, in imagination, to brush aside the snow and rejoice in the finding of spring's first crocus.

Wistfully, through the written word, Margo had watched as Molly and Cameron, whom she could not remember in person, had grown from youth to maturity. Almost she could see Cameron's thick, fair hair and blue eyes and Molly's tossing mane, as black and curly, it seemed, as her own. Margo could picture their injuries, described by Kezzie, laugh at their predicaments— Cameron learning to ice-skate in skates too large, stuffed with paper; Molly determined to ride a calf. She studied the crude drawing of the log cabin, coloring in new rooms as Kezzie reported their addition to the original structure. She studied the wisps of thread and scraps of material Kezzie sent, at Margo's pleading, so that the child in the east could picture more completely the children in the bush and how they were clothed.

In imagination she had taken the buggy ride to Prince Albert for supplies, had bundled herself against the cold when the sleigh made the same trip. She had rejoiced with Bliss's residents when, at a certain crossroads, a small hamlet had sprung up, with a post office, a store, a smithy, and, soon, a granary, and was named, appropriately, Bliss. None of Kezzie's often vivid accounts of hardships, blizzards, discouragements, could change Margo's impression of the place called Bliss. Until she could go to heaven, Bliss would do!

With her father lying dead in his coffin in the drawing room, with the weight of the family businesses hanging like an ominous cloud over her head, with the responsibility for the running of Heatherstone on her shoulders, and with Winfield waiting impatiently to become a bridegroom, Margo's youthful dream of Bliss dissolved in the tears that now fell on Kezzie's letter.

Molly, it seemed, as Margo resumed her reading, was in a fair way to marry the new, young minister who had come to the recently established church at Bliss. Cameron, Kezzie reported, was managing a superior farm just a few miles away in Bliss; he was, after all, in his mid-twenties. *And still single*, Kezzie wrote, as she had before. *As you know, women here are hard to find— single women, I mean—and not everyone wants to become a pioneer bride. What's more, Cameron seems to have this idea that God is going to send along the right one, and he needn't worry about it. You see, Margo,* and Margo could almost hear Kezzie's frustration, *this entire family has the idea that God is*

150

*in control of things. I must say it makes for peace, even in try-
ing times, and seems to give a contentment that I, for one, can't
really understand. But I would like to. The older I get, the more
I need peace, Margo. But certain things go along with it—confession, for one. Well,* another sigh, Margo supposed, *some things
are easier said than done.* Now what, Margo thought, could darling Kezzie find so hard to confess, when she had been such a
good woman? Hadn't she been, since childhood, a staunch member of the Established Church? Dear Kezzie!

Margo finished reading her old nurse's letter, folded it, and
put it away until such time as it could be answered. Somehow
she would have to make time before the wedding to write Kezzie
and tell her of Hugh's death, her forthcoming marriage. . . .

With a sigh equal to those of her faraway friend, Margo, with
a wrench, put aside her dreams of someday visiting Kezzie and
her family, laid aside, forever, any hope of a buggy ride to Bliss.

hunk! Thunk! The dropped handfuls of dirt thudded on the coffin containing the final remains of Hugh Galloway. Wet dirt . . . clay, molded by the gripping hand into a solid ball, plastered itself to the rain-splashed box, to melt apart in the downpour and drip back to the earth from which it had been gathered.

Under the circle of umbrellas, Hugh Galloway's prestigious acquaintances and few friends huddled, eyeing the dead man's only offspring with varying reactions. A few, knowing how very little Margo understood of the vast Galloway estate, shook their heads; some, envious of the same vast estate and its money, gazed darkly; a few, noting Margo's isolation—alone except for one supporting male—were touched with sympathy.

But all emotions faded quickly as the dreary words "ashes to ashes and dust to dust," half-washed away in the smothering rain, signaled the end of the ceremony without additional misery.

Margo, alone, glanced back at the coffin already blurring in the sheeting rain, her anguished tears lost in the rain running down her face. With friends and acquaintances fading from view as they spread out toward their various means of conveyance, with the world around eerily silent except for the slicing down-pour, she walked in a world alone it seemed, and she shivered. Then, with Winfield solicitously tucking her hand into his arm and drawing her under his umbrella, she clung, as to life's last hope, to him. Thank God for Winfield!

"Don't look back," he murmured in her ear. "Look ahead. Think of the future—the life we'll build together, the things we'll do, the places we'll go. Why, in one week, darling, you'll be my wife. Think about that." Even in the hour of sorrow, even with their feet all but mired in mud, his tones were thrilling. Margo managed a smile. "There, that's better," Winfield said, handing her up into the Galloway carriage.

Settling himself beside her, Winfield's sense of satisfaction in ownership revealed itself as he noted, with disapproval, the soiling of the carpeted floor. "Griffin will need to substitute another carriage to get me home tonight. If this rain continues, it has to be an enclosed one. In a week," his tones were tender again as he took Margo's hand, removed the sodden glove and rubbed warmth into her stiff fingers, "I won't be leaving you—ever. In a week we'll be together."

Margo, emotionally drained, couldn't tell whether her shivers were from the cold and wet or the romance and intimacy Winfield's tones implied.

With her hair draggled around her face, her hat drooping, rain running down her collar, with Winfield's arm around her shoulders, Margo found herself wishing for the loving arms of Kezzie Skye. Though it had been many years, she was so wrapped in the loving care of her old nurse, so sure of it still and missing it so fiercely, that her heart filled with longing. Now, with marriage, any trip to see the aging woman would be forever out of the question. Margo found another reason to shiver, another reason to cry.

Winfield tighened his embrace. "Are those tears?" he asked tenderly. "In just a little while, my dear, we'll be safe and warm by the fire in your father's study . . . with Fletcher Wren bringing us the good news, the wonderful news, of your inheritance.

Now, doesn't that cheer you? You are free, Margo. At last you are free."

But was she? Not free to trade the heavily sprung, ornately gilded, comfortable carriage for a lopsided buggy bound for Bliss. Responsibility for the Galloway estate would keep her tethered, richly, plushly tethered but not free. The precious bonds of marriage would keep her tethered.

Years of harboring a secret dream of someday being reunited with Kezzie died painfully. With one last pang Margo laid them aside for the mature role that lay before her.

Even now her letter to Kezzie was on its way, reporting her father's death—it would shatter Kezzie, who had given a lifetime of devotion to Hugh Galloway—and her forthcoming marriage. For the first time ever, she had concluded her letter without the earnest though childlike pledge, "I'll see you soon, Granny Kezzie."

Warm again and dry, her hair—always curly but today riotous and unmanageable—sternly tied back, Margo seated herself in her father's dark-paneled study, Winfield taking a chair at her side. The rain sliced silently against the windowpanes, and Casper attempted to arrange the drapes to allow for more light. Even so, the lamps were lit against the room's pressing darkness.

At Fletcher Wren's request, four members of the staff had been summoned to be on hand for the reading of Hugh Galloway's last will and testament. Each came separately, emphasizing the difference in status: Bridget, cook, in pristine white, sailed in like a galleon before the winds and took a chair with supreme dignity; Dauphine, housekeeper, scarcely more regal in her black bombazine with white collar and cuffs, nodded stiffly to the lawyer and took a chair; Bailey, Hugh Galloway's personal attendant and always self-effacing, a wisp of a man in black almost too overpowering for his pale face, entered noiselessly; Casper, butler for Heatherstone, Canada's, duration, a white-haired, soldierly man of considerable presence, gave Margo a keen look, let his eyes slide over Winfield at her side and, with an audible sigh, seated himself with the others.

Fletcher Wren cleared his throat, fiddled with the papers in his hand, ran a finger around his shirt collar, cast a glance at Margo that had all the earmarks of apology, and began to speak.

Watching the rain on the window just over the lawyer's shoulder, grieving again over the casket that had seemed so . . . abandoned in the desolate cemetery, the trite legal phrases made little impact on Hugh Galloway's natural heiress.

I, Hugh Cavalier Galloway, being of sound mind . . .

A sound mind, a sharp mind. The mansion in which they sat attested to the man's abilities, his investments, his taste. By some manner of means Heatherstone, Canada, unlike its mirror-image Heatherstone, Scotland, missed being a mausoleum. Though it had its formal rooms, much of it was comfortable, pleasant, even homelike—except for this particular room. To Margo her father's private quarters spoke chillingly of the many visits made here to curtsy daintily, to perhaps sit with ankles crossed and skirts neat, to exchange a few words, to be dismissed into the care of the maid who had brought her. Nevertheless, she had resisted Winfield's plans to lighten and brighten the study and make it his own special retreat; she felt more like sealing it off and leaving it as it had always been.

To my faithful staff . . .

Margo was not surprised at her father's generosity toward the four seated here, the four who had kept the house running after Sophia's death as smoothly as when she was alive. Dauphine's stern face flushed; Bridget's ready tears brimmed over and needed a quick dab to keep them from splashing the spotless bosom toward which they ran. Bailey looked visibly relieved; Margo had an idea he had not looked happily on Winfield's wishes to have him stay on as his, Winfield's, valet. Casper, straight-backed and straight-faced, crumbled in both when his pension, with words of appreciation, was made known to him.

Dear Casper. Margo was certain she could persuade him to stay on, at least until a new routine was established and life was flowing smoothly for the new master and mistress—Mr. and Mrs. Winfield Craven.

Fletcher Wren hesitated. He coughed. He fumbled with his papers. He ran his fingers through his hair, his elbow bumping the prisms of the hanging lamp and setting them to tinkling. Even in the dim light his flush was evident, and he put forth his hand to steady the lamp and quiet the sound whose jubilation, it seemed, was muted along with all else on this dreary occasion. Margo sighed, and Winfield, ever attentive, leaned toward her, drawing her shawl more closely around her shoulders and smiling encouragingly. *Almost over*, the smile said.

Apparently Fletcher Wren had made up his mind to hurry on. It was the mention of her name that brought Margo's attention into focus.

"'To Margaret . . .'" With flushed cheeks Fletcher Wren, in legal terms, outlined Hugh Galloway's bequest—a stipend or fixed sum to be paid periodically and the privilege of living at Heatherstone until such time as she might marry. "'To Margaret also,'" Fletcher Wren read, rapidly now, "'for reasons she may ascertain should she care to do so, I leave my small holdings'" and the lawyer gave the legal description—section, township, range—of a certain piece of property in the district of Bliss, in the Northwest Territory, "'presently in the care of my old servant and friend, Kezia Skye.'"

None of it made sense to Margo. Stipend? Northwest Territory? Kezzie?

Silence reigned, but an electric silence that had routed the dead quality of the room. No one moved; every eye looked at the lawyer.

"'In order,'" Fletcher Wren hastened on, stumbling a little, "'that the Galloway holdings remain in the Galloway family and name, I leave the remainder of my possessions to my nephew Wallace Galloway of Kirkcudbright.'"

Through the inventory of Galloway holdings—railroad, shoe factory, mine shares, various buildings, Heatherstone itself—Margo's mind reeled. Her ears heard and reported, but her brain refused to grasp its message.

Wallace? Heatherstone? Everything to Wallace? Wallace of the pimply face and the cruel hands? Heatherstone to Wallace? Round and round it went until the lamp joined the spin, until the room spun crazily in the desperate dance.

Just before the lamplight blinked out, just before the buzzing in her ears faded and darkness carried her off into oblivion, Margo saw the twisted face and furious eyes of Winfield Craven.

Cameron set down the box of supplies his mother had ordered and sorted through the papers and letters he had picked up at the Bliss post office.

"Not much for you today," he reported, "except for a week's supply of papers. But there's a letter here for Mam—from Margaret Galloway. I dread giving it to her."

The envelope the young man held in his hand was edged in black.

"Oh no!" Mary's hand flew to her mouth as if to deny what was clearly spelled out—someone had died. Who else but Hugh Galloway? For the last few months Margaret had been sending increasingly serious reports concerning her father's health, no doubt hoping to prepare his old nanny for this very time when final word should come.

"Do you think you should go on over with me?" Cameron asked, with a line of concern between his brows.

"I don't think it's necessary, son," Mary decided. "She's known it's about to happen. And you can be as much comfort as she needs. Oh, how I wish she'd turn to the Lord for her comfort!"

Cameron tucked the fateful letter into his pocket, gave his mother a hug, and turned to go.

"You're right, of course. I'll do my best, but yes, her heavenly Father could be much more comfort than either her earthly daughter or grandson. From what you've told me and from what I gather from listening to Mam, this blow is about as heavy on her as if one of her own flesh and blood had died."

"Yes," Mary said, knowing it was true but never having been jealous of it, "she has loved Hugh Galloway deeply. This will hit her hard. To think that she should have outlived him. She's older by, oh . . . I believe she was in her mid-teens when he was born and she was taken on at Heatherstone, helping to look after him and going on to become full nanny."

"And even more than that to Mr. Hugh's child—granny, isn't she?"

Mary sighed. "It was so hard on her to leave Margaret . . . Margo, she calls her. She was born, you know, on the ship coming over—"

"I know, Mother. I well remember." Cameron counted the shipboard experience among his first memories. Now, lest his mother dip into the grief of her own bairn's death and burial at sea, Cameron hugged her again, picked up his hat, and turned to go.

"I'll do my best. Now, do you have eggs for me? One of these days I'll stock some hens on the Bliss place—Galloway place, that is. Mam isn't able to look after chickens, that's for sure, and I haven't the time. I'm blessed just having her there with me, doing what she can, and she is always good company. She does bake a wonderful oat cake!"

Leaning back comfortably in the buggy, the reins slack in his hands and the horse stepping out toward the Bliss-Galloway place, Cameron wondered again what it was that held his grandmam in such a clutch that she should grow pale of face, ragged of breath, and desperate of countenance, yet stubbornly resist surrendering to the claims of Christ.

His thoughts swung to Mr. Hugh and Mam's devotion to the man. It was a devotion based on far more than the Galloway estate provision for Kezzie's old age, though that spoke clearly of the gentleman's reciprocation of his nurse's love.

How deeply moved Kezzie had been when, about three years before, "her" Mr. Hugh had written to tell them he was coming for a visit and requested that it not be revealed to anyone back east—Margaret, Cameron supposed. To the surprise of all, Mr. Hugh had been intent on purchasing property, not a homestead that would require his presence for a certain amount of time each year but a place that someone was desiring to sell. Such a place was available, and right here in Bliss—none other than the Bliss place itself.

Old Mr. Bliss, having homesteaded many years ago and having worn himself out in the process of proving up his land, needed to move back east to a daughter who could care for him in his crippled condition, and he had been a ready seller, counting himself unbelievably fortunate to have cash in hand. Except for personal items, everything had been left for the new owner—cattle, horses, machinery, and, of course, the buildings.

Of next importance was to leave the property in good hands. Cameron, then twenty-two years of age and looking for an opportunity to homestead for himself, had listened to Mr. Hugh's arguments and arrangements and felt his fortunes to be wonderfully blessed and himself favored by the plan. He, Cameron, would farm the Bliss place as if it were his own, actually receiving a salary just like dozens of other Galloway employees, perhaps hundreds of others. Though Cameron hesitated at first to give years of his life to something that would not in the end be his, still he rationalized that, with the funds accumulated, he would be in a position to purchase his own place when the time came. Just when that would be, he had no idea—Mr. Hugh had made no mention of himself retiring here. And now he was, apparently, dead.

Cameron tipped back his hat, put a boot up onto the dash, and considered what this letter would mean to his own future, if it did indeed bring news of Mr. Hugh's death. Perhaps the place would be sold. If so, perhaps he could be the purchaser. The thought widened his blue eyes and silenced the jaunty whistle abruptly.

He could hardly love the Bliss place more if it were his own, he realized, and something in him stirred with a hope he had not known an hour ago. The new owner, probably the only child of the deceased, Margaret herself, could not be expected to have an interest in the place, much less live here permanently. Soon, in one way or another, his—Cameron's—future would be decided. If it was to leave the Bliss place, he would find a homestead though it might mean moving some distance away from Bliss and his loved ones. It would be hard on Mam. Not long for this world, her frailty was obvious. Could she survive another harsh winter? Would the sad news of the letter be a means of pointing her toward the Savior who waited so patiently for her? Cameron urged the horse to a trot and soon saw the well-loved outline of the Bliss place ahead.

Surrounded still by bush in spite of much clearing of fields, meadows, and garden space, the buildings were almost snuggled in a leafy embrace. The original Bliss cabin had eventually been replaced by a well-planned, well-built structure furnished for comfortable living, with the kitchen at the far end, the remainder divided into bedrooms. Poplars from its own land had been carefully squared and so tightly fitted that very little chinking had been necessary. Left to color naturally outside, the inside was whitewashed regularly, keeping it bright and, even in dark weather, light, with its deep windows entirely adequate for the purpose—too many homesteaders fretted the winters away in depressing dimness. Each fall storm windows were added to help keep out the cold. It was a comfortable, welcoming house that, with the coming of Mam to stay with him, was indeed a home. Just whose home, now, was questionable. Perhaps the letter would tell.

Mam was in her rocker when Cameron laid the letter in her lap. Her old hand trembled as she held it.

"Mr. Hugh," she whispered.

"Let me open it for you," Cameron said gently and did so, replacing the single sheet of paper in his grandmother's hand.

"Read it, laddie. I'm afraid I can't see . . . just now." True, her eyes were full of tears.

Cameron read; read of Mr. Hugh's final days of illness, his death—a blessing, Margaret admitted, ending months of suffering. He read of Margaret's despair and her loneliness, in spite of Winfield Craven who, she wrote, "was her rock of Gibraltar at this time."

Winfield Craven, he read, had pointed out the advantages of an early marriage. Winfield Craven, Margaret said, would take on himself the tremendous responsibilities of the Galloway estate and holdings. Soon, Cameron read, Margaret would sign her letters Mrs. Winfield Craven.

Cameron's voice died away. Kezzie sat staring into space, back across the years, Cameron supposed. But when she spoke, it was not of Hugh Galloway.

"Did she say," Mam asked tensely, "'I'll see you soon, Granny Kezzie'? Did she finish her letter that way?"

"No, Mam. She finished it, 'Love always.'"

"Then," Kezzie said, and the tears started down the withered cheeks, "I'll never see my angel girl again. And what's more—you'll never see her. Mary will never see her. . . ."

"Perhaps she'll come yet," Cameron said, trying to comfort his grandmother. "No doubt she'll inherit everything, including this place—"

"She doesn't even know about this place."

"But she will. And it may give her an excuse to come . . . perhaps to sell it."

But it was meager comfort. Cameron knew as well as Mam that Winfield Craven, known by letter better than Margo could have imagined, would not spend his time and energy and interest on a small Galloway holding in a place far away, reached only by many days of miserable travel, and with only rude accommodations upon arriving.

No, Kezzie was right to loose forever her dream of yet sharing something of life with Margaret Galloway . . . Margo. Seeing the sad acceptance of it in Kezzie's drooping shoulders and dropped head, Cameron knelt beside her chair, took her hand in his, and once again urged, lovingly, "Mam, don't you see how much you need Jesus? Only He can comfort your heart. Why, Mam, why won't you pray with me?" Cameron had long ago faced the possibility of his precious Mam's death and had tossed reluctance and hesitation to the winds. There was no time to lose, and there was eternity to win, an eternity with the Lord. And so he lovingly and faithfully pressed on Kezzie, again, the claims of Christ.

And, again, he saw the dear face stiffen, saw the blue eyes close, as if in pain, understood the wordless shake of the frizzled gray head.

With his arms around her, Cameron offered up one more prayer for the salvation of his grandmother. "Whatever the means, Lord," he prayed silently, "bring her to yourself."

C old the atmosphere in which Margo came to herself after her collapse in her father's study. Cold, cold the eyes of Winfield Craven.

In fact, those eyes had brought it all back with a rush—the reading of the will, the stunning bequest of little or nothing to herself, the entire estate to Wallace. Her plummet into darkness had been marked by the cold eyes of Winfield. Furious eyes. Now that she was awake and aware, the face seemed less furious, but the eyes remained as cold.

Needing him so much, Margo reached a hand, beseechingly, toward him. It was taken and held, after a moment, by Dauphine.

"You've given us such a fright." The usual stern countenance of the housekeeper was softened by concern. Casper was closing the door on the other servants who had, apparently, stood around helplessly until life and color surged back into the pale cheeks of their mistress. And yet not their mistress.

With consciousness came remembrance: Heatherstone—handed over to Wallace. Margo's eyes flew to Winfield. What she saw there was as clear to her as though it were spelled out: Margo the pauper was not nearly as attractive as Margo the heiress.

"It was the shock," Dauphine was saying. Fletcher Wren, hovering in the background, had the grace to look ashamed, as the means by which the shock had come. He shuffled his papers, looked around blankly, and seemed relieved when Casper appeared with his hat, coat, and umbrella.

"I'm sorry, my dear," he mumbled in Margo's direction. "If I can be of help . . . perhaps explain. . . ."

Margo made no response, but her closed eyes may have spoken for her. Fletcher Wren made a hasty retreat and, one felt, closed the door gladly behind him.

"Help me up," Margo managed, and Dauphine did so.

"Sit here, Miss," the housekeeper advised, leading a trembling Margo toward a comfortable chair at the side of the fireplace. "Or do you feel up to the climb to your room?"

"Not yet," Margo said, and anyone who knew her would have noticed the set to her shoulders and the resolute tone of her voice. There was no use putting off what had to be done. "You may leave us," Margo continued. "I'll call you when I need you."

Casper offered a rug, which Dauphine tucked around Margo; then, with grim glances at Winfield, who stood at the window looking out at goodness knew what, the housekeeper and butler left the room.

"Winfield."

Slowly the man turned; reluctantly his eyes met Margo's.

"Yes." No hyperbole now. No passion of eye or suggestion of tone. Not even the pretense of his former avowed devotion, and for that Margo was grateful. It made it much easier to do what needed to be done.

If she hadn't felt so ill, she might have played with him a little. "Winfield," she might have said, "darling. After all, we have our love. Surely that's all that matters."

She wasn't prepared to say it, wasn't prepared to deal with Winfield's stumbling escape from bonds that were now obviously odious to him. And unnecessary.

So she said, quietly, "In view of my uncertain plans, Winfield, I think it's best that I be free."

Having said it, she was surprised how true it was and what relief it gave her. Her future might be uncertain, but it certainly didn't include an alliance with Winfield Craven. In spite of sorrow over her father's death, in spite of the shocking news of Wallace's inheriting, in spite of her own bleak hopes, she felt a surge of relief that made her almost giddy again.

"Yes, yes. Of course. I fully understand." Even as he spoke, Winfield was moving toward the ring Margo had taken from her finger and was holding out to him. As it dropped from her hand to his, so easily, so finally, a riffle of hysteria broke the surface of her calm. Hearing the sound, Winfield's handsome face flushed, then darkened. Pocketing the ring, he spun on his heel and made for the door.

"I wish you good day, Madam," he said stiffly, "and good luck."

"And," Margo couldn't help but respond quietly, "better luck to you."

───

At Margo's express wish and with Fletcher Wren's approval, the staff stayed on. All except Bailey, Hugh Galloway's personal attendant, who, with his pocketed inheritance, made his quick way back to his home in England.

But life at Heatherstone was at a standstill. After years of Hugh Galloway's vital presence, after his months of illness and death, after plans and preparations for a wedding, Heatherstone seemed in a vacuum where the days and weeks slipped by, one much the same as another.

Margo, with distaste, disposed of the wardrobe she had accumulated with Winfield's suggestions and guidance, walked each day in the nearby park, read a great deal, and waited. Waited for she knew not what. Waited for healing, perhaps; waited for comprehension of the incomprehensible will and its revelation; no money . . . no future, except through Wallace's gratuity . . . no Heatherstone.

To be deprived of father, lover, and home in one moment—it was almost too hard to grasp. Eventually Margo came to grips, or tried to, with the most puzzling part of all: the bequest of a "small holding" in Bliss. Why would her father leave this remote property to her? No sensible reason presented itself to her except that Kezzie was there. Perhaps, anticipating her bewilderment, her father had added that cryptic sentence, "for reasons she may ascertain should she care to do so," with something in mind. But what? She cared, almost frenziedly, to understand, to be able to solve the staggering mystery. And why, she eventually wondered, did her father say the Galloway estate was to be left in Galloway hands? Weren't her hands Galloway hands?

Slowly, in her thinking, Heatherstone and all the Galloway resources slipped away. They were no longer hers. What was hers was a miserable piece of bushland.

There came a day when Fletcher Wren stopped by to report that he had heard from Wallace Galloway and that the new heir was on his way to take up residence in Heatherstone, Canada, and would, in fact, be here within the month.

Consulting with Dauphine, Margo saw to it a suite of rooms was prepared for the new owner. Cook, alerted to Wallace's arrival, searched out her best Scots recipes. Casper, quieter than usual, saw to the grounds, the stables, and much more. All was in readiness.

On the appointed day Margo dressed as usual, without extra care or adornment. Remembering Wallace as she did, she actually felt supremely casual, almost disdainful, toward him, and would put on no display to impress him. Older now, more sure of herself, she felt confident of her ability to handle him should she be required to do so.

Waiting in the drawing room, Margo heard the low voices at the door as the men entered, as Fletcher Wren spoke briefly and left. She heard footsteps as Casper and Wallace approached the drawing room with its open door. Turning casually from her position at the fireside, Margo was agreeably surprised by her first glimpse of her cousin. There was a definite improvement—growth, school, and time itself, had all had a part in it.

Wallace strode directly toward the girl—woman—he hadn't seen since she was thirteen, seven years prior. Well dressed as he was, even impeccably so, his clothes fitting his tall, thin frame perfectly, he clearly embodied the assurance that wealth and position bring.

The pimples were gone, but the face was unhealthy in color; perhaps it was the lighting. He was clean-shaven, the mode at the time, and Margo had the momentary thought that here was one man who would have benefited from a beard. She hadn't time to think further; Wallace was bending gracefully over her hand. In spite of herself, Margo felt a surge of relief, for in her memory clear and sharp remained the frightening nip on the ear made by the boy Wallace years ago.

If Wallace remembered, he made no mention of it. Rather, he greeted her with "Cousin Margaret. How good to see you."

Margo murmured a response, happy that he had released her hand; his hand, slender and white, was moister than she cared to encounter.

"Welcome, Wallace, to Heatherstone. It's your home now, of course."

Wallace glanced around approvingly. "It's like home—that is, Scotland—and yet it isn't. I'm sure I'll be very comfortable. And you, too, cousin. Let me make it clear, right from the beginning, this is your home, too."

Margo had to appreciate the announcement, while regretting that it was necessary.

The tea cart was ushered in by a maid who glanced at her new master with curious eyes, bowed briefly, and retired. Margo was happy for the distraction, seating herself at the tea cart while Wallace took a chair opposite and stretched out his long legs and appeared to make himself at home.

"You do that well," Wallace said with a smile. "Like one to the manor born, of course."

In spite of herself, Margo flushed. Wallace agreeable, Wallace mannerly, Wallace self-assured she was unprepared for.

"Yes, cousin," Wallace was continuing, "we shall do beautifully together, I'm sure."

Margo felt herself relax; she had been more tense than she knew. Here was a civilized man, a man of good breeding.

"Well, of course," she said, "I was my father's hostess for several years, ever since my mother's death, of course."

"And you shall be mine," Wallace said gallantly.

"Milk?" Margo asked. "Sugar?"

"Just a little sweetness," Wallace said, leaning forward. His tapering fingers took the cup, and his eyes, close now, looked straight into Margo's momentarily as his knee, in its fine worsted, came into contact with her knee and stayed just a moment too long. Stayed a moment too long, and with too much pressure. "Yes, a little sweetness will do just fine," he said.

Leaning back and crossing his elegant knees, Wallace smiled and said smoothly, "I think we shall rub along together very well."

Picking up her cup, Margaret heard herself saying, with just the proper amount of surprise, "Why, didn't you know? I shan't be here."

"Not be here?" Wallace sat up straight, his tea slopping.

"No. My father left his Saskatchewan property to me, and I shall be leaving directly for the Territories."

M olly tossed her hat aside, ran a free hand through her springing black hair, and felt it lift and blow free in the breeze caused by the increase in the horse's gait. With her other hand, she jockeyed the reins, urging speed from the surprised mare.

Not that there was any need to hurry. But life, to Molly Morrison, was a joy to be experienced, and she faced it head on, eager and fresh and tending to be impatient with caution and deliberation.

But Parker Jones was deliberate, if not cautious. The young minister was undoubtedly still feeling his way in this, his first pastorate, learning as he went. But where things of the heart were concerned, Molly felt there should be free rein, a glad embrace, not the earnest thoughtfulness that Parker Jones exhibited!

Having made up her own mind—where love and marriage and Parker Jones were concerned, and with a nature that tended toward impulsiveness—Molly was submitting to some hard lessons.

I know he loves me—I can tell, Molly thought now, and it was such a happy thought and sent such a surge of pure joy through her vibrant young body that she laughed aloud, and the trill equaled the spring birdsong for joy. There was no one to hear, and the mare, trotting at a clip to keep pace with her mistress's heartbeat, flicked her ears and quickened her step.

Then, realizing that hurrying wouldn't bring a faster resolution to her frustrated love life, and settling for it, Molly accepted that Parker Jones must be allowed his own time and way in what was obviously a matter for serious consideration to him. She grimaced and resigned herself to more patient waiting.

"Do you think," Parker Jones had asked just last week, strolling on a Sunday afternoon, relaxed after delivering his sermon, and content after a good meal with Molly and her family, "that you could settle for the life of a pastor's wife?"

Settle *into* it, he means, Molly supposed, knowing herself well. Would it mean wearing her hair in a bun? If so, forget it! Her riotous curls might be tied back and pinned down, but be obedient to decorum? Never. Dress soberly? Watch what she said? Molly sighed, even now biting her tongue and stifling the impetuous response that surged in her thoughts, eager to be voiced.

Could she settle for it? Molly knew she could. Any price—to be the wife of Parker Jones! Seriously though, Molly felt honestly—and prayerfully, having taken this important matter to the Lord many times—that not only could she take on the role required of her if she married Parker Jones, but she could also feel a sense of the rightness of it . . . feel fulfilled, even as did Parker.

Passing the woodsy acreage on which the small log "parsonage" had been built—land donated for that purpose by her own father from his own homestead—Molly cautioned herself not to fly in at the gate, which was her natural impulse. No, she had already embarked on the pathway to self-control and maturity, which would be her lot should she indeed win Parker Jones. A hard path, for Molly Morrison, but one that would make a woman of the girl, a wise woman of the unformed girl; a loving, giving, caring, serving woman whose spontaneity would never be completely dimmed and whose bright outlook would never fade, no matter the hardship or trial.

No, she wouldn't automatically turn in, but if Parker Jones should beckon. . . .

Sadly, Parker's buggy was gone from the yard. Making calls, no doubt . . . perhaps on Grandmam. Molly had, on more than one occasion, shared her burden for the salvation of her Mam with Parker Jones. And more than once he had stopped by the Bliss place, to share a cup of tea and an oat cake, and to—cautiously, Molly supposed—introduce the subject of Jesus Christ and His love.

"You'll have to be—" Molly had wanted to say "pushy," but knowing Parker Jones and her own anxiety to see Mam saved *soon* in the face of her old age and declining health, she had substituted "persistent."

"You won't hurt her feelings," Molly had assured her friend and pastor. "We've all been very earnest with Mam . . . we can't bear to think that she might . . . might die, and not be ready. We couldn't bear an eternal separation." And Molly's eyes had filled with tears that spoke more eloquently than her words.

But Parker Jones's buggy was not at the Bliss . . . Galloway place. Molly could hear Cameron whistling somewhere in the dark depths of the barn as she reined to a halt and, with her usual zest for life, tumbled from the buggy. Going to the back of the rig, she gathered up the mail and the box of supplies she had picked up for her granny and her brother and turned to the house.

Kezzie stood in the open doorway, obviously enjoying the spring weather and the hint of lilacs from the bush budding at the corner of the house. She opened the screen door, relieved the burdened girl of the mail, and returned with it to her rocking chair.

Molly stretched her young body, her arms over her head, once again gathering up her hair into some semblance of order. Kezzie's head of frizz, duplicated in her daughter Mary even to its original color—red—was tamed to a tight curl in her granddaughter and black as a crow's wing, like Angus's. Molly's eyes were the same blue as her grandmother's, but in her the sparkle had not faded, nor the dance slowed. Had Kezzie, Molly sometimes wondered, subservient and loaded with responsibility all her life, ever been free to sparkle and dance? She, Molly, was so blessed! Not remembering the old home and the old ways, still she counted herself fortunate to be free . . . to be all that she could be. That women were still severely hampered in many ways was not a serious drawback to Molly. Rarely had she been thwarted; instructed, guided, trained—yes, but always free. The word, so important to her father, rang in her heart. Free from bondage, in this new and brave land; free, in Christ, from the bondage of sin. Molly Morrison was a liberated woman!

But Mam, darling Mam, whom she had missed knowing for the first half of her life, was certainly bound by . . . something. Free to be free, the only freedom she knew was from the old bonds of servant and master where this world's values were concerned. She still went in bitter bondage where her soul was concerned, a source of sorrow to her loved ones.

Kezzie's eyes were riveted on the expensive envelope in her hand. That it was expensive Molly knew from her perusal of the catalog and the "Papeteries" section. Hurd's Irish Linen, she supposed, or Royal Superfine, or Crown Imperial, or Harmony Stationery, and all "cream wove or with superfine cream finish" (Molly wondered what that meant—the only cream she knew anything about came from cows or was rubbed into dry skin). As Kezzie drew the single page from the envelope, Molly identified it, to her own satisfaction, as "Gold Edge Papeterie," with its vaunted "tinted ruled octave paper and fine gold edges, round corners, baronial envelopes to match." That it came from a tinted box, Molly knew, too. Why would one need to own it, when looking at it gave one such satisfaction? Contemplating her proposed life as a minister's wife, Molly happily settled for the latter and felt none the poorer for it.

But what, this time, had the faraway object of her Mam's devotion written? That it wasn't bad news she could surmise from her grandmother's face. But neither was it good news. Perplexed for the moment, Molly watched the aged face and its conflicting play of emotions.

"Good news?" Molly finally asked.

"Yes . . . I guess so. Yes, of course. She's comin'."

"Coming . . . to Bliss?" Molly was dumbfounded. The rich, pampered, stylish Margaret Galloway was coming to *Bliss?*

"For goodness' sake, why?" Molly asked bluntly.

"This land—the Bliss place," her Mam said, "it's hers now."

"Well," Molly said, perplexed, "so are dozens of other properties, if what I've heard is correct."

Molly knew Hugh Galloway had died; Margaret's letter had been sent immediately confirming that. Now, apparently, she was writing to tell of the will's disposition. But come to Bliss? With so many other options, so many more important responsibilities? Besides, there was her marriage. . . .

"Do you mean after the wedding?" Molly asked, small alarm bells ringing. It would be one thing to entertain Miss Ritzy Galloway, another to include a husband, a man unknown even to Mam. And on their honeymoon? What a honeymoon! A train trip, a bush hideaway—

"Apparently there's been no weddin'," Mam said and seemed a little confused. "Listen, I'll read it to you. It's verra brief."

Lifting the "linen wove" stationery to her fading eyes, Kezzie read, "'Things here are such that I've made up my mind to make a change. This is no longer home. I'll explain when I arrive, for it seems the only'"—here the writer had struck out the word *only* and substituted *best*—"'the best option, to come to Bliss. My father's property there, the will says, is mine. I understand it's under the caretaking of your grandson Cameron Morrison. There is no time to write back, Granny Kezzie, for my plans are made, and I will leave as soon as I can make the necessary arrangements.'

"She'll be here . . . two weeks from tomorrow, if there are no delays. Bein' summer and all—or nearly so—the train should come straight through." Kezzie looked blankly at the letter in her hand.

"Is this troubling you, Mam?" Molly asked gently. "Isn't it something you've longed for?"

"In a way . . ." Kezzie quavered, swallowed, and continued. "Yes, yes, of course. I've dreamed of holding my angel girl in my arms again before I die. On the other hand—"

"You're afraid we're not fancy enough for her. That's it, isn't it, Mam?"

Kezzie hesitated. "No, no, of course not—it wouldn't matter to Margo." She hesitated, glanced at Molly, down at the letter, back to Molly. "Well, yes, maybe that's it," she added lamely, and Molly knew instinctively it wasn't the problem at all.

"We'll all pitch in and help," Molly promised, brushing her Mam's soft cheek with a kiss. "Now, I'm off home. Don't you worry about a thing, you hear?"

Kezzie blinked, brought her thoughts and attention back to Molly, and managed a smile. But it was an uncertain smile, and Kezzie's eyes looked strained. Perhaps even alarmed?

Molly met Cameron in the yard.

"Hey," he said, knowing his sister well. "What's the trouble? Things not going well with . . . you know who?"

Molly smiled faintly. "They're not going particularly swimmingly, to my way of thinking, if you mean Parker. But that's not it. Cameron," Molly lowered her voice, though there was no chance of Kezzie's hearing the conversation, "that girl—Margo—is coming."

"To Bliss?" Cameron sounded unbelieving. It was a development he had not foreseen. That someone—a representative of the Galloway estate—should eventually come by, he half expected. That he would need to be prepared to give a reckoning, he expected. But that it would be to the "heiress" herself, now that was a surprise. Cameron whistled.

"My future looks a bit uncertain," he said. "I knew there had to be a change sometime, however. Well, I'll take it a day at a time. She's welcome to get someone else to run this for her . . . or, better yet," Cameron's tanned, square face lit up, "maybe she'll sell. I could meet her price, I believe, or her terms. Say, wouldn't that be great?"

Molly mounted the buggy with much less zest than she had alighted from it and drove home thoughtfully: Mam troubled and uncertain; Cameron building hopes on the faint possibility that the Bliss place might yet be his. Loving them both, Molly laid aside her own uncertain future to take on the burden of prayer for her grandmother and her brother.

26

Margo had marveled at the prairies. Nothing she had heard had prepared her for the vast stretches of open spaces of the northwest. In her mind's eye she could see the humped backs of the buffalo, and she felt a strange sorrow over their decimation. Once, at a small town, she saw a massive pile of buffalo bones, the first crop, she was told, for many homesteaders. Sold for fertilizer, they brought about seven dollars a ton. Often, around a small town's station, ragged, aimless men lingered—former buffalo hunters, and at a loss since the passing of their way of making a living. Indians, also, poor and thin and pathetic, lounged around the stations, selling handmade items that the white man sometimes found interesting.

It would take a very special woman, Margo felt, to agree to live in such isolation as she saw from time to time from the train window. Small huts, called soddies, since they were built from the sod of their own land—dark, sometimes windowless, ugly, *lonely*—dotted the prairie, with only gophers, rabbits, and hordes of mice for company. But such blue sky Margo had never seen, and once, stepping from the train at an isolated stop, the wind had blown across the greening land, and endless miles of grass had bent and swayed to its orchestration in a silent grace that was sheer beauty. Margo had caught her breath, feeling very small indeed, and had crept back onto the conveyance—made by man and creeping painfully and noisily across the same land—and acknowledged the sovereignty of the One who ordered, "Let the earth bring forth grass . . . and it was so . . . and God saw that it was good." It wasn't difficult to believe in Creator God, on the prairie.

Nevertheless, she breathed a sigh of relief when the green arms of the bush made their appearance. Almost, it seemed, they reached out to her. Could Margo find some semblance of reason and sense for the turn her life had taken—in the bush? Here, in the deep and secret vastness of the bush, would there be some light shed on the reason behind her father's strange will and his stranger message that she might find out "why" if she cared to? Was her heart leading her to Kezzie? Was it possible that, as well as comfort, she would find understanding?

If not, and this turned out to be a dead end, she could sell the property, return to the east, and make a new start with the funds obtained. It was the only resolution Margo arrived at.

Stepping down, finally, to the platform in Prince Albert, the bustling, busy northern center of civilization, Margo knew only vaguely that here French Fur Traders and Mountain Men had coexisted with the Indians a century and more ago.

Here, Margo also knew, Angus and Mary Morrison had ended their long trek from Scotland's bonny braes by a disastrous ocean trip and a long, wearisome overland passage by boat and by trail across Canada. Here Granny Kezzie had been summoned, and here she had stayed. Accustomed to the sounds and sights of a large city, Margo looked around with wonder, almost as she would look on a new world and a new species.

"Miss Galloway?"

Margo turned and found herself looking into dark eyes in a plump, dark face.

"I'm Sadie LeGare," the stranger said, "friend of Angus and Mary Morrison. Your train is considerably overdue—"

"There was some kind of repair work going on . . . frost had thrust the rails out of line, I understand."

"It happens," Sadie LeGare said with a twinkle. "Now, if you feel comfortable about it, you're to come with me until one of the Morrisons, or someone from Bliss, comes in. They've been checking daily, so I s'pose it won't be long you'll have to be waitin'." Sadie LeGare lifted inquiring brows.

"Thank you," Margo answered, relieved. She had been feeling very alone, and very far from home. "My things—"

"I'll see that they are stacked for the time being. Pierre, my husband, will get them, or whoever comes for you."

"Bliss," Margo asked when the two women were walking together, "is it some distance?"

"About twelve miles," Sadie LeGare said, hefting the one small bag she had decided to carry; Margo had identified it as containing personal items that would be important to her toilette.

"Mrs. LeGare," Margo asked, "how did you know me . . . or had you asked others first? There were several disembarking with me."

"It was no problem," Sadie LeGare said promptly. "Not only because of your dress . . . you look the part of Margaret Galloway, to my thinking. Our fashions here, of course, are several years behind yours. But—more than that."

Sadie LeGare turned her squinted gaze on the mass of dark hair and the delectable complexion of the young woman walking at her side and added, "I don't know, really. There's a resemblance . . . but that's silly, I guess. You are about the age of Molly—"

"She's two years older, Gran . . . Kezzie . . . always told me."

"Well, she's young and strong and built like you. Fresh and vigorous, full of life. Two young women would have much in common. You'll like Molly."

"I trust so," Margo said somewhat primly, willing but at the moment feeling strange and wondering just how much she could possibly have in common with a bush-raised girl.

Thankfully Margo turned in at the small frame house, scrupulously neat, that was the LeGare home. Gratefully she accepted the use of a bedroom and a basin of warm water and the assurance of privacy should she care to bathe and rest.

Sitting on the edge of the bed, the steaming basin and snowy linens on a pine stand, Margo breathed deeply and looked around; never in her entire life had she seen anything like it: simple, almost barren, small, clothes hanging on nails along the wall, a rag rug on the board floor, homemade curtains at the one window. If she had been transported to the moon, she felt, it couldn't have been more foreign.

Having completed her bathing and freshening up, she was at a loss about what to do with the basin of water. Looking around, she saw no signs of any exit except the one through which she had entered, and it led into the living quarters of the home. Opening the door, she asked hesitantly, "The basin . . . what shall I do with it?"

"Just leave it. I'll get it later." As she spoke, Sadie LeGare opened the back door and tossed out the contents of a dishpan; with a squawk, a dozen chickens dashed for its contents. Even on the edge of town, it seemed, people raised their own food; Margo could see a large garden just beyond, greening nicely.

"Come, sit down," Sadie invited. "I'll get the tea ready. I know it will be refreshing after such a trip as you've had." And she directed Margo toward a comfortable overstuffed chair in the part of the room obviously designated as . . . drawing room? Parlor?

"You'll find the Morrison place more . . . commodious. Pierre helped them build the first phase of their home, and it's grown from there. They've done so well, you'd be proud of their accomplishments, if you just knew how raw and rough things were in the beginning. We, Pierre and I, feel ourselves so blessed, here in our home. God has been good to us."

Margo almost burned herself on the tea she gulped in astonishment. If this was blessing, she'd been living in Gloryland. And hadn't known it.

The tea and fruitcake were barely consumed when there was the sound of a rig outside and a masculine voice ordering "Whoa!"

"That's the Morrison buggy," Sadie LeGare said after a glance through the open door. "I wonder who's come for you. Molly came yesterday, and the day before that—"

Mrs. LeGare was setting aside her cup and reaching for Margo's as she spoke. Before she could reach the door, the screen was thrust open, and a man strode in. Looking toward the light of the entrance, Margo could see the outline of a tall, well-built male, broad shouldered, with shirt sleeves rolled up, immediately sweeping a hat aside. The sun, behind, lit the fair hair with a touch of fire, like a halo in the darker room.

"So—you've arrived," the voice said. "Miss Galloway, I'm Cameron Morrison, welcoming you for my grandmother and apologizing for her that she couldn't be here in person."

Cameron Morrison stepped into the room, away from the blinding outline of light. His eyes, as blue as Kezzie's, were fixed on the face of the newcomer in frank appraisal.

Margo raised her eyes to a square, bronzed face as masculine as any she had ever seen. The nose was strong, the eyebrows straight, the mouth firm. But it was the blue eyes and the depth to them that held her transfixed. Margo Galloway, trained in some of the country's best schools, gracious hostess and elegant, self-possessed dinner companion, was wordless before the keen, warm gaze of Cameron Morrison.

With Margaret's things piled around them, before and behind and on her lap, the man Cameron Morrison vaulted (there was no other term to describe the vigorous motion) into the buggy and picked up the reins. Even with her burden, the buggy tilted with his weight. Cameron Morrison was a big man. Big but without an ounce of flesh to spare. Big and healthy and, obviously, filled with the joy of . . . about to say "life," Margo paused in her assessment, remembering Kezzie's letters and repeated reference to her family's personal relationship with Jesus Christ. Margo was hardly comfortable with addressing the Almighty as God, let alone heavenly Father, Jesus Christ, and Holy Spirit. Such familiarity made her uneasy. Thankfully Granny Kezzie seemed to find it as unreal as Margo herself. Surely a man as masculine as Cameron Morrison would find such familiarity with one's maker as unmentionable as all Margo's other acquaintances had.

But Cameron Morrison was saying, "Thank God you're here safe and sound. According to Mam—that's Kezzie, of course—it's not proper for young females to travel unaccompanied. And so we all prayed faithfully for you. Other than being a little tired," the blue eyes looked down on Margo in kindly fashion, "which is perfectly natural, you seem to have come through unscathed. Once in Bliss, with Mam, and our good fresh air and lots of rest, you'll be as right as rain, I'm sure."

"How long until we get there?" Margo managed, feeling young and gauche and, somehow, furious because of it.

"Two hours or so. Depends on whether we hurry. And I don't see why we should. This is one beautiful road. Well, not the road itself, which tends to be rutty after a rain such as we had last night, but look—have you ever seen such green?" Cameron gestured toward the bush that crowded the road, cut back occasionally to accommodate a way into someone's property.

He was right. It was the new green of spring. Margo became aware of the freshness of the air and found herself breathing deeply.

"Pure perfume," Cameron said. "No pollution by man. Let's hope it stays that way. I know it's pristine—that is, hardly touched—so that it comes as near to Eden as is possible here on this old earth."

"You sound . . . you sound . . ."

"Foolish?" Cameron asked with a grin.

"I was going to say contented."

"I suppose I am," Cameron said. "I like what David said—"

"David?"

"The psalmist," Cameron responded, and Margo felt herself flush at her ignorance. She hoped this man—so strong and vital and masculine—would not be a spouter of religious banalities. Would that be his one flaw? For that he was near perfection in all other ways Margo was blindingly certain. She hoped rather desperately that she would immediately discover a human frailty and that it would, once and for all, still this strange tumult in her heart.

"The psalmist?" she asked now, and waited for his trite and stilted "testimony."

"It has something to do with fat paths." Cameron's grin was fleeting, but it was there. Was he teasing?

"Fat paths?" Margo asked cautiously, intrigued in spite of herself.

"Fat paths, happy hills, and singing valleys."

And that was all. Margo sat, stewing, in silence.

Finally, "It's Psalm 65 if you should care to explore it for yourself," Cameron added.

"Fat paths?" Margo burst out with after a moment's silence. "That's the reason you are a contented man? *Fat paths?*"

"Would you prefer shining paths?"

What was wrong with the man! Why couldn't he just preach to her and get it over with!

"The path of the just," Cameron all but sang out above the clip-clop of the horse's hooves and the occasional creak of the rather ancient buggy, "is as the shining light."

With these thought-provoking words ringing in her ears, with a strong shoulder pressed occasionally against hers by the jouncing of the rig, with the wind gloriously fresh in her face and the sound of a meadowlark piercingly sweet filling the blue sky, with Granny Kezzie awaiting her coming with loving arms, and with an unknown but suddenly appealing future ahead of her, Margo found herself believing that the path, if not fat, seemed on the verge of plumpness.

"Just ahead," Cameron said, "is Bliss."

28

The small hamlet appeared as if by magic. The rig rounded a bend in the road, the bush fell away, and ten or twelve buildings appeared, bulked around a crossroads.

"As a town, it'll never amount to much, I suppose," Cameron said, "and that's because the railroad doesn't come through here. Still, we were happy to have our own town with church and school. As for supplies, Prince Albert isn't all that far away and has much more to offer—flour mill, dentist, doctor, lawyers, and so on. And of course, the Lands Office. It's gotten so that, to homestead, you have to go farther afield, though there's still plenty available in the Territories. Your father's place is the original Bliss place, and it happened to become available when he came here wanting to buy. Most places—as you've seen when we drove past—are not nearly so well under cultivation, being much more recently claimed."

"I noticed," Margo said. "Such tiny cabins—"

"My folks started off like that. What they have, they've worked for, believe me. But we've been happy and contented, and I remember the good times more than the bad. It was a tough time when my mother was so ill. That's when I did my first serious praying."

"That's when Kezzie came."

"Yes, and how we've loved having a grandmother, Molly and I. Did you know she lives with me now? Well, of course you know, hearing from her regularly."

"I knew, but what I didn't know was that it was on land owned by my father."

"I see," Cameron said thoughtfully. "So this has all been a surprise to you."

With the buggy turning in at the one and only building that could possibly be a general store, Margo was spared an explanation of her surprise regarding her father's property and his will.

Leaping from the buggy as lithely as he had gotten into it, Cameron came around the rig to offer his hand to Margo.

"Might as well get down and stretch," he said. "It's another three miles home. But we'll stop first at my folks' place—that's two miles from here. They are eager to meet 'Margo'." Cameron smiled.

"Where's Granny Kezzie?" Margo asked, walking beside the tall man toward the false-fronted building.

"At my . . . your place." Cameron made the correction quickly. "She's not really able to climb in and out of a buggy anymore. Once in a while we lift her into the wagon and have a chair in there for her to sit on, and take her home, maybe for Christmas or some special day, like a birthday. Sometimes we have everyone over to our . . . your place, but Mam isn't physically able to fix meals for a crowd. She takes care of me, though, to the best of her ability, and it's great to have her with me. These are days I'll always cherish, I can tell you that."

Cameron was holding open the door and ushering the newcomer into the store. One end was given over to food supplies, and here a man was checking a list held in his hand; a small pile of goods was before him on the scarred counter. Both he and the proprietor looked up and watched the approach of Margo and Cameron with interest.

"Hey, Cam," the proprietor said.

"Cameron," the customer said, politely and warmly, and both men shifted their gaze to the woman at Cameron's side.

"Hey, Barn," Cameron replied in kind, and "How are you, Parker? Struggling over what you can afford, I guess. Miss Galloway, I'd like you to meet our right Reverend Parker Jones. He's a good man, but just to make sure, we keep him on short rations. This other character is Barnabas Peale. Gentlemen—Miss Galloway."

Margo offered her hand, to have it soundly gripped and shaken.

"Welcome to Bliss," each said, while the minister quickly removed his hat.

After a moment, "Barn" went about filling the list the minister handed over to him. "Do your best with it," Parker Jones said. "You know my salary as well as I do . . . and my tastes."

"Yeah. They run to the cheap—beans, mostly."

Parker Jones turned his attention to Margaret. His smile was sweet, for a man, and Margo's first and natural impulse to criticism and perhaps skepticism because he was a "man of the cloth" melted away, and she found herself quite liking the man without knowing him.

"They like to make light of my housekeeping abilities, Miss Galloway," the minister said sadly. "I'd like to see how well they'd do by themselves. Cam, here, had to call into service his aging grandmother to take care of him, and Barn, poor, desperate man, just married for the third time."

Cameron didn't linger; he picked up what mail had arrived for his household and his parents' and turned to go.

"Mam is waiting to see her dear Margo," he explained, and his tones came across as tender ones. The other two nodded, murmured their good-byes, and Margo and Cameron returned to the buggy and the final lap of their journey.

The town of Bliss—what appeared to be several business establishments, including a barbershop and livery stable, interspersed with a few small houses and, at the end of the street, a white frame schoolhouse—soon disappeared as the buggy was enveloped once again in bush.

"The church?" Margo asked, thinking of Parker Jones and his congregation, of which, she supposed, Cameron was a part.

"The school serves as the church here, as in many places across the Territories. We just double up on its usefulness. It's a good plan. The schoolhouse is central to everything in these new districts and is often the first building to go up. Canadians are serious about good education."

"Parker Jones—he keeps house for himself, I gather."

"Now he does. He started off, about a year ago, living around with the church families; a month here, a month there. Not good. He had a terrible time, no place to study, bunking with the boys of the family. And then there's this: people shouldn't know every intimate detail of their pastor's life. Just imagine every woman in the congregation having washed your underwear, for instance, or knowing your best pair of socks is full of holes."

Margo couldn't restrain a laugh at the very thought of Parker Jones suffering such indignities.

"So, what was the solution?"

"We built him a house . . . cabin, of course, mostly called shack hereabouts. One that's big enough for now and can be added onto should the need arise. You'll hear it here first," Cameron said with a grin, slanting Margo a look, "but my sister, Molly, is already decorating that cabin—in her mind, of course, and, I imagine, in her dreams at night."

"And how does Parker Jones feel about all that, or does he know?"

"Oh, he knows, all right. His dreams—nightmares, possibly—probably have to do with making his small remuneration stretch to feed one more mouth. I can't call it a salary; whatever comes in in the offering plate, that's it. People are good about taking in garden stuff, baked goods, and so on. And he seems to have a knack of dropping in for a call near mealtime. But who am I to fault him for that? I hated being a bachelor so much I prevailed on Mam to take pity on me. It's not only the meals and all the work they mean, it's the company. Especially in winter. But there—I don't imagine you'll be here that long. Make a quick visit, check on your investment here, and get back to civilization, right?"

"Well—" Margo hesitated. The buggy seemed a poor place to talk business. "We'll need to discuss . . . everything."

After a keen glance at Margo's face, Cameron offered, "Of course, I expect that. Anytime, Miss . . . by the way, is it all right if we just dispense with formalities? They seem out of place, having known you through Mam for so many years, and with the ties my father had with yours, and with his more recent business dealing with me. What do you say? I'm Cameron to most people and just plain Cam to a few—take your choice."

"Cam . . . Cameron, of course. And you have a choice, too—Margaret, as most folks call me, or Margo, as Kezzie has always called me."

"Who do you think of yourself as?"

"Margo."

"Margo it will be. Well, Margo, here we are at the Morrison homestead."

And it was as "Margo" Cameron introduced her to Mary, then Angus when he had made his way in from the barn. Their welcome was warm and sincere, not surprising after Sadie LeGare's friendly greeting and Cameron's easy camaraderie.

"Come in . . . come in! We've looked forward to meeting you, especially since your father visited us a few years ago."

Margo was ushered to a comfortable seat, and conversation ran naturally along the lines of her father's last illness, old memories, and earlier connections. Never had Margo been made so welcome, never had she felt so comfortable.

The door slammed, and everyone turned toward the sound. The doorway framed a girl—young woman. Perhaps she had been running; perhaps she was excited. Her piquant face was delicately flushed, her black-lashed, blue eyes were sparkling. And her hair, smokily riotous, had escaped the ribbon that had tried to restrain it and curled in pure abandon over her forehead and around her ears.

Automatically, Margo reached a hand to her own head to tuck up the stray curls. For one fleeting moment, gone as quickly as it came, she had the giddy sensation that she was looking into a mirror.

29

The moment went as quickly as it came. Like a lightning flash on a dark night, for one split second giving startling clarity, so the moment came and went, as if it had never been. And indeed, had it?

Apparently she was the only one to have seen it; the others were busy with introductions and comments. Margo looked at the most recent family arrival, Molly, and saw her only as a young woman about her own age; probably older, if memory served her right. A girl with boundless energy, vivid face, and a mass of unruly, blue-black hair. Countless people have unruly, blue-black hair in this world, Margo realized. Molly's father, Angus, for instance. Though Molly's excessive curl was like her mother's and her mother's mother, the color was her father's. Angus's thick thatch, however, was touched with gray now. More than once Margo had heard her mother make reference to Angus Morrison's "thatch" and Mary's red "mop." Margo, a lonely child with no relatives near, had pressed her mother for accounts of the old Scottish home, every phase of life there, the momentous move to Canada, the disastrous sea voyage, her own birth and the birth and death of Mary Morrison's baby, or "sma' one," as Kezzie called her. For Kezzie, too, recounted the story, making it live for Margo until she almost felt that the absent Morrisons, Kezzie's family, were her family, too.

"And she never had a name?" Margo liked to ask, hearing again that Mary had never even seen her bairn but called her angel.

"Like you call me," Margo would say, cuddling close to Kezzie, to have her curls fondled lovingly and a kiss placed on her forehead.

"For such y'are," Kezzie would declare, and Margo thrived on the assurance in Nanny . . . Granny Kezzie's tones.

"Mam is so anxious to see you," Mary was saying now, "so we won't try to keep you. But Sunday, if Mam feels well enough, you'll all come over for dinner. Our pastor, Parker Jones, will join us—"

Margo noted Molly's quickly heightened color and the flash in her blue eyes.

"Dinner," Molly explained, "is our noon meal, you know. Our evening meal is supper. And bush protocol doesn't call for dressing for dinner, either." Molly's impish smile took any sharpness from her voice; neither did the farm's simple way of life come across as anything but natural and good. Margo was feeling more and more at ease. She would accept and adjust to rural ways; after all, they would be her way from now on. What would the Morrisons say when they learned that she was to become a resident of Bliss? If she were to suddenly burst forth with "I'm staying on, you know," what would their reaction be? Unbelieving, most likely, a rich girl's whim. But if they understood her reduced means and the absolute necessity of making a go of it somewhere other than at Heatherstone, after their first shock would they accept her as plain Margo, as dependent on the land as they were?

Taking the last mile of the trip with Cameron from the Morrison homestead to the Galloway place, Margo tried, hesitantly, to introduce the subject.

"If I stayed . . . would there be room at your . . . that is, the Bliss place, for me?"

Watching the bronzed face intently, Margo saw no telltale emotion, good or bad. But the moment of silence hung heavily between them before Cameron spoke.

"Your father had the Bliss house enlarged; it's quite roomy. We always kept a room ready for him, though he never came back after that one trip. It'll be your room now, of course, and for as long as you wish, naturally. But I doubt that you'll want to stay on into our winter. Bush life, for a sort of a lark, is fine . . . for a holiday. You'll appreciate civilization all the more for having experienced life in the bush. Sponge baths, for instance, or a dip in a zinc tub; keeping a fire in the cookstove all the time just for the simplest kinds of meals; making bread a couple times a week . . . gathering garden stuff for supper; a path to the . . . ah. . . ." Cameron's description of life in Bliss faltered.

"I understand," Margo said quickly.

If only *he* understood. It didn't matter how crude the lifestyle; not matter the inconveniences. She had no choice. It was life in the bush on the farm deeded her by her father or the impossible situation at Heatherstone with a groping Wallace and no hope of anything better.

He didn't understand! He didn't know that Wallace's gross insinuations had spoiled forever her Heatherstone home. He didn't know that the defection of Winfield Craven, upon learning of her penury, had released her from any last tie with the former life.

He didn't understand that . . . that something unexpected had touched her heart at the moment she laid eyes on him. Something that even now tripled the beat of her heart and shortened her breath. Something that caused Heatherstone to fade into insignificance and Bliss to blossom with happiness and hope.

No, this, in particular, Cameron didn't understand. And thank goodness! How foolish could one be! Never had she imagined such a scenario: herself, weary and rumpled from the long trip, wrenched from all former things and unsure of the future, coming face-to-face with a man—a stranger in all but name only, but vital and masculine and magnetic—and, in that instant whirled off into depths and heights of emotions such as never for one moment suspected or experienced in her engagement and marriage plans.

"I just thought it well to prepare you," Cam Morrison was saying now. "I'm sure you've never known such primitive ways. Actually, it may end up seeming like a sort of memorable visitation. I hope so, anyway," he finished lightly.

Unseen by Cameron, Margo frowned. How was she going to explain to him that there would be no going back?

And would Cameron, when he found out, give up his place as resident farmer? If so, who would take his place? The farm must be kept productive; it would be her only source of income. She—Margo Galloway, one-time pampered child of the rich—was as dependent on the land as any poverty-stricken settler in the Territories. The sponge baths, the kitchen range, the bread baking, the garden planting and tending, the *path*—all were to be as much a part of her life as that of the latest immigrant from the ghettos of Europe.

And when Cameron Morrison learned that this poor little rich girl was to be his employer, and a live-in one at that—

The final leg of the buggy ride was never to be remembered as Margo plunged into a half-frenzy of despair. Having met Cameron and realizing he was no *servant* such as she'd known but a man who would have goals and aspirations of his own, she saw how futile it would be to expect him to stay on, working for someone else. Especially a woman, especially when that woman had little or no funds to pay wages.

"Here we are . . . and there's Mam, bless her, waiting on the porch."

At Cameron's words Margo's worries fled for the time being, and she turned eager eyes on the house coming into view. But the sturdiness of the buildings and the beauty of the setting were ignored in favor of her first glimpse of the only grandmother she had known. Nanny, nurse, friend, all wrapped up in the dear, stooped figure awaiting her in the heart of the Canadian bush.

If this isn't home, cried Margo's heart, *where on earth would I find it?*

30

When Cameron had unhitched the horse, watered her, and turned her into the corral, he returned to the house. As he opened the door quietly, his breath caught in his throat in a strange way: seated in her old rocking chair, Kezzie, her withered cheeks wet with tears, was bent over the figure of the graceful girl who had flung herself with complete abandon on the floor and buried her face in the aproned lap. Kezzie's bent fingers stroked the tangled hair with remembered gentleness.

"Whoosh, whoosh," she was murmuring tenderly, in what Cameron was sure were remembered tones.

Feeling that he had intruded on a scene too private and too precious to be shared, Cameron turned to go. His movement caught his grandmother's eye.

"Come in, laddie," Kezzie invited. "Wee Margo is one of us. This is her home in ways more than ownership."

If I ever saw a lamb come home to the fold, Cameron thought, *this has to be it. How will Mam bear it, when separation time comes?* Well, that would be two or three months away, he supposed, months that were vital to his own future. He wouldn't wait too long to bring up the subject of the homestead's purchase; surely that would, quickly and happily, settle Margo's business in Bliss. And settle his own uncertain future happily and quickly *if* she agreed to sell to him. Aside from the fact that he could make only a partial payment, needing terms for the remainder of the purchase price, he could foresee no problem. And who, if anyone, would have the full amount to give her? With her wealth, a small arrangement such as this one would be of little consequence. To her. To him, it would be everything. So much of himself had gone into the Bliss place, with so many tentative dreams concerning it, that it would be hard indeed to turn it over to anyone else.

"Wee Margo" buried her face even deeper in Kezzie's lap and clutched the ancient knees in a tighter grip. Something—perhaps years of loneliness—was spilling itself out. Spilling out and being wiped away.

Cameron backed away. "I'll tend the fire," he said quietly, "and start supper."

The large room that served as the living area for the home's inhabitants—braided rug surrounded by comfortable furniture, lamps, and books, and across the room a kitchen/eating area—absorbed the soft sounds of loving comfort at one end and the muted thumps and clanks of Cameron's domestic efforts on the other. When Cameron pulled the roasting pan from the oven and the fragrance of the crisp-skinned chicken filled the room, he looked through the gathering dusk to see Margo sitting back on her heels, looking up at Kezzie, sunshine on her face. For a moment Cameron thought it was a glow from the girl herself. With a shake of the head at his own foolishness, he recognized it as a touch of the setting sun through the lace-curtained window.

Nevertheless, it was as they sat at the table, under kerosene lamplight, with her dark eyes puffed and her nose shiny, that Cameron, for the first time all day, gave Margo his full attention. Before she had seemed a rather rumpled but perfectly outfitted doll; he now saw the girl herself. And was strangely, suddenly, jolted. Before he might determine what this strange reaction was, he checked it firmly.

"More chicken?" he asked quickly, offering the platter.

If Margo hadn't taken that moment to raise her eyes to his, all might have returned, safely, to normal, and Cameron might have persuaded himself that he had been mistaken. Now, caught in the web of her lashes, he looked and couldn't stop looking.

Here was no coy miss; here was no façade; no games were being played such as he had experienced with other young women. Gazing into the honest, vulnerable face, before the thick lashes came down over the tear-washed eyes, Cameron gave an almost visible start.

"Thank you," Margo said. "It's so good. It's *all*," and her eyes swept not only the table but the entire area, "so good."

Cameron's gaze dropped to his plate, blankly. His mind seemed equally blank, as time stood still. Then, *Oh no!* he groaned soundlessly. *No no no no no no!* The mindless denial went on, *No! No!* and he never knew that one final "No!" escaped his grim lips until he saw the surprised faces of Kezzie and Margo.

"That is—no, thank you." Then, to the puzzlement of those watching, he proceeded to spoon gravy over his potatoes until, with a start, he realized the savory goo was spilling over onto the tablecloth. *I've lost my wits as well as my heart,* he thought.

The eyes Cameron raised to his grandmother were eyes of despair. With a deep breath, Kezzie put her hand over the hard, brown hand clenched beside his plate.

"Laddie," she said gently, and oh, so knowingly, "it's all right. It'll all come out . . . satisfactorily." But whether she meant the gravy seeping into the tablecloth or the warm sensation creeping into his heart was not clear. In either case, it was up to him to get rid of it.

Pushing back his chair, he said, "Clumsy of me. If you've finished, I'll serve the pudding later. Right now I'll clear the table and put this to soak. It'll wash out . . . with a little effort, it'll wash out. Won't it, Mam?" The eyes he turned on Kezzie were imploring.

"Put it to soak for now, laddie. That's the wisest thing to do."

"I'll help," Margo said. And though she'd never done such a chore before, some basic woman-instinct gave her joy in handling the family's china and deft fingers in piling the soiled plates in a dishpan of hot, sudsy water.

"Don't," Cameron said, more harshly than he had meant to, and he softened it immediately with, "Please don't. I'm used to such chores. I'd feel better if you'd just go sit with Mam." But even the smile with which he said it did not change the resolute tone of his next words: "Mustn't forget . . . you're the owner of this domain, and a lady."

"Still—"

"You like Mam's blancmange, I understand. It will remind you of Heatherstone and her time there with you. Simple as it is, she insisted on making it for you. It'll not be served in the cut-glass crystal that you're accustomed to, and the spoon will not be solid silver. . . ." He tried to sound wry; instead he sounded grim.

Again Margo raised those clear, honest eyes to his, and Cameron faltered. This time, her gaze held a small speculative look, as if to say, "Why is he doing this—reminding me of Heatherstone and its luxuries?"

I'll have to be very careful, Cameron warned himself, *that in my defense against her, I keep from going overboard.* And smarting under the obvious fact that a defense was necessary, he served up the blancmange in breakfast bowls rather than the daintier sauce dishes Mam expected.

"The cream, laddie?" Kezzie asked gently, looking down at the lumped concoction in the crockery in her hand. "And the jelly?"

Lips tight, Cameron recovered the bowls, added the cream that was whipped and ready, then a dollop of Mam's brilliant pin cherry jelly.

199

"You'll not have had pin cherry jelly, Missy," Mam explained to Margo when once again the dessert was placed in their hands, this time with a serviette.

Desperate to escape, Cameron excused himself. "It's time to start evening chores. No matter how pleasant the company . . . in fact, no matter how poor the health or bad the weather, chores have to be done. Day in and day out . . . summer and winter . . . in sickness and in health. . . ." Cameron's muttered explanation died away as he made his departure. "I'll do the dishes when I come back in, along with the separator parts," was his parting shot.

Kezzie was staring into her pudding. But she could only do that for so long. Eventually, raising her eyes, she met the straight, calm eyes of her bairn and understood their look completely.

"He's right, you know," Kezzie said gently. "He belongs here . . . you belong at Heatherstone. What you are thinking—it's not possible. And Cameron knows it, even if you don't. Don't play with him, lassie." Kezzie's voice was pleading. Loving both of them, she could see only misery ahead. "Why are y' here, anyway, when y're supposed to be gettin' marrit?"

It was much easier to tell, sitting at Kezzie's feet. Laying aside the remainder of her pudding Margo crept back to put her arms on Kezzie's knees and tell the entire story: her father's illness and death; Winfield's pressure to marry; his abrupt departure to better prospects; Wallace's arrival and his loathsome suggestions.

"Then, lassie," Kezzie said, "y're runnin' away, aren't y'?"

Margo looked surprised, thinking about it. "I don't think of it as that," she said finally. "I think I'm running *to* something."

"And what's that, lassie?"

"A future . . . my future."

"In Bliss, lassie? All those things Cameron has been spoutin'—strikin' out blindly is what he's doin'—they're all true. Life here isn't easy, much as it has improved and the worst over with. You can't know what you're sayin'."

"I think I do, Granny. You haven't heard everything yet." And Margo gave the details of her father's strange bequest.

"So it came to that," Kezzie whispered, and put her head back and closed her eyes.

"To what, Gran?"

But Kezzie made no explanation. Rather, she stroked the tumult of hair in her lap, her face strangely pale.

"So you see, I have no choice," Margo finished, raising her head and looking firmly at her old nurse. "I can't go back; I can't abide living with Wallace. I have no money to speak of—a 'stipend' only and that until I marry. I'm . . . I'm a pauper, Gran. And I don't understand why. Papa said . . . in the will he said I would be able to understand should I care to do so, or something puzzling like that. What did he mean, Gran, what did he mean?"

Kezzie sat in frozen silence, her face, if possible, whiter than before.

"You can tell me," Margo said slowly, studying the white face and closed eyes and hearing the ragged breath. "You can tell me . . . if you will."

Kezzie struggled to her feet, her frizzy hair wild about her face, her eyes as wild as her hair.

The twisted lips, as Kezzie loosened herself from Margo's arms on her knees and turned toward her bedroom, whispered what sounded, to the astounded girl, like "Never . . . never . . . never. . . ."

Margo was up bright and early, charmed from sleep by some unknown bird's song. Dressing hastily she opened her door to a quiet house. But there was a fire in the kitchen range, and what looked like a pot of porridge simmered on the back lids.

Having watched Cameron, the previous night, dip water from the stove's reservoir, Margo took the enamel basin from its stand at the side of the door, dipped water, which was comfortably warm, and returned to her room for a sketchy wash. Briefly she thought of Cameron's reference to a "zinc tub" and decided she'd settle for that before another day went by.

Struggling with her mostly unmanageable hair in front of the small mirror, Margo remembered yesterday and her first, startling glimpse of Molly Morrison; she frowned. How strange! Common sense told her that the heritage of each of them could easily be traced back to . . . well, perhaps to the Romans and the invasion of England and Scotland by Hadrian, centuries ago. His soldiers could not have built and maintained the stone wall and the many stationary camps, mile-castles, and turrets without great numbers of them. And, being human and far from home, it was not unlikely that, from alliances with the women of the area, dark-haired and dark-browed offspring were born, the coloring to emerge from time to time across the years since. Yes, that was the explanation, that accounted for the color. But the curl! Who was responsible for the curl!

"Oh, bother!" Margo muttered with vexation; she tied her own "mop" back severely with a ribbon and wished Molly Morrison good luck with her so-similar problem.

Making her way again across the silent house, Margo dumped her bathwater in the slop pail beside the washstand, set the basin in its proper place, opened the door, and stepped out.

It was the parkland at its best. Birds flashed around with burst of color and song; the grass was springy underfoot; the bush was sparkling with dew. *It would not be hard to fall in love with the bush country!* Margo felt its magic and did not resist. Knowing her future was sealed in this place, she did not resist the impulse to happiness and satisfaction. Would they—happiness and satisfaction, peace and comfort—be found here?

Considering, Margo's gaze went automatically toward the barn and the faint sounds emanating from it. Soundlessly she crossed the wet grass, entered the open door, studying the dark interior. It was the sight of three cats ranged behind the swishing tail of a cow that gave her a clue to Cameron's whereabouts. Even as she watched, a stream of milk spurted, straight and true, toward the cats. Never moving except to open their mouths, they received the foamy offering placidly. Margo's laugh, as happy in its way as the birds' songs, caused the flow to cease abruptly and the cats to turn their slanted eyes toward her, stand, tails erect, and rub their heads against her hand as she bent to fondle them.

"Good morning, Princess," came the muffled voice from the side of the cow.

So that was how it was to be, she thought, with a sigh. Stepping around gingerly, Margo watched as Cameron stood, lifting a brimming pail, and turned toward her.

"Good morning," she responded and, knowing there was nothing to be gained by waiting, added, "We need to talk."

"Of course. At your service."

"Well—not here." Margo felt disadvantaged on such strange turf. "Could you step outside?"

Walking beside her, his old hat on the back of his head, his blue eyes squinting into the morning sun, Cameron was the picture of health and masculinity. Stiffening her resolve, Margo looked around for a likely place of business.

"Sit here," Cameron said, gesturing toward the woodpile, and Margo seated herself on the chopping block, Cameron nearby on an upturned chunk of poplar.

"I love the smell," Margo said simply, and Cameron's eyes softened, in spite of himself.

"You mean the wood," he said smiling, "not the barn."

"The wood, of course. The wood, and the woods, and . . . everything has a fragrance all its own. One could grow accustomed to it, I suppose. Does it lose its charm?"

"No."

"Cameron," she began, "for your sake, as well as mine, I need to discuss the . . . the . . ."

"The Bliss place?"

"This place of bliss."

Cameron's eyebrows lifted. "You make hasty decisions," he said.

"I guess I do," she said, surprising herself as she recalled her vacillations in regard to marriage to Winfield. "Anyway, at present, Bliss seems a refuge for me—"

"The intended marriage," Cameron asked casually, "it didn't come off?"

"It's off; no doubt about that. Off, and over."

"Is that why Bliss is a refuge for you?"

"Partly. It seems like a new beginning."

"For you. What about the place, Margo? What about the future? I'm sure that's what you want to talk about. And it's what I need to hear."

Margo took a deep breath and started in. The Bliss place, she told him, was indeed hers, the only thing that was hers. What's more, she had limited funds with which to run it. She would have to make it pay, to survive. Without money to pay wages, was there some arrangement—half and half, perhaps, on whatever the farm brought in? And would he, Cameron, be willing to stay on with such an arrangement?

Having finished, Margo waited tensely for Cameron's answer.

Cameron was slow in responding. A calf, somewhere, bawled; a cat rubbed itself against Margo's ankle, and a late-rising rooster crowed.

"You've taken me by surprise," Cameron said, finally. "But I have a solution for you. I'm ready to get my own place—can't work forever for someone else. Let me buy you out, Margo. I can put down a fair amount . . . enough to get you home again and keep you until you get settled; something will open for you among your father's business partners. Life can go on for you much the same as always, I'll be bound."

"I haven't made myself clear, Cameron. I'm not going back. Not ever. I'm here to stay. Sink or swim, survive or perish," she said firmly, "it will be in Bliss."

Looking into those dark eyes, now fiercely determined, Cameron had no choice but to take a deep breath, rise, brush himself off, and say, "Then I'll need to make my own decision. And that will take some praying. If this is what the Lord wants for you, he'll be faithful to show me what he has for me."

Before he picked up the milk pail and walked away, he asked, "You've prayed about your decision, I suppose?"

"I'm not in the habit—" Margo began stiffly.

"Perhaps you should be," Cameron said mildly, but seriously. A faint smile lit his face. "Oftentimes the Lord is leading when we don't know it. I have a feeling that's so in your case, 'wee' Margo. I'm certain it will all turn out for the best, for all of us. And if you're looking for a refuge, consider wings."

"Wings?" Margo asked uncertainly.

"God's wings. 'In the shadow of thy wings will I make my refuge,'" the stalwart man quoted and seemed none the weaker for it in his listener's eyes.

Wings, Margo thought as Cameron swung off with his pail of milk, the cats following, tails aloft. *What a comforting place to be, hidden away under wings.* The only things comparable that she had known were Kezzie's arms.

And these, she realized with a pang when she went into the house, were hers only for a time . . . a brief time. For Kezzie, in a wrapper, sitting in her rocking chair with a cup of tea in her hand, seemed frighteningly frail. The morning sun through the window was merciless, etching lines not revealed before and emphasizing the poor color of the sagging face.

But Kezzie smiled her fond smile, and Margo stooped to place a kiss on the withered cheek. Who could blame them if each found the moment another time for tears? Margo laid her cheek on the white, frizzy hair for a moment and knew the trip was worth it for this alone.

Kezzie had set the table, and bread was toasting on the range top. A coffeepot bubbled, and the porridge, when the lid was removed, steamed invitingly.

"Cameron will get milk from the icehouse," Kezzie explained to an exploring Margo. "And butter and cream. You'll want to get acquainted with your icehouse, Margo. What a blessing that's been. I don't know what homesteaders do in places where there's no winter and no ice."

Margo discussed her need to learn the farm's workings at the breakfast table.

"It will be a good time for us to get our own chickens," Kezzie suggested. "You can care for them . . . gather eggs. . . ."

"The garden," Cameron said. "You might begin to think about berry picking. It's early, but strawberries are coming on."

"The cows . . . the team of horses . . . the plowing," Margo said, impatient with egg gathering and berry picking. "Hitching up—"

"Whoa!" Cameron responded, laughing. "It will all come, in time. I *have* decided one thing—I'll stay on through harvest. I couldn't, with a good conscience, leave with the summer and fall work ahead. When the harvest is in, that will be the time for me to turn it over to someone else and leave."

"If you leave," Margo said, her breath catching.

"If I leave. But I think I may want to, Margo. I can't be a hired man all my life." Unspoken, as he watched the vivid face, was the urgent goad to remove himself from this girl's presence for her own good. Vulnerable, she was, and well he knew it. Vulnerable and wounded in love and open, he felt sure, to being taken advantage of. All the more reason to remove himself. Cameron Morrison and the poor little rich girl? A most unlikely alliance, for sure and certain. No, no. The moment the thought had presented itself, he had soundly rejected it. And too bad . . . too bad. What a choice person she was.

The rest of the week flew by. Unaccustomed as she was to kitchen duties and the never-ending preparation of food, it seemed to Margo that dishes were barely done from breakfast before it was time to pare potatoes or some such thing for the noon meal. The longer afternoon, which might have allowed a breathing space as far as meals were concerned, was crowded with a dozen other tasks pressing for attention. There was so much more than swishing through the house with a dust rag, dressed in a frilly apron, or serving tea to one's company. Company, when it came, had business in mind. Molly dropped in once to deliver mail but also to fill a can with cream from the icehouse. "We have been making the cheese and butter for both households," she explained. "Now," and she eyed Margo speculatively, "you may want to handle it here."

"In time, lassie," Kezzie responded for the hesitant Margo. "Just now it's biscuit-learning time . . . sock darning . . . setting hens to nest. . . ."

"I get the picture." Molly smiled and turned to take her departure. There hadn't even been time for a cup of tea together. "We'll visit Sunday," she said. "Bliss people, for the most part, recognize it as a day of rest, and thank God for it. Will you go to church with Cameron, Margo?"

Margo fumbled for an answer. "Ah . . . do you go, Kezzie?"

"Nae, lass."

"Then I'll stay with you."

"Well, then, at the dinner table—at our house, you remember—we'll just have to go over the sermon for you. We preach to Mam regularly, don't we, Mam?" Molly's words were crisp, but her eyes were loving as they rested on the old face so marked by the cares of this world and the old eyes, so soon to look on the next world, and Margo felt there was serious thought behind the half-teasing words.

Molly kissed her grandmother tenderly and whirled away, a blur of vitality and purpose.

"That's our Molly," Kezzie said proudly.

"You know, Mam—" Margo found it easy to adopt the title the rest of the family used for Kezzie, and reserved the Granny/Nanny words for their close and personal times, "I had the strangest sensation when I met Molly for the first time—"

Kezzie looked at her sharply.

"She seemed . . . familiar, somehow." Weak words, to express the blindingly bright recognition of herself, for one brief fraction of time.

"You're both young . . . pretty . . . full of life. . . ."

"It was more than that, Mam," Margo pursued stubbornly.

"The dark Scots . . . what else could it be? Your eyes are brown, lassie; hers are blue."

"I know," Margo said, somehow unsatisfied and wondering why.

If Sunday was a day of rest, as Molly had reported, it certainly didn't start off that way. Breakfast routine was the same; Cameron went off to chores the same as always. Margo fed the ducks and geese; Cameron "slopped" the pigs. But there the routine changed. Rather than proceed with farm tasks, Cameron brought the team and wagon to the door, slipped into his room, and emerged a transformed man. Gone the blue denims (thankfully, Margo thought, never the "bib" or "apron" variety); gone the cotton cassimere overshirt (as opposed to undershirt, Kezzie had explained at mending time); gone the worn Wellingtons or rubber boots that Cameron wore almost exclusively outside, changing at the door for felt pacs, or padding around in sock feet.

If she had thought him handsome before, Margo's breath was as good as taken away by her first glimpse of Cameron in his "Sunday-go-to-meetin'" clothes. Unless she was sadly mistaken, the well-fitting navy blue suit was made of German Vicuna cheviot cloth, very closely woven, very smooth, soft surfaced. The coat was undoubtedly satin piped throughout, with every pocket stayed and with arm shields of velvet. And all sewn, of course, with silk and linen. His shoes were of satin calf and featured the dongola top and the new coin toe with tip and had never seen the inside of a barn.

Straightening his neatly dotted pongee silk Windsor tie before the washstand mirror, Cameron turned to catch what Margo supposed was a foolishly approving look on her face, and she blushed.

"Clothes don't make the man," he said with a grin and clapped the latest style derby on his head.

"Mam knows just about when I'll be back," he said. "We'll load her up—that's why I have the wagon. I'll just pick her up, chair and all, and we'll go have dinner with the folks."

More bemused by him than ever, Margo watched the wagon trundle away. "Your Prince Albert stores," was her single comment, "seem to be better supplied than I realized."

"The catalog, lassie. Much more convenient than P. A. I guess the 'wish book' carries everything one would want. Some people call it the prairie Bible and study it more than they do the 'good book' itself."

Settling herself at Kezzie's knee, as of old, Margo asked for the stories of "olden days."

209

Kezzie's mind, still sharp, had not only retained the facts of her early days in Scotland with the Galloway family but had absorbed the very savor . . . the essence of those days. Margo interrupted from time to time. As an adult, hearing it all again, she asked questions that were important now—about her ancestors, her parents' marriage, about Heatherstone, Scotland. . . .

When it came to the sea voyage, Kezzie's tale faltered.

"Oh, go on, Granny Kezzie . . . do go on. I've wanted to hear it all again for so many years. No one else can give me all the details, and I need to be refreshed about it. Tell me again about when I was born . . . about that miserable doctor . . . about that sad, sad day when you and Papa stood with Angus and Molly and Cameron, and baby 'Angel' was buried at sea."

But Kezzie's head was back against her chair, and her face was white again, and she barely managed, "Not today, lassie," before struggling to her feet and turning to her room.

Margo was chastened. She had asked too much. It must be Mam's age; never before had she hesitated over the touching account of birth and death.

I need to make allowances for the changes time has made, she realized.

Margo hadn't heard the old stories since Kezzie had left Heatherstone almost eight years before, and many of the details had faded. Sophia's accounts had been from an entirely different viewpoint, and anyhow, as Margo grew older, they had ceased altogether. If Kezzie couldn't, or wouldn't, recount those times for her, her slim hope of making some sense of her father's bequest looked bleaker than ever. What had he meant? If Kezzie, her father's faithful friend and servant for many years, couldn't shed any light on the cryptic words, then who could?

It was a happy, even joyous, group that gathered at the Morrisons' oak table, the added leaves extending across one end of the comfortable room that was living/sitting/drawing room, parlor and kitchen, all in one. Mary had left a large roasting pan in the oven when they went off to church, and the roast and fresh garden vegetables—baby carrots, onions, tiny potatoes dug carefully from the hill—topped with rich, brown gravy, couldn't be surpassed.

After the blessing was said by Angus, and the bowls and platters were being passed around to hearty chatter and much good humor, Margo grew silent . . . watching, listening. Here was a family circle the likes of which she had never experienced but often dreamed of. Always eating alone, in the nursery, during childhood, occasionally dressed to come down for a few special moments to meet guests; joining, finally, not long before her mother's death, her parents for a quiet, elegant dinner; enduring the meals alone with her father after her mother's death, with little to say and no laughter at all—it all seemed so bleak now, so empty. Sitting now, an outsider, at what seemed a charmed circle, Margo warmed her lonely heart at the Morrison fires and wished they were her own.

Sensing her mood, perhaps, Angus turned to her, at his side. A man in his early fifties, large, like his son, though a little stooped, with a smattering of gray in his ink-black hair and a fine network of wrinkles around the dark eyes, he was, obviously, a man of great physical attraction—like his son. And obviously a gentleman, due, Margo had heard, to her grandfather's recognition of the boy Angus's abilities and possibilities and the Galloway investment in his education. Margo's father had had a high regard for the absent Angus, always spoke highly of him and kept in touch across the years. Sophia's opinion of Angus had been . . . Margo tried now to puzzle out her mother's opinion of Angus. There had been a dreamy quality to Sophia's recollection of Angus; her brief comments concerning him had always ended with a sigh. Now Margo wondered. . . .

"Am I like my father?" Margo asked abruptly, "or my mother?"

With conversation swelling around them, Angus studied the face before him, smiled, and said, "Neither one, lass. You're yourself, and a lovely self it is at that. Your father must have been proud of you."

211

At that moment, Margo tensed, her face going still. Startlingly still. So still that Angus set down the tumbler from which he had been about to drink and asked, "Are you all right?"

"Your finger," Margo said. "The little one. It's—" her voice was strange—"it's bent . . . curved."

"And so it is." Angus seemed relieved that there was, after all, no problem. "Both of them," he added, and held up his two hands, open, with fingers splayed. The two little fingers were indeed unusually bowed.

"Born with them," Angus explained. "So was my father; so was Molly. It's a trait that seems to run in the family."

A great roaring filled Margo's ears. Angus's startled face dimmed away momentarily; the happy dinner sounds faded to an indistinguishable murmur.

So this is why he sent me here. Molly clenched her curved little fingers with the others into fists in her lap. *So this is why Papa sent me here.*

No, not Papa. Never again Papa. Hugh Cavalier Galloway—cruel, vindictive, venomous Hugh Galloway—had deliberately sent her here, and for this malicious purpose.

F ine," Margo muttered tautly. "I'm fine." And with trembling hand she picked up her tumbler of water and put it to lips quivering in spite of her fierce effort to still them.

But Angus Morrison was looking at her queerly. "My dear," he said, "perhaps you should lie down," and he reached out his hand with its distinguishing curved little finger to lay it gently on her arm.

As though that curved finger were a branding iron to mark her irrevocably and irretrievably as someone other than a Galloway, Margo jerked herself from Angus's touch. Then, at the sight of the pure astonishment widening his eyes, she managed a smile.

"Forgive me," she said thickly. "I'm . . . I'm not myself." Almost, the descriptive phrase, innocently but aptly spoken, sent her into a fit of hysteria. *If I'm not myself . . . who am I?*

Perhaps he—this black-headed, curly-locked man with the dark eyes and the bowed fingers—could tell her. Undoubtedly, he could tell her. In her moment of soul-shaking distress, Margo came near flinging the bitter words at the craggy Scotch face,

213

the face her mother had described over the years with what Margo now thought had been nostalgia: *Who am I?*

But even half blind with fury and pain, Margo saw the clear lack of comprehension in Angus's eyes. *Perhaps he doesn't even know,* she thought with surprise. *It's possible he doesn't even know!*

Mary looked up from her end of the table, her face filling with alarm and concern. Hurrying to Margo's side she put an arm around Margo's waist and led her away to a bedroom where she urged her to lie down.

The last thing Margo noticed as she turned from the table were the bewildered faces of the family and Parker Jones. "I'll just sit here a moment," she managed. "I'll be fine. Please . . . please don't worry about me. It's just a . . . an indisposition—"

The blue eyes above her were sympathetic; Mary's voice was kind as she offered, "It's probably a reaction, lass. All that you've been through—it's caught up with you. Your father's death, that long trip, the excitement of seeing Mam again. Not to mention all the work you've been taking on."

How to tell Mary that she had loved the work, loved the farm, and that she had felt that she was truly at home in Bliss. How to tell her that she was beginning to fall in love with her son!

And now it was all lost, lost to her before she had ever really owned it. Margo felt hot tears run down her cheeks and couldn't check them.

Mary pressed Margo's head, the hair now in wild disarray, against her breast. *Doesn't she see, can't she feel the similarity?* Margo thought. *Hasn't she pressed Molly's head of identical curls in just this same way, countless times?*

No, she doesn't see, she concluded. Or, if she did, it was not to be explored. Never to be explored.

And there's no need for her to know, for any of them to know, her thoughts ran on. *I'll get out of here and leave them as they were. Leave them all with their hearts and lives intact.* Momentarily she indulged in the bitter wish that she might thrust the same knife of pain into Angus and have him suffer even as she was suffering. But to spare the others, she would, she must, leave them in their ignorance. Yes, and in their bliss. And not for their sakes only but for her own sake.

Margo drew about her whatever remnants of pride she had remaining. She would be no illegitimate embarrassment to this family and to herself! She would be no tagalong appendage to this happy group! Life, for the Morrisons, would resume its sweet flow, spared the humiliation that would surely shatter them all, should they discover Angus's (and Sophia's) perfidy.

Now her whirling thoughts turned to her mother. Not only had recent events taken Margo's fiancé from her and shaken her very roots concerning home and father, but now her memories of her mother were sullied. It was startlingly clear: Sophia . . . and Angus!

It was all too much. Margo whimpered out her anguish in the arms of her newfound friend and grieved for one final loss: these arms, too, would be denied her.

For that she would leave Bliss was the one certainty Margo had.

⁕

It was a silent trip home; it had been a silent leave-taking or at least a muted one. Kezzie was visibly shaken; even Molly's vivaciousness was curbed. Of the haze surrounding their farewells with their loving pats and murmured words of comfort, one thing stood out clearly: Pastor Parker Jones's prayer.

"Just a moment," he had said, as Kezzie, Margo, and Cameron were about to leave the house. "Let's look to the Lord concerning this." Everyone bowed their heads, and Margo, who was not accustomed to prayer of any kind, was moved in spite of herself. Surely, if there was a God on the throne, everything would turn out for the best.

Margo found herself clinging to that thought as she jounced along on the wagon seat beside Cameron, Kezzie seated in the rocking chair behind them, looking white and worn.

"Want to talk about it?" Cameron said, and at her shake of the head, he added, "Let me know if I can help," and he placed his big hand momentarily over hers. In spite of the distraction of her wits, Margo felt the small thrill that sped from Cameron's grip, up her arm, straight to her heart. Almost casting herself into his arms, she restrained herself somehow, gave him a watery smile, and cherished the thought of his touch and her spontaneous reaction.

With the afternoon sun warm on her back, the by-now familiar birdsong lifting occasionally from fence post and bush, with Nanny Kezzie within arm's reach and the most desirable man she had ever met at her side, Margo's spirits rallied. Her mindless reaction to something so simple as a curved finger seemed to border on foolishness. Perhaps it was the invigorating air she drew into her lungs, perhaps it was her passionate desire to fit into life in the magnetic beauty of Bliss, but Margo began to feel embarrassment over her strange outburst. What had possessed her? There would be, surely, no need to abandon Bliss and all it held for her. The thought poured like sunshine into her heart, and she lifted her head, dried her eyes, and squared her shoulders.

"Good girl," Cameron said, noting the change, and his approval was music to her ears. "It was, we all know, a cruel blow—to be more or less disinherited—"

"It isn't that so much," Margo said hesitantly, "it's wondering why. Papa . . . Hugh, said something about leaving the estate in the Galloway name and in Galloway hands." And, in spite of herself, Margo looked down at the hands clasped in her lap; that brought to mind her curved little fingers, and an involuntary shiver ran through her.

"Well," Cameron explained rationally enough, "when you marry, you won't be a Galloway. Right?"

"Of course!" Margo felt considerably cheered and reassured. Truly, she had come to believe, here in Bliss the money didn't matter all that much. It was the puzzle . . . the mystery . . . of the unexplainable will that troubled her.

Before she could lay it all to rest, she decided now, she would have to talk with Kezzie. Kezzie, she believed, held the key to the entire matter. And Hugh knew it. Needing a father so badly, Margo regretted her earlier castigation of Hugh. She had, indeed, come to a conclusion that was unfounded. Or founded on such flimsy evidence as two small curved fingers!

Oh, how she wished she might lay her head on the broad shoulder that was just going to waste at her side. Instead, she smiled up at the eyes so seriously searching her own and felt the warmth of Cameron's smile as it lit up his face, clear to the toes on her dangling feet.

"Feeling better?" he asked.

"Yes, indeed. And sorry for the . . . the . . ." Margo didn't quite know what to call the recent incident. "That prayer, by Parker Jones. Perhaps God will work all this out, to His glory and . . . and for my best. I'm beginning to believe that."

Now Cameron's eyes were the watery ones. Accustomed to Hugh's rigid discipline, Margo marveled at a man who could show emotion. "That's the best news of all," he said from the depths of those emotions, and he reached and took Margo's hand in his.

It was enough. For the moment, it was enough.

⌐———◦

Kezzie had needed to rest when they reached home—the place of Bliss. And then there were the evening chores in the barn and pigsty. Margo was by now familiar with the routine and did her share almost automatically. When Cameron called her "Pardner," she felt the glow. What a day it had been for glows, shivers, tears, and smiles. Now was the time for glowing, it seemed, and Margo did it well. Did it well and never knew that Cameron, stepping outside and away from her, looked up at the evening sky, raised a hand to shift the hat on his head, and mouthed a soundless, "Whoa!"

One quart flour
One cup sour milk
One tsp soda
One-half pound lard
One-half pound chopped raisins or currants
Roll two inches thick and bake in a quick oven. Split open, butter, and eat hot.

Margo had toiled and fussed over the measuring, mixing, and rolling. Now she fretted about the heat of the oven. She took unnecessary peeks at this, her first baking. Tea cakes. Not like any she had eaten previously, she was sure, but a tried and true recipe that Kezzie recommended. Her family, she maintained, loved them.

"They should be done in time for tea," Kezzie offered from her chair at the other end of the room. "Come, sit doon and rest. Y've been at it since dawn, lassie."

Margo tossed aside the floury apron, smoothed her hair at the washstand mirror, and laughed to see the flour on her nose. What a day it had been!

Monday . . . and washday. Ignorant but game, Margo had struggled through, with Kezzie's advice and help.

"For once," Kezzie had said, "Cam can get on with the chores. Usually he helps with the wash."

He still helped. There was no way Margo could hustle the great pails of water needed for the numerous piles of clothes sorted out onto the floor of the kitchen area. The copper boiler alone held about twenty gallons, all carried from the well, filling the boiler, which was placed on the front lids of the wood-burning stove. Galvanized tubs were brought in and placed on a bench, also brought in, and half-filled with cold water to which was added hot water from the boiler. Then, of course, the hard yellow soap had to be shaved and dissolved down in a small pot of hot water. Finally, she was ready to get to the actual washing itself.

Special needlework was done by hand; wool and silk items were done separately. White goods were put into the tub for scrubbing, then lifted by means of an old broom handle and transferred to the boiler. "Dry clothes are never put into the boiler," Kezzie explained, "because the hot water sets stains."

Soaking, bleaching, starching, bluing, wringing, all were exhausting. Thanks to Kezzie, dinner cooked at the same time— a pot of beans simmered on the back of the same stove that boiled the white clothes on the front lids.

Pinning a final batch of clothes on the line, Margo declared she would never again toss clothes as casually into the wash as she had done for a lifetime; somehow she'd eke another day's wear from them! And to think—tomorrow was ironing day.

Clothes washed and hung and drying, there was the routine to go through in reverse. Out went the water, pail by pail, to be dumped as far away as one could stand the pull on one's arms; out went the tubs, out went the boiler. There was a wet floor to mop, the stove top to blacken. Only then could Margo draw a breath, collapsing onto a kitchen chair.

"What's for dinner?"

It was Cam, in from the fields. Margo hurried to set out bread and butter and fill glasses with milk to accompany the piping hot beans. "I suppose," she muttered, half-vexed, half-proud, "I'm *bustling!*"

The tea cakes, later on, were a brilliant idea. Not only were they designed to teach her some baking skills but the fresh delicacies would call for a few moments of rational, civilized living—teatime. Kezzie was all for it, stating that the pantry, fortunately, held dried currants.

When the pan was in the oven and Margo had removed her apron and tidied her hair, she turned toward Kezzie with the decision to have the talk, say the things, ask the questions that had to be faced. It was natural and good to drop onto the rug at Kezzie's feet, smiling up fondly at her dear old nurse.

"Granny," she began, using the pet title from childhood, "please. . . ."

"Yes, wee angel," Kezzie said tenderly, reaching out a worn hand to fondle the lively curls, brushing them back from Margo's temple.

Margo took the hand in her own. "Granny," she began again, "ever since Papa said what he did—about Heatherstone staying in Galloway hands—and ever since he said. . . ." Margo paused, her throat tightening.

"What did he say, lassie?"

"He left me this property here, and he said I'd understand if I cared to, or some such words. I think he said I could find the reason . . . if I cared to. Of course I care to! I can't go on not knowing. There's some sort of secret here, Granny. Why . . . why did Papa send me here? Why did he say what he did? You've got to be the one and only person to tell me, to shed some sort of light on this puzzle. To give me some sort of healing for the frightful ache I feel."

As she talked, looking into the old face and holding the worn hand, Margo saw the face whiten, felt the hand tremble.

"What is it, Mam? What is it that makes you upset?"

"Lassie . . . lassie," Kezzie whispered, "leave well enough alone."

"I can't. I won't. Tell me, Kezzie, tell me!" There was enough of the noblewoman in Margo's voice to remind Kezzie of her status and her life of service.

Kezzie's throat worked spasmodically; her mouth opened and shut strangely. But no words were forthcoming. Margo gave the hand in hers a little shake.

"I need to know," she said, more gently, but still with that touch of authority that Kezzie recognized.

Trying to speak, Kezzie's face grew whiter, if that were possible, and words seemed unable to be uttered. Greatly touched, Margo almost backed down. But if Kezzie didn't tell her, *who would?* Her desperation drove her to say—and it may have been the pleading note in her voice that moved Kezzie the most—"Gran . . . Gran . . . tell me—"

Gran tried; it seemed she honestly tried.

Margo loosed Kezzie's hand, raised herself from a sitting position to her knees, and leaned over Kezzie's lap, bringing her young face and beseeching eyes close to the ancient face and the closed eyes.

"Tell me, Granny—" Margo forced herself to utter what her heart had been struggling with for twenty-four hours, "is Angus Morrison my father?"

Just before Kezzie's head fell forward in a half-faint, the withered lips twisted and opened.

"Aye," Kezzie whispered, tears squeezing from beneath the eyelids. "Aye, lassie. He is indeed. But lassie . . . he dinna ken . . . he dinna ken."

Leaping wildly to her feet, Margo ran blindly from the room, from the house, her mindless passage taking her through the lines of laundry, into the bush.

With her white clothes trampled in the dirt of the yard, with her proudly made tea cakes burning in the oven, Margo flung herself face down and dug her hands with their telltale curved little fingers into the damp leaf mold.

Cameron Morrison was her half-brother.

34

Supper, what there was of it, was a miserable affair. Kezzie had retreated to her room and refused anything whatsoever, though Cameron brought a cup of tea and a piece of toast to her. It was Cameron who fixed the meal for himself and for Margo, who appeared, shaken, drawn of countenance and curiously specked with what looked like leaf mold, to wash herself at the washstand, ignore her tumbled hair completely, and set herself, at Cameron's invitation, at the table.

"What's wrong, Mam?" he had asked Kezzie earlier.

"Nothin' to concern y'rsel' with, laddie," Kezzie had answered, and no amount of persuasion could change her.

"Well, then," Cameron pursued, "maybe I should get Mother, or Molly—"

"Nae, lad. There's nothing anyone can do. I'll be a'right."

Sitting at the table, watching Margo pick at the scrambled eggs and bacon, Cameron was more troubled than ever. That something serious had happened between the two of them he could clearly discern; just what, had him mystified.

"Something's gone terribly wrong, Margo," he said, finally. "I'd be blind not to see it. I can't imagine what could be so bad between Mam and you. She's adored you always. I believe you feel the same about her. Can you tell me about it?"

"No."

"I can't stand to see you both suffering like this. You're young and strong"—Cameron's voice took on a concerned note—"but Mam is old and nearing the end of her days. I don't want to have her spend them in misery . . . in fact, it appears that this is going to shorten what time she has left. Isn't there something I can do . . . you can do . . . ?"

"I wish there were," Margo said dully, with the futile wish to turn back the clock, back to a time before she knew the truth about Angus . . . about her mother . . . about herself . . . about Cameron.

"Just know this," she said. "I haven't deliberately hurt Kezzie. It's nothing . . . nothing I've done." *Except to ferret out the truth,* she thought to herself. And, feeling as she had toward Cameron, how relieved she should be that the truth had come out before . . . before. . . .

But the weight on her heart said otherwise.

"I can comfort her," Margo said now, "and trust it helps."

With that she excused herself from the table and made her way to Kezzie's room. There the make-believe grandmother and the pretend granddaughter wept in each other's arms.

"I'm sorry, lass," Kezzie whispered over and over. "It would have been best if y'd never known." And though part of Margo agreed, another part—the secret corner reserved for Cameron—cried out in repudiation.

It would have been best if she'd never come, she told herself. And yet she had been forced into it by the terms of Hugh Galloway's will. He had literally taken her life, turned it, shaped it, and changed it forever. He had left her no alternative but to retreat to the bush country and the place he had, she supposed bitterly, prepared for her. Perhaps, knowing Wallace, her father had even hurried her decision by bringing him from Scotland.

Why had Papa . . . Hugh . . . hated her so? She felt she understood now—he had looked on the proof of his wife's infidelity every day of the child's life and suffered. And, finally, he had devised a diabolical scheme to all but annihilate her.

How had he managed to treat his wife as gallantly and properly as he had? "Gran," she whispered now in Kezzie's ear, so close to her lips, "did my mother realize that Papa knew the truth?"

"He never let on, lass. He knew how much she wanted a bairn. Perhaps he knew he couldn't father one—his first marriage had been childless, y'know. It may have been the one thing he couldna gi' her. Never blame Hugh, lassie. He was a great and good mon, with high principles . . . a true aristocrat and gentleman. If you only knew—" But here, it seemed, Kezzie's lips were sealed. Margo, try as she might, could find no redeeming feature about the man she had considered her father, except that he had treated her decently and raised her properly. Only—at the end, she thought bitterly—to crush and destroy her.

———

By morning Margo's mind was made up; she knew what she must do. And, difficult though it was, the decision brought a measure of peace to her.

While Cameron was doing the milking, Margo went about the by-now familiar task of fixing breakfast—porridge, of course, for this Scotch family. Cameron, when he came in, gave her a keen glance, and settled himself soberly at the table.

"Heavenly Father," he prayed, "as we thank Thee for this food, we also ask Thy guidance and grace for this day. Bless this wee lamb that Thou hast brought among us, and bring her, too, into the fold." There, he had said it. Boldly and without embarrassment, as seemed to be the Morrison way. His words spelled out Margo's situation—a lost lamb, a stray without a shepherd—and plainly asked for her rescue.

He couldn't have put it better. Feeling so lost, so alone, Margo found a quick longing in her heart for that sheepfold, the safe, protected fold where the Morrisons were sheltered. A swallow of coffee did little to rid her of the lump that had risen in her throat.

"Cameron," she said quickly, "I've decided to sell the place after all. And you shall have it, if you want it. What do you say?"

"What I say is," Cameron answered slowly, "how come?"

"You want a place; I need the money. It's that simple. It seems like a perfect arrangement and shouldn't take long to accomplish. I suppose a trip to Prince Albert will do it. When do you think you can get away?"

"Whoa!" Cameron said, a frown line appearing between his sunburnt brows. "There's no hurry, is there? Let's take time to think this over." His hesitation over the very thing he had so wanted was strange indeed.

"There's no reason to wait. No," she insisted, "I can't wait."

"You have plans, then?"

"Ah . . . tentative, I suppose you'd say." Truth to tell, Margo hadn't gone that far in her thinking. *Leave, just leave!* had been the one thought consuming her.

"Does this mean," and Cameron's lips tried to turn up in a hint of a smile, "that you've given up on Bliss?"

"Bliss," she answered matter-of-factly, as though they were discussing chokecherries, "is where you find it. What's in a name, anyway? It could be . . . Snicklefritz, as far as I'm concerned." The foolish name, pulled from the air, brought no smile to Cameron's face, nor to Margo's.

Under the silent study of that dear face, Margo's eyes stung and her bravado faltered. To recover, she said quickly, "I'll go see how Kezzie is."

"Will you . . . have you . . . told her?"

"No, and I don't think I will yet. After we get the business part done . . . when there's no backing out, then I'll tell her. I think she'll understand."

"I wish I did," Cameron said roughly, as Margo hurried away only half hearing, away from the troubled look on Cameron's face.

Nor did she hear his urgent, "Father in heaven! Stop her, Lord! Keep her here, if it please You, Father, as it would please me."

Their business transaction taken care of, most of Cameron's hoarded wages transferred to Margo's account, and arrangements made for payments to be made at harvesttime over the next few years, Margo and Cameron mounted the buggy for one final ride together to Bliss. Though the deed crackled in Cameron's pocket, and a train schedule crackled in the Chatelaine bag made from the same rustling taffeta as Margo's skirt, there was no satisfaction on either face and no joy in either heart.

Put a little crape on the bridle and an armband on our sleeves, was his gloomy thought, and you'd have a right fair funeral cortege.

It's as final as a funeral, was her thought, leaving Granny Kezzie, the others, and . . . Bliss, forever and ever.

"Surely," he said finally, "you've given some thought to what you'll do, where you'll go. And surely," he added, again in that rough voice so unlike him, "we have a right to know. Well, perhaps not a right—"

"Well, of course you do. You've all been most kind." Could she continue? The lump in her throat made it difficult.

She delayed further conversation while she took a handkerchief from her bag, coughing delicately into it and, hastily, wiping her telltale eyes.

But Cameron was pursuing the subject. "You'll go back to Heatherstone, of course. I understand you have a home there for as long as you care to stay. That's a sensible idea—"

"No," she interjected quickly. "I told you, I'll never go back to Heatherstone. I think . . ." she was thinking even as she spoke, "I'll go to Winnipeg. Yes, that's where I'll go—Winnipeg, 'Gateway to the Golden West.'"

"And what will you do in this golden gateway place?" Cameron flicked the reins, the muscles in his jaw tight though his tone was casual.

"First," she said, her voice wobbly but gaining confidence as she worked out her future for the first time, "I'll find a . . . a genteel place to live. With what you've paid me and with the small income . . . stipend, it's called . . . from my . . . from the Galloway estate—" Her confidence seemed to be faltering, along with her voice.

"There, never mind," Cameron said, giving the flushed face a keen glance, then reaching over and giving her gloved hand a quick squeeze. He might as well have squeezed her heart, so tight and pained did it seem. But of course a brother could offer such comfort and kindness to a sister.

"You'll have to think of a sensible story to tell Mam," Cameron said. "It certainly doesn't sound very sensible to me. Truth be told, it doesn't make sense at all. Frankly, I'm not a bit sure Mam can survive it. Have you thought of that?"

"I'm sure she thinks it's best . . . all the way around."

"You're not making a bit of sense again." Cameron, now, sounded angry, and he jerked the reins unnecessarily so that the horse jumped, sidled, and settled into a fast trot, taking up the attention of both of the ancient buggy's occupants.

———

There was no use putting off the fateful moment; every day, every hour, every minute made the farewell harder.

"Granny," Margo said, settling herself beside Kezzie's couch, "I'm going away. I'm going somewhere away from all this terrible situation."

"Oh, my angel," Kezzie moaned. "Just when I've found y' again. How can I bear it? First my Mr. Hugh, now you. Couldna y' linger a wee while? I'll no be here forever, y' know, lassie."

"Don't, Granny, don't. I can't, I just can't stay. Don't you see? That . . . that man—Angus Morrison! I can't bear to look him in the face!"

"Ah, lassie," Kezzie's voice was distressed, "y're wrong, sae wrong! Angus is a guid mon, a . . . a Christian mon—"

"Christian! To let his family believe him to be such a fine, upstanding man, when all the while . . . oh, it's too wicked to mention!"

"Lassie, lassie, y're wrong! You mustn't think such things! Oh, God in heaven, what have I done?" Kezzie's cry was pitiful.

"I despise him! He's ripped away every true, dear thought of the man I always knew as my father and left in its place himself, a creature who sins and runs away and leaves the consequences for others to suffer! I despise him, I tell you!"

Kezzie, pale and shaken, was silent for so long that Margo said anxiously, "You see, Gran, why I've got to go. I couldn't hide feelings like that. I'm afraid if I see him again, I'll spew out all this misery, and then everyone—Mary, Molly, Cameron—will be as miserable as I am. I've got to get away and get away soon."

When Kezzie could speak, she said clearly, "Call Cameron. I've got to talk to Cameron."

"You won't tell him!"

"Nae, I willna' tell him."

Cameron came from Kezzie's presence to say simply, "She wants me to bring my mother over here."

"Mary? Why, Cameron? Did she say why?"

"She says," and the young man's face was touched with a quiet wonder, "she's ready to make peace with God. You don't know, lass, how we've prayed for this time to come. It seemed there was an unbreakable barrier holding her back from the love God offers her. Oh, to think she's ready to accept His great gift at last!" There was a spring in his step as he left.

Margo peeked in on Kezzie; her eyes were closed, perhaps she was asleep. Certainly she looked worn, growing more frail almost daily. *I suppose,* Margo thought, *if one needed to make peace with God, one shouldn't wait.*

Peace! Did one need to die to obtain it? How about the living? Wasn't there some balm for hearts like hers? Knowing the

Morrisons, Margo could only conclude that yes, such peace was possible. A phrase from the Bible came to her from the days when a governess had religiously set a portion of Margo's day for the reading of a Bible passage; Margo had been struck then by the scene it painted, and she recalled it now: "All thy waves and thy billows are gone over me." *That's me,* Margo cried, *that's me!*

But wait! Dimly she remembered a fascinating story about how Jesus, in just such an overwhelming situation, had stood up in a little, tossing boat and commanded, "Peace, be still." As a child Margo had thrilled to the glorious "Then He arose, and rebuked the wind and the raging of the water; and they ceased, and there was a calm."

Opening drawers and removing her effects and placing them in her trunk, Margo felt the troubled waves surging over and around. And true, the pressing greenery of the bush, in some respects, resembled the tossing sea. But where was Jesus when He was needed? And would Granny Kezzie, in what were possibly her final moments, come to experience His peace for herself?

The dog barked its welcome, and Margo heard the rattle of the buggy and the jingle of harness as Cameron and his mother drew up to the door. Believing this was a private, personal matter between a mother and her daughter, Margo continued her sorting and packing, though it was with reluctance and despair that each garment was readied for departure.

There was a tap at the door. "Margo," Mary called, "Mam has asked that you join us."

"Are you sure, Granny," Margo asked, kneeling at the side of the bed, Mary on the other, "that I should be here? This praying . . . I don't know much about it."

"Perhaps y' should, lass. Perhaps if I'd prayed wi' y' earlier . . . well, I didn't, and I had my reasons." Kezzie was propped into a half sitting position. Her white hair floated freely around the white face; the blue eyes, though fading, were set with determination.

"Mary, my own bairn, I've somethin' to say to you. It must be said . . . though I had hoped to live and die withoot sayin' it."

"Must you, Mam? Must you?" Mary asked with entreaty in her voice. "I can see it's all been too much for you. You know I love you . . . nothing can change that."

"I must say it," Kezzie continued, with a half sob in her old, quavery voice. "I must ask your forgiveness . . . and then, maybe . . . God's."

"Oh, Mam!" Mary couldn't watch, couldn't listen, without feeling her mother's distress and weeping, too.

"I never thought to tell it," Kezzie went on. "But now, if I don't, wee Margo will go awa' by hersel'—no Mam, no father, no mither, no one . . . and I canna bear it."

Don't tell, Margo felt the silent scream rising in her throat. "Don't tell! Don't ever tell her . . . about her husband . . . and my mother! I'll go away! I'll never breathe a word of it—"

Kezzie seemed to rally, to gain strength as she proceeded. The Scots seemed to fade from her speech, and her words were clear.

"I've done a terrible thing, an unforgivable thing, though I didn't intend it to be a bad thing. At the time, I didn't have time to think . . . I just acted automatically. It was on board ship . . . comin' over."

At the reminder Mary's eyes darkened. "Ah, Mam—must you?"

Kezzie plowed on steadily as though she hadn't been interrupted. "You, Mary, were in labor, terrible labor. You don't remember all about it . . . you faded in and out of consciousness. The hours went on and on, down there in that crowded, foul place, 'til I was near to faintin' from it all. At the same time, Mrs. Hugh went into labor too soon, having fallen down the ladder. Mr. Hugh wanted me with her; I needed to be with you. So I went back and forth."

Mary's head was bowed onto the hand she held as she kneeled at the bedside. Her tears flowed freely. Margo couldn't help it; her own eyes teared up with sympathy and with love for the two women obviously living through a dreadful ordeal. The ordeal that had left her alive and taken Mary's baby.

"Mr. Hugh sent the doctor down, insisted that he go. But he was ruthless . . . diggin' into you with his dirty hands, haulin' your poor wee bairn out regardless of life or death for either of you. I was there. I saw it all. You never knew any of it; you were as good as dead. In fact he pronounced you dead, wiped his hands on the bedding, and left. Angus and the bairns were kissin' your hands and face, Angus was near to faintin', and all the folks in the hold were silent, some weepin' with us."

"I know, Mam. I know all this; I've been told time and again. Please, let's not live it all over again—the burial . . ."

"Hush, lass." Kezzie's voice was growing weaker, her face whiter, if that were possible. "You don't know it all . . . you haven't heard all of it. No one has, though Mr. Hugh knew the rest of the story. The only one to know the rest of the story."

At the mention of her father's name, Margo lifted her head and fixed her puzzled gaze on Kezzie's face.

"Yes, Mr. Hugh knew, though he never mentioned it and no word of it ever passed between us. Still, he knew."

"Knew?" Mary's voice expressed bewilderment. "Mr. Hugh . . . knew?"

"I took your newborn bairn, wrapped it in something or other, and took it with me. I had to get back to Mrs. Hugh. And, Mary," for the first time Kezzie's eyes filled with tears, "remember—I thought you were dead. You had been pronounced dead. There was nothing more, at the moment, that I could do. And Mr. Hugh," Kezzie's slavish obedience to her Mr. Hugh had shaped her decision, "needed me, and expected me. He was stayin' with his wife. I just had time to lay the bairn down when Mrs. Hugh began bearin' down. Within minutes her bairn was born. Mr. Hugh was at her head, comfortin' her, strokin' her hair, and I took his wee one, wrapped it quickly, and laid it alongside the other babe. But not before Mr. Hugh saw it. Oh yes, he took a quick and smilin' look at his first and only child. But oh, Mary—" Kezzie's story broke on a sob, and it seemed she might not be able to continue. Margo reached to console her, but Mary—Mary was sitting back on her heels, still holding her mother's hand, her eyes drying as she looked, startled, at her mother's twisted face.

"The bairn—Mr. Hugh's bairn—" Kezzie whispered, "was dead."

"What . . . what are you saying?" Mary asked, tense now.

"I had a split moment to think, Mary. You were dead, your babe lived. Mr. Hugh lived, his babe was dead. Loving him as I did . . . and loving the babe—"

In a flash Margo saw it all: Kezzie's love could no more have been denied her than a fish could live out of water. She, Margo, was born to Kezzie's love.

"Loving your bairn, Mary. Even then, loving your bairn."

Yes, Margo thought, and loving her Mr. Hugh.

Mary's face was dead white . . . sick white. "Mam . . . Mam," she managed, "what have you done . . . to us all?"

"I did," Kezzie said thickly, "the only thing I could think to do. And the only thing that would have made any sense, if you had indeed been dead. Can you see that, Mary?"

"My baby," Mary was whispering, "buried at sea—"

"Nae, love. Living . . . alive." Kezzie's hand, holding Margo's, pulled her closer, and her eyes were fixed lovingly on Margo's face.

"Your Angel, Mary."

35

From one side of the bed, Mary raised incredulous eyes to the girl kneeling across from her, eyes in which understanding was dawning, eyes that were brimming with love, so long buried and so newly born, that Margo's own breath was, quite truly, taken away.

With a cry not far different from the first wail of a newborn, Margo reached across the bed, her curly-fingered hands outstretched. For a moment the two pairs of eyes—blue and, like her father's, brown—gazed into depths never seen or imagined before.

Across the body of the grandmother who had separated them, thinking she had done the best, hands were not enough. Mary and Margo, somehow, were wrapped in each other's arms. The sounds, mewing, cooing, broken, told what words could never say. Only Kezzie's eventual shifting drew mother and daughter apart, and then it was so that Margo could slip around the end of the bed and into her mother's arms again.

It was from that position that the continuation of the story was heard.

Kezzie told how her Mr. Hugh, having glimpsed his son and being told he was dead, had watched silently while Kezzie, baldly and boldly, had laid Mary's baby in Sophia's arms.

"He went over and touched his bairn briefly and lightly," Kezzie said, remembering that sad moment, "and let me prepare him for burial. I had to refer to the dead child as a girl; Angus knew his babe had been a girl. Mr. Hugh stood alone on the deck while his son was slid into the sea. His hat was off, his hair was blowin' in the wind, and he looked so forlorn. But though I knew he knew, he never, ever, let on."

Having made up his mind, apparently, that what Kezzie had in mind was acceptable, Hugh had never revealed the imposture to his wife. Often, Kezzie said, she would catch his eyes on Margaret, all across the years, with gentleness. Always he had been concerned for her, but with his ingrained inhibitions had never been able to show his feelings. His will, finally, had been his way of making amends.

"He insisted that I be allowed to stay on with the family at Heatherstone; often he stood up for our relationship, which did indeed exceed the usual ties of nurse and nursling. He always felt that he had done the best for you, lassie, by havin' me there for you. And I had no hesitation about tightening every bond, though Sophia never understood. You were my own wee angel, and I gave you the love and attention you deserved. Always—" Kezzie's voice broke—"I was aware that I had deprived you of your rightful family and them of you. The pain . . . at times, was almost more than I could bear. Havin' done what I did, I had to live with it. Mary . . ."

Mary looked up at her Mam, then reached and took the hand held out beseechingly.

"She's had a good raisin', Mary, everything she could need or want. Except you. Oh, my own dear bairn . . . can you forgive me?"

Now daughter and granddaughter turned to the weeping, shaking figure on the bed. Embraces said what words need not.

"One thing more," Kezzie said, when eyes were dried and rational talk was possible. "It's Angus. Lassie . . . I couldna stand by and hear those untrue words about that guid mon. Angus, remember, doesn't know even now . . . nor do Molly and Cameron."

Kezzie was exhausted. Her pallor was such that Mary and Margo were alarmed.

"Here, Mam," Mary said, "let me settle you comfortably for a little rest. You're emotionally drained, and I don't know whether you can stand much more of this. But it's all over now—"

"Not yet, Mary. There's more to be done. You've forgiven me—but God—"

Kezzie was weeping again, and these were the tears of a heart's repentance for sin.

"This is why you haven't asked God to forgive you, isn't it?" Mary asked. "It was unmentionable, wasn't it? And yet, Mam, God knew all along."

"Aye, He knew. And I knew He knew. It's been a sorry burden on my conscience. But how could I repent and keep on sinnin', that is, livin' a lie to y' all? Nae, I couldna. I remember, Mary, a portion of Scripture one of you used one day when you were preachin' at me—oh, yes, ye did that regularly, bless y'—and it was Paul preaching to the Gentiles that they should repent and turn to God, and do works meet for repentance. Remember that verse, Mary? Do I have the meanin' right?"

"Yes," Mary said steadily, "it means to prove your repentance by your deeds."

"And I couldna do that. I knew He wouldna save me if I continued on in my sin. But now, Mary ... I need to be forgiven and shriven."

Mary smiled at the old-fashioned word but saw her Mam's earnestness.

"I have good news for you," was what she said, but it was no news to Kezzie, who had had it explained to her many times across the years by one Morrison or the other. "The promise is, 'If we confess our sins, He is faithful and just to forgive us our sins, and to cleanse us from all unrighteousness.'"

With a wavery but beatific smile on her face, Kezzie folded her hands, closed her eyes, and made her confession.

"Oh, God," she prayed, humbly and sincerely, "I'm a sinner. I'm sorry ... so sorry. Please forgive me and grant me eternal life with you. And now, I receive your Son, Jesus Christ, as my Savior. I confess Him as Lord, and I'll follow Him and serve you, all the days of my life—any that you might see fit to allow me. Thank you, Father. Oh! Thank you, Father!"

What had begun solemnly enough ended with pure joy as the reality of the great transaction went from faith to fact.

Margo, listening with fascination, found herself, at first, following the momentous words along with Kezzie. Somewhere—about the place where she confessed Jesus as Lord and Savior—rote became reality, and when Kezzie was breathing her joyous "thank you," a similar joy was welling up in Margo's heart.

"Now," Mary said tenderly, "we are all part of another family—the family of God."

It was all too much . . . it was all too wonderful; Margo felt she could never contain the joy. What she felt, she saw reflected in Mary's worn face, in Gran's old face, and knew they shared the moment fully. To think of it! Never would she be lonely and alone again. Besides an earthly father, she had a heavenly Father, and He had pledged never to leave her nor forsake her, or so Mary was assuring her.

Cameron could stand it no longer.

"What's going on in here?" he demanded, opening the door. No one needed to tell him of the spiritual transformation; their bright countenances spoke for themselves. It was the best news he could have had.

Of the other amazing development—Margo a member of the Morrison family—all three tried to tell at once.

The cows bawled their need of attention while Cameron ignored them and drove like Jehu to take word to Angus and Molly.

While Kezzie slept the sleep of exhaustion, her face peaceful and her heart light, the Morrison family went over the incredible story . . . again and again. Angus's arms, often around his two girls, were as a blessed haven to the one who had, so recently, declared her contempt of them.

"Mother," Cameron asked, "is it possible you've forgiven Mam for what she did? I can't imagine anything more painful—"

"I've wanted so much for Mam to give herself to the Lord, and I've prayed for that so many times. Here she was, asking God to forgive her, and I was struggling with this terrible . . . pain—almost a horror of unbelief for what she'd done—when I remembered what Jesus said. 'If ye forgive men their trespasses, your heavenly Father will also forgive you: but if ye forgive not men their trespasses, neither will your Father forgive your trespasses.' That settled it. He helped me to forgive her, fully and freely. I may never understand it, and I suppose I'll always grieve over all the years we didn't have our girl with us. But yes, I've forgiven Mam, and with God's help will never let bitterness spoil this for me."

Now there was time for Margo's side, told simply and openly. Now was the time for comparing little fingers and laughing and crying. Now was the time for putting two curly black heads on each side of Angus's curls and laughing and crying.

Finally, reluctantly, Cameron rose to answer the insistent demands of the milk-laden cows. Angus turned to accompany him, and Mary, Molly, and Margo turned as one person toward the kitchen and their need for sustenance. One more time, Margo put her arms around her loved ones.

"Just think," she marveled, near tears again, "after all the years as an only child, I have a sister and . . ." though it brought a pang to her heart, she voiced it, "and a brother."

Amid the smiles, Cameron drew back, the by-now familiar frown between his sunburnt brows, the by-now familiar word on his tongue:

"Whoa!"

The faces of the other four turned toward Cameron.

"What do you mean whoa?" Molly asked pertly.

"Her brother. She said I'm her brother. You heard her."

"So?" Molly asked impatiently.

"I'm not her brother . . . never her brother."

"We know that," Molly said.

"But does she?"

"I . . . I don't understand." Margo's face expressed her bewilderment. Her hand, clutching a chair back, expressed her alarm. Was one member of the family about to disown her? Hard as it was to even think that Cameron might be her brother, his rejection, for whatever reason, would be shattering.

Cameron was looking at Margo searchingly. "I don't believe you know," he said slowly. "And if not, it would answer so much—I'm not your brother, Margo," he said. "I'm not Molly's brother. I'm not a true-born son of Angus and Mary."

"Not . . . not a Morrison?" Margo asked stupidly.

"Oh, I'm a Morrison, all right. But two or three times removed from this branch. My father, a distant cousin, died on a fishing expedition, and my mother died when I was born. Angus and Mary took me in and raised me as their own. I thought everyone knew. Obviously," he said, a certain light in his eyes, "you didn't know."

"No," she said as steadily as she could considering that her breath was ragged in her throat, and her heart was thudding to an erratic beat.

Watching the wordless interchange, Molly whispered, "Well, what do you know!"

Angus, with a smile and a shrug, said, "I'll tend to the cows, lad." Not too old to be remembering the ways of young love, he added simply, "The horse and buggy are still at the door."

Cameron held out his hand and Margo took it. Together they stepped out into the shadows of the northland's long evening. And though her black and curly hair reached almost to his chin, "Come, wee Margo," he said. "Come explore Bliss with me."

239

Ruth Glover was born and raised in the Saskatchewan bush country of Canada. As a writer, she has contributed to dozens of publications such as *Decision* and *Home Life*. Ruth and her husband, Hal, a pastor, now live in Oregon.